Matthew Iribarne

Astronauts & other stories

SIMON & SCHUSTER

New York   London   Toronto   Sydney   Singapore

SIMON & SCHUSTER
Rockefeller Center
1230 Avenue of the Americas
New York, NY 10020

Book design by Ellen R. Sasahara

Manufactured in the United States of America

1   3   5   7   9   10   8   6   4   2

Library of Congress Cataloging-in-Publication Data
Iribarne, Matthew.
Astronauts and other stories/Matthew Iribarne
p.   cm.
Contents: Astronauts—Make them laugh—Sudden mysteries—The gift—
The sun in the sky—A dream, not alone—The clear blue water—Ross
Willow's new and used cars—Wedding dance.
1. United States—Social life and customs—20th century—Fiction. I. Title.
PS3609.R54 A94 2001
813'.6—dc21   2001020545
ISBN 0-7432-0380-1

"Make Them Laugh" has previously been printed in the *Chicago Tribune.*
"Sudden Mysteries" has previously been printed in *The New England Review.*

For my Father

Acknowledgments

DEEPEST APPRECIATION to those whose friendship and support were essential to the writing of this book. Their contribution is gratefully acknowledged, with additional thanks to: Greg Changnon, Michelle Carter, and Nishka Chandrasoma, for thoughtful reading; Bhargavi Mandava, Tom Franklin, and Roy Parvin, for insight and encouragement; Sonia Pabley, Marie Florio, and Tara Parsons, who worked on the collection's behalf; Phyllis Wender, my agent, for her tireless advocacy, walking me through with intelligence and care; and Marysue Rucci, my editor, diligent and perceptive, offering much inspiration.

With gratitude to the Ledig House International Writers' Colony, the Ragdale Foundation, and the San Francisco Foundation, for their generous assistance while working on these stories.

Contents

Astronauts

Richard could hear the birds, their twitter and chirp and loud songs. He sat on the roof of his grandmother's house and stared down at the valley. His brother Stephen sat next to him, leaned back on his elbows. The sun passed behind the clouds, purple in its setting, and it was hard to believe that above him and his brother were the astronauts floating in their tiny silver capsule. The astronauts, talking into their radio and saying how beautiful it all was, looking up at the earth and down at the stars. "It's in the papers," Stephen said, and Richard knew that he was thinking of the astronauts too. There was the breeze that came up against them, the smell of the grass all around.

Now all these years later, waiting in the hospital to see his brother who had been picked up by the police wandering along the freeway in his finest suit, it seemed like a long-ago dream, something that had never happened. He knew the story, that his brother had stopped taking his medication, he didn't even have to be told this much. Richard had been at work when he'd gotten the call, his sister telling him that Stephen was at the police station, but on his way to the hospital, where they would keep an eye on him until he came out of this latest terrible spot.

Everyone knew Stephen here. Stevie, they called him, although Richard hadn't ever called his brother that. *Stevie will be glad to see you,* they said. *Stevie is such a good soul.* It was the first time Richard had come to the hospital, despite the fact that Stephen had been here twice already. But this time, as his sister told him, he would have to drop by and sign the papers, she was stuck in the office and she needed him to do this, just this once. So here was Richard, his stomach all screwed up, hating that his brother could be such the dolt, but feeling the world for him too. The nurse came into the waiting area, told Richard he could follow her now.

Richard pushed his way through the heavy doors, then another set of heavy doors. He looked around at the patients. These were young people, mostly, recovering from various addictions or dealing with the same kind of illnesses as Stephen. A boy with skinny arms who appeared to be no more than fifteen or sixteen stared at him with glassy, blue eyes, an obese woman in a red sweater kicked up her shoes and gave him a smile. "He's in there," the nurse said. "But first I need you to stop at the desk." Richard emptied his personal belongings into a bowl behind the counter, the nurse locked the items up and told him Stephen was over in the room to the left.

Richard went to the room, found his brother still wearing his suit. "Hey Richard," Stephen said, as if this were the most normal thing to be here. "Tough break, huh?"

Fuck yeah, tough break, Richard said to himself. He gave his brother a hug and stepped back. "The freeway?" he said.

"Yeah. I guess I was pretty out of my head."

"And what about the medicine?"

Stephen rubbed his hair, agitated. "I don't know the answer to that one," he said. "Did I *say* I knew the answer to that one?" Then he made two fists and sat down, glared at the ceiling and Richard noticed there were no windows in this room, only the soft chair and poster of the clouds passing over the green tree with the words *Into Each Life.* God, he thought, his sister was supposed to be here, was the person who usually dealt with these problems.

Until recently, Richard had stayed out of the messes his brother had made. But now, since returning home from his marriage that had fallen to pieces and taking the job at the hardware store, he had no choice in the matter, not really. He'd come home, as his sister liked to say. Just as we all came home, eventually. Richard leaned into the smooth, cool wall. "So what usually happens now?" he asked.

Stephen smiled. "Lithium, then observation, then more lithium, and maybe a little basketball to show I'm still one of the living."

"Basketball is good."

"I'll dunk over their sad asses."

Richard checked the hallway for his sister, pushed himself

away from the wall. Hard to believe that his brother was only six years younger than he was, twenty-eight to his thirty-four. He felt more like his brother's father at times, would find himself fighting the urge to ask him what the hell he was doing, that this wouldn't happen if he'd only stick to the medicine. But Stephen liked to believe he was fine, even though he couldn't keep a job and would do these strange things whenever he stopped. There was the morning the police found him sitting on his neighbor's porch like some kind of Boo Radley, rocking back and forth. And the night he ended up in the recreation center sitting in the middle of the court holding the basketball to his chest.

"I'm going to need my toothpaste," Stephen said.

"Elaine will take care of it."

"My razor and socks."

"She'll pick it up."

Elaine had taken the responsibility for Stephen when all the business had started, done the research and made the diagnosis before any doctor. She was younger than both of them, but acted like the angry mother who resented that she had been put in this position. *You might want to know your brother is in the hospital,* she would tell Richard each time it happened.

"I need to make this mental list is all," Stephen said. He moved close, Richard could smell the cola on his breath. "They don't let you carry pens here."

Richard sat down in the chair opposite his brother and pushed his fingers into his eyes. He wanted out, right now, in this very moment. This was too much, his brother sick like he was—the windowless room and poster with its withering proclamation. When their mother died in the car wreck was when this entire mess started. Then their father from the lung cancer two years later and that was the clincher, when Stephen began telling Richard about the voices in his head.

"Sell any hammers today?" Stephen asked. He laughed through his nose, always seemed to find this question hilarious, as if selling hammers was the funniest business in the world. A year ago, Richard had been working for a Los Angeles graphic design firm, lost the job when the company declared bankruptcy. Then the business with his wife started, her telling him she was unhappy, him only wanting to take any job that would pay him while he got his head screwed back on. So here he was in the hardware store in Sacramento, answering the most mundane questions about how to attach a rain gutter, or hang a picture frame in the best way. But mostly he worked the cash register, and even this was bad enough, having to take each nail out of the bag and count it.

"Seven hammers," he said, although he had no idea. The truth was, they sold more screwdrivers than hammers, that people already seemed to have hammers, like people had spoons or chairs, they were just there. He smiled, tried to include himself in on the joke. "And seven nails too."

"That's perfect symmetry," Stephen said. "Let's hope there were seven walls for those seven nails."

"I'm sure there were."

"Good," Stephen said. "Good."

Richard considered his brother. He had a headful of curly,

thick hair, eyes that were soft and brown, pensive. But when he was in this state the eyes seemed to shoot electricity, each synapse of his brain creating a greater charge. And this suit, ridiculous and soiled, the tie crumpled, loosened. The last time he'd seen him dressed this way had been at his wedding four years ago. And the funerals, but that had been in a different suit, when Stephen had been smaller. The medication had had this effect, putting weight on him so that his face appeared to be more blocklike, less shapely.

Finally, Elaine appeared, and Richard had never been happier to see her. She wore her work clothes—the brown skirt and white blouse, the shiny black shoes with the heels. She clumped into the room and tossed down her purse. "The freeway, Stephen?" she said. "The freeway?"

He shrugged. "I'm crazy."

She took his hands.

"So I'll be out in the waiting area," said Richard.

Elaine glanced back at Richard. "Sure then," she said. "Sure."

THAT EVENING at home, Richard called his ex-wife Sandy in Los Angeles. He was feeling extra alone, figured she might have some kind words to say after going through the experience of seeing his brother at the hospital. He knew he shouldn't have been calling her, that it was better to make the clean break. But he needed her right now, he told himself, he needed her voice in his ear, that was all that he needed. He called her at the number he'd been given, the apartment across town from where they'd lived. A man answered and Richard hung up—he tried the number again. The man. "Is Sandy there?" he said, his chest filled heavy.

The man hesitated like the dumb ox Richard knew that he was, went to get her. "Who the hell was that?" he asked, as soon as she came on.

"Hello to you too."

"Well?"

"Is it any of your business?"

Of course Richard knew that it wasn't, but all he'd wanted to do was tell her about Stephen and have her listen as she used to, hear her say this was the way life could sometimes be, however unfair it was, however awful. He'd wanted to hear her explain that there was a lesson in here somewhere, that that's what life was for—lessons. But what was the lesson in this? The ox at her apartment with the ink barely dry on their divorce papers, less than three months since they'd agreed to end everything, even as Richard still had his doubts that it was truly over when she'd said it was a done deal, they had nothing to offer each other, it was time to move on. "My brother is back in the hospital," he said.

Her breath dropped in its concerned way and he sat back and waited for the words to wash over him, to bring him back to the place they'd once been, where he could know that despite everything else that was wrong in his life he had this compassionate woman who could see the larger things.

"That's too bad," she said.

Yes, thought Richard. *Go on.*

"But you have to know I can't offer you anything now."

Richard stared out the window at the camellia bushes and the way nearly each flower had gone brown. He felt the urge to go outside and shake the bush, pull down every dead camellia from its branch. *How about that for moving on?* he'd like to tell Sandy. Not a dead flower here on this bush but all on the ground. Mashed into the dirt, like his heart that was falling, falling, into this great nothing of despair. "I just thought I'd tell you," he said dumbly.

"Well," she said. "I'm sorry Richard. But don't."

He hung up and went to the window, then outside to the bush before heading toward the street. He walked then around the block. Not once, not twice, but fourteen times. He counted each turn, watched the angle of the moon as it seemed to change shape, however slightly, with each rotation. *I am the moon,* he said to himself. *Moving around and around my house silent as the space all around me.*

HE STOPPED BY the hospital the next evening. Stephen was there in his T-shirt and shorts, having given up the suit. He gave Richard a handshake and ran his stubby fingers through his hair. The eyes seemed less jittery, his speech a touch slurred. Slurred was good, thought Richard. That meant the medication had started to kick in. "What's the word, Stephen?" he asked.

"Too much fun," said Stephen. "Television every night and breakfast every day. What more could a man ask for?"

"Are you doing all right?" Richard asked.

Stephen shot him a glare. "I'm fine. What the hell brings you by?"

"I wanted to know how you were is all," he said. They sat in the same visiting room with its heinous poster, Richard glanced at the blue floor and table with the rounded corners, felt the embarrassment of trying to pretend he hadn't been away for as long as he had. "So everything is fine."

"Fine?"

"Yeah. You're doing all right?"

"It's in the papers," Stephen said, and Richard remembered sitting with his brother on their grandmother's roof so long ago, wondered if Stephen remembered it too. But he gave no indication, simply gestured to the hallway and the boy with the skinny arms who peeked into the room. "I'm doing as fine as fine can be, and what more could one ask for in these wonderful accommodations?"

"Not much, I suppose."

"Yeah?" said Stephen. "Not much, huh?"

Richard looked at Stephen and saw him once again as the small boy on the roof, his hair combed over his forehead and eyes so wide. It was how he'd imagined the astronaut's eyes as they stared upon the earth with their sense of wonder and awe, and when his brother's eyes had gone dead as they had Richard couldn't exactly say.

"I wish I'd come sooner," he said.

"What's that?"

"Sooner. I've been gone for so long."

Stephen got up. "Yeah, well," he said. And he walked out from the room, brushed past the skinny-armed boy and down the hallway.

RICHARD met Elaine in the parking lot. She was walking up from her car staring down into her purse, didn't even see Richard until she was the foot or two away. *"Richard,"* she said, clearly startled. Her eyes were red, the lines in her face suddenly pronounced. "This is something."

"I thought I'd visit."

"It's just a surprise."

They stood there, Richard pushing his hands into his pockets, a car slowly went by. Out on the field a man ran with his black dog, giving a sidelong glance at these two figures standing in front of this anonymous, dark-windowed building. And Richard supposed it was a surprise his being here, never showing more than the passing interest in Stephen and all the troubles he'd ever known. *But I lived four hundred miles away,* he wanted to explain. *I've come home—as you would put it—these things are easier now.*

"How's he doing?" Elaine said.

"Fine," said Richard. "He's doing fine."

He got into his car and steered out of the lot, drove past the man running with his dog, along the empty road. Stephen, he thought, sitting on the roof with him all those years ago as they looked up at the sky. And he knew what he would do, that when he got home he would draw up the plan, map out the route that would take him and his brother across the country to New York—upstate—the place his parents had been born and where they'd moved away from, to end up in Sacramento, pleasant and warm, the land of opportunity, the state capital, after all. He would mark the lines with his pencil, trace the route. On top of the map he'd write the words, underline them twice. *To Grandmother's House,* he would write.

STEPHEN got out of the hospital two weeks later, Richard and Elaine met him in the waiting area as he came out with his composed face after having adjusted to the new doses of the medication. "Ladies and gentlemen," he said, stepping through the door. "Meet the Beatles."

They escorted him to the parking lot. Elaine had arranged to drive Stephen home, although Richard had wanted to take him to discuss the final details of the trip they'd been hashing out. Stephen had agreed on going, only insisted that they stop every two hours because he had to piss like clockwork. Elaine thought the trip was a bad idea from the start, said that what Stephen needed was a routine and not a vacation. It was probably true, but Richard knew this much, that he had to get away and that he needed to bring his little brother, it was something that had to be done was all. It filled him with an excitement, this trip, something he hadn't felt since the early days of his marriage to Sandy, when the world was opened wide like the gates to the greenest field. It was the unknown, his own flesh and blood, his chance to make good on the one part of his life that perhaps, he could make good on.

"Second thoughts?" she said at the car, and Richard told her he didn't have any. "Because you should. Have second thoughts that is." She opened the door for Stephen, let him in. "Richard," she said when she came back to him. "I don't want him to get hurt is all."

"I know."

"And you *have* to promise me he won't get hurt."

"I promise."

She got into the car, rolled down her window. "It won't be easy, you know," she said.

Richard nodded.

"As long as you know that."

"I know."

She backed away, Stephen gave his brother the open-fingered wave. Richard grabbed for his keys. The next day he would tie up the loose ends at work, take care of the last-minute business with Mr. Jacobsen, the owner of the store. Richard had hoped Mr. Jacobsen would let him go, force him to find something, anything, better than this job. But this was one of the problems with the hardware store, his manager and coworkers so flexible and accommodating. He had pictured himself throwing down his apron and walking out the door, making the clean break. But as the time got closer and he mentioned he would be leaving, Mr. Jacobsen had told him, "Good for you, you get two weeks off anyway." It was the first, and Richard hoped, the last, foil to his plan for this trip, ending things and starting anew all the way around.

TWO DAYS LATER Richard stopped by Stephen's apartment—a state-subsidized complex on the far side of town. Stephen was waiting with his suitcase and sunglasses, said he was ready, had been ready, since six o'clock in the morning. "Now it's nine," he said, shuffling near the car. "It's funny how quiet it can be so early, how it keeps getting noisier and noisier the later it gets."

"I'm sorry you waited," Richard said. "I thought we agreed on nine."

"We did," said Stephen. "I was up was all."

They loaded the car with the suitcase and Richard asked him if he was sure that would be all he would be bringing. Stephen tilted his head. "I got everything I need. Really."

"Okay then," said Richard. They got into the car and pulled away from the apartment. "Well let's say good-bye."

Stephen rolled down his window and stared back at his apartment. "It's all okay," he said. "It's a vacation is all."

"It is."

"A drive back to our youth."

"Indeed."

"Hello youth."

"Put all your troubles in a bag."

"Can we get pancakes?"

"Of course."

They pulled onto the freeway and the late-morning traffic was light as Richard had known it would be. His brother turned on the radio and closed his eyes. There was the wind blowing through Stephen's window and the feeling in Richard's heart that something good was happening right now in this very moment, that here was the beginning of his new life as he'd imagined it would be, right there before them.

THE FIRST HOTEL was a mess. It was in Nevada and the door stuck so that Richard had to kick it open. The pool was empty, bats flew all around the courtyard. But it was past midnight, every other hotel was booked, and all Richard wanted was to sleep. They tossed their suitcases into the room, Richard sat in the yellow chair while Stephen took his medicine, used the toilet. When he came to the bed he was out in minutes. Richard used the bathroom while his brother slept, considered the faucet in the sink that was simply the bolt, the mirror cracked along its edges.

He tried to sleep but the sleep didn't come. It didn't help that the couple next door were going at it and that the air conditioner was noisy like a truck, that the headlights shined in from the interstate highway. *This isn't good,* Richard thought as the grunting next door continued. His brother snored as he fell into a deeper sleep. Richard covered his head with the pillow, it seemed that when sleep finally came his brother was shaking him, telling him it was morning and time to leave.

"What time?" Richard said.

"Almost ten."

"Ten? Jesus."

"Yeah. I went out to the balcony, watched the cars."

Richard kicked off his covers and stepped onto the floor. The air conditioner continued to make its noise, but the couple was no longer. "Did you hear the racket next door?" he asked.

"Racket?" said Stephen.

"They were screwing."

"Damn, no," he said. "I missed that, of course."

Richard took a quick shower and they headed out, stopped at the restaurant down the street for some breakfast. Stephen took his pills and drank his water, Richard watched him. "Can you feel them working right away?" he asked.

Stephen scowled. "It's not like that," he said. "It builds up, gradually." He placed the pills on his tongue, took a drink of water with two gulps. "Subtle like aspirin."

"I like the sound of that," said Richard. "Catchy."

The waitress came and Stephen ordered his pancakes, speaking slowly. Richard ordered eggs and toast and a black coffee. They handed her the waxy menus and Stephen sat back in his seat and stared at the waitress as she walked from their table.

"She was pretty," he said.

Richard peeked back. "She was okay."

"No. She was pretty." He rubbed his left eye with his fist. "So you could hear them going at it last night?"

"I could. It was awful."

"I always miss those kind of things."

They looked out at the various people at the tables. Most were men in plaid shirts, eating as if the food on their plates was some kind of business to tend to, like everything else in the world. It occurred to Richard that his brother wanted to talk more about these sounds coming from next door, that his sexual experience had likely been little to none and that he only wanted to hear about the details.

"It was just a lot of grunting," Richard said.

"Grunting," said Stephen, thoughtfully.

"Nothing more."

"It's something."

"No it's not," Richard said.

He watched one of the men in the plaid shirts get up from his seat and stick a toothpick in his mouth, lumber to the register.

"You ever kiss a girl?" Richard asked.

Stephen's eyes took on a worried quality. He moved his water glass in a circle, picked it up and took a long drink. "A lot," he said.

"Okay," said Richard. He held his hands together, knew that to continue would only disturb his brother further. He knew the signs.

"She *is* pretty though," he said. "The waitress."

"You could say that," said Richard. He reached for his napkin, the waitress darted from table to table with her fixed smile. Stephen turned the blinds at their table and stared out the window, pointed to their car and told Richard it was funny to think it would take them all the way across the country. Richard regarded the car, knew that if he had another night like the last one he wouldn't make it much further.

"You snore," he said.

"I don't snore."

"You snore, and from now on you sleep on your side."

"Fine," said Stephen. "I'll sleep on my side."

They ate their breakfast in the same rushed way as those around them, finished their meal and Richard paid. On the way back out to the car, Stephen told him that he wanted to sit in the backseat because it reminded him of being a kid and driving this way with their parents, Richard said what the hell, they *were* going back to their youth. Stephen slept for a good hundred miles, when he woke he pulled out a book from his suitcase about the Vatican art collection.

"What are you doing reading that?" Richard asked him.

"I want to see what the pope owns," he said.

They stopped every two hours, either at the gas station or along the side of the road. Stephen took his medication with water from the bottle, put on his sunglasses and gazed out at the landscape. Occasionally he would see a deer or rabbit, yell to Richard when these moments happened. "It does exist," he'd exclaim. "Nature, that is."

The hotels got better. Nebraska had a fish tank in the lobby, a television with all the cable channels. Iowa had a refrigerator filled with complimentary candy and soft drinks, a bed that vibrated. But still, these hotels had no pools. "I need to swim," Stephen said. "If I don't swim then how can it be a vacation?"

Finally, in Ohio, they were able to get a hotel with a pool. Stephen swam for a good hour while Richard sat on the deck and paged through the book on the Vatican, read about all the art the Church happened to own. Leonardo da Vinci. Caravaggio. Even Matisse. As well, the countless Greek and Roman statues, the Egyptian artifacts. Stephen came out from the water, stood on the deck's edge and held his hands together. "Man that pope has some stuff," Richard yelled to his brother. Stephen shivered. "Why do you think they call him the pope?" he said, and he jumped back in. Richard put the book down and walked to the edge of the pool. He set one foot in, then the other, slowly lowered himself into the water.

THEY WENT TO the restaurant that evening across the street from the hotel. Stephen ordered a steak and potato, Richard a Caesar salad and iced tea. They were mostly quiet, as they had been since that breakfast all the way back in Nevada many days ago. It had become a part of the routine, Stephen taking his pills and Richard glancing around the restaurant and occasionally commenting on the plates of food being brought to the tables.

Stephen still pointed out the women, had an eye for the ladies, that much was clear. But whenever the moment came to actually *talk* to these women, he clammed up and stared down at his feet, became agitated and fearful. Richard knew this feeling, had never had the gift of banter with anyone, let alone women. He'd been lucky enough to meet Sandy at work, had

had the time to build a relationship that didn't smack of pursuit. He'd liked her from the beginning, had played his cards close to his chest and only made the move when he was absolutely certain it would be reciprocated.

But today, relaxed from the sun with the smell of chlorine rising from their bodies, Richard was charged, his head light, ready to try something he normally wouldn't. With the waitress for instance. She came up to the table to check on how things were and Richard said that everything was just fine Darling, *Darling*, for Christ's sake, something he'd never said even to Sandy in all their years together. But this was the new Richard, he thought. Flirting with pretty women was a new part of who he was. The waitress snapped her gum. "Uh huh," she said, sticking her pencil into her apron and walking away.

"What was that?" Stephen said. "Darling?"

"I wanted to try it," said Richard.

"Well you tried it all right." He looked over at the waitress. "I think you embarrassed her."

"I didn't embarrass her," Richard said. "She hears it every day."

He kept his eyes on the waitress. "No. I think you did."

The waitress swung back by the table.

"Excuse me," said Stephen.

She considered him with folded arms. Her mouth was generous, her lips full. "What is it?" she said.

"I think my brother has something to say to you."

Richard put down his knife and fork. "What?"

"I think you do."

"What do I have to say?"

"I think you know," Stephen said.

"Oh come on."

"Richard."

She glanced from brother to brother. "I got other tables."

"Exactly," said Richard.

The waitress walked away and Richard gave Stephen a kick under the table.

"What was that all about?" he said.

"You were supposed to apologize."

"For what?"

"You know what. *Darling.*"

They ate the rest of their meal in the usual silence, Richard reading the book on the Vatican art while Stephen concentrated on the newspaper crossword puzzle. The waitress finally came back. "Will there be anything else?" she asked.

Richard said they were fine, Stephen stared up at her.

The waitress wrote the check and leaned close into the table. "Now honey," she said to Stephen. "You have some kind eyes."

That was all it took for Stephen to go as red as the apple before picking, to go back to the crossword puzzle with his forced deliberation. "I am sure he thanks you," Richard said, and the waitress turned her attention to him.

"You on the other hand," she said.

"I know," said Richard. "My eyes aren't very kind at all."

"They are," she said. "But in a different way. Your brother, his eyes are gentle and calm. Yours though, they seem like they're filled with some other things too."

"Other things?" Richard said, even while he thought he could have gone on to tell her that his brother's eyes were only gentle and calm because of the medication. He smiled, the fact being that here he was talking to the woman he'd called Darling and that perhaps this was a part of his new life. "How would you like to have dinner?" he asked, then he laughed, because he realized that's exactly what they *were* having, that this was a waitress he was talking to and that dinner was probably the last thing she wanted. "No," he said. "Not dinner. How about a walk, though?"

Stephen looked up from his crossword puzzle, his face screwed up with something Richard could only interpret as anger.

"With you?" the waitress said.

"Sure," said Richard, and Stephen slammed his pencil down. "Or with us."

"Us?"

"Me and my brother."

The waitress shook her head. "That sounds funny."

"I'm sure it does."

"No," said Stephen. "You go. I need to finish this puzzle anyway."

The waitress pointed to Stephen's vials of pills. "I seen you taking those," she said. "Depression?"

Stephen twitched a smile.

"My sister has that. Pretty far gone. You though, you seem all right."

"I am," he said.

Then the waitress reached over and gave Stephen's shoulder a pat. "I'm on my break starting right now," she said. "I'd like to talk about how it is. Just outside while I have my smoke." She caught Richard's eye. "If you don't mind."

Richard shrugged. "No," he managed to say.

"Good. So?"

Stephen pushed the newspaper aside, gave his brother a panicked face. The waitress slipped off her apron and tossed it behind the counter, Stephen followed her outside and they sat down on the bench. Richard watched her put the cigarette to her lips, Stephen take the lighter from her hands and hold it out for her as she brought the cigarette to the flame.

HER NAME was Reese and she lived on the other end of town with her two cats and mother and sister. The sister was manic-depressive, and Reese was afraid, afraid because her sister couldn't do much more than trudge around the house in some kind of mild daze. "That's why it's so good to see your brother like he is," she told Richard.

Richard nodded. They stood outside the hotel across the street where Reese had agreed to meet Stephen for a late-night walk. It had been her plan, and Stephen was in the room putting the final touches on his hair, patting it down with the water and shaving himself for the second time that day. After he'd come back to the table from Reese's break, he'd sat across from Richard, told him, "I think I'm in love."

"You're not in love," Richard said. "You're in lust. But not in love."

"No," said Stephen. "She's sweet."

"*Sweet,*" Richard had said, leaving the tip and going to the register. On the way out, Reese had come up to Richard and told him the plan they'd made for the late-night walk, asked how this sat with him. "What am I, his father?" he asked.

"No," she'd said. "I know you're his brother."

So here she was standing in front of the hotel, wearing her T-shirt and jeans, her brown hair hanging to her shoulders and freckles on her neck suddenly visible. She leaned into the fence and looked up at the stars in the sky, plentiful here in this small Ohio town with the name Richard couldn't even recall. "My boyfriend says my sister's a nut case but I know better than that."

"She's not a nut case," said Richard. "None of them are nut cases."

"I know," she said. "Sometimes I hate him. My boyfriend that is."

"Well, it's never easy."

"You know?" she said.

"I know."

Reese glanced at the hotel room window, its shadow of Stephen as he surely primped in front of the mirror. His brother was not prone to vanity, but Richard had seen it, here and there. In high school he might wear his best shirt for the dance he'd come home from alone, not to mention the suit he'd put on for his curious freeway saunter. Richard slouched over the gate next to Reese. "I was married," he said. "Four years until it ended three months back."

"Oh, I'm sorry," Reese said, and the door opened and closed as Stephen came out from the room. "But you should have learned by now that people leave people. My father, for instance—that I can barely remember." Reese stepped back from Richard, Stephen came toward them with his hair pressed up from the gel. "But as my mother likes to say, God gave us feet and here is one of the reasons."

Richard opened the gate for Stephen who smelled like the aftershave. "Reasons?" he said.

Reese took Stephen's arm in hers, turned. "To leave," she said.

REESE kissed Stephen. It was a tiny kiss, only a peck really, but it was still a kiss, and Richard saw the whole thing from his window as he sat on the bed in the dark and watched them stand in front of the gate. He thought about Elaine telling him to promise her Stephen wouldn't get hurt. Yet here was his brother getting hurt, although he didn't know it yet. Because here is how it always started, here it was, the beginning of the end. He knew how it would be, Stephen waltzing into the room with the stars in his eyes, the drive the next morning with his brother so quiet, the sadness of going away.

But he didn't stop them. He simply sat with his hands on

his knees and watched how Reese held him, turned her head up so that her hair fell down. How funny, he said to himself in the darkness. How funny that Reese might have been his own chance to break away from the memories of Sandy—while there was Stephen—barely able to talk to women, that had probably not even kissed until tonight, under the streetlamp with Reese as she wrapped her arms tightly around his body. They broke away, Stephen did his dazed walk back to the hotel.

When he came to the door Richard lay back on the pillow and feigned sleep. "Don't forget to write," Reese whispered, like the joke that it was meant to be, these two ships passing in the night. But then Stephen was telling her that he would indeed write, much too loudly. "I will," he said, almost yelling. Then in the whisper, "I will," he said again.

Stephen closed the door and went directly to the bathroom, Richard sat up and stared out the window. Reese was across the street lighting her cigarette. She breathed in the smoke, wandered past the restaurant parking lot, down the sidewalk and away from the hotel. Richard kicked off his sheets and got out of bed, knocked on the bathroom door. "Reese walking?" he said.

"Richard?" said Stephen. "I thought you were asleep."

"I was. But now I'm awake." He placed his hand squarely onto the door, the wood rough and knobby against his palm. "So," he said. "Is she walking?"

"Her car is broken."

"Broken?"

"That's what I said."

Richard put on his pants and shoes. "Well I'm going to drive her then."

"What's that?"

"I'm going to drive her."

The bathroom door opened and Stephen came out looking more peaceful than Richard had ever seen him. He had the hotel towel draped over his shoulder, the hairs on his chest curled up and gave him the appearance of being the man that he was. He leaned into the jamb, smiled. "She'll be fine, Richard. Really."

"It's late."

"We're in the middle of nowhere. Everyone knows everyone."

Richard tucked his shirt into his pants. "I'll be back in a flash." He picked up the car keys from the dresser and left Stephen standing there in the middle of the room, got into his car and backed it away with the skid.

Reese was two blocks from the hotel when he spotted her. She held the cigarette between her fingers, it made its glowing trail. He pulled up alongside her, rolled down the window. "You should get a ride," he said.

"Oh Christ," she said. "I'm fine, really."

"No, you should."

She tossed the cigarette and got into the car, pointed straight ahead. "Just keep driving and you'll be there in less than a minute."

"It's close?"

"I told Stephen."

They drove and Richard regarded her knee, the roundness of it. Watching her kiss his brother had stirred something deep inside him, left him missing Sandy more than he could ever remember missing her. He wanted to start new, that was all that he wanted. And wasn't it in the kiss that the new began, the princess to the frog, Judas to Jesus, George Bailey to Mary? He placed his hand on her knee and she looked at him as if to say, What, what, *what* are you doing? "I'm alone, you know," he said.

She turned her face to the window and he took back his hand. "You're getting close."

"Tell me when."

"My boyfriend says he needs to watch me."

"Your boyfriend is full of shit," said Richard.

She kept her eyes out the window. "You don't know him."

"Your sister isn't a nut case. Your sister is a good person, like my brother. You love your sister more than you would ever love your boyfriend. You could hit him sometimes. This much, I know."

He slowed, she nodded to the house surrounded by the bushes. The porch light was bright and glowing. "That's me," she said. Richard pulled up to the curb in front of her house, gripped his steering wheel tightly. "Well thank you for the ride," she said. There were the freckles that lined her neck, that followed themselves down the front of her chest. "You didn't really have to do that."

"No," Richard said. "It's fine."

Then she put out her hand, and Richard took it in his. "You shouldn't feel alone," she said. "You have your brother."

"Like we could ever really talk."

"You could."

"Maybe."

Then he kissed her, and kissed her again, tasted the sweet and pungent smokiness, the roughness of her tongue. How long had it been, he thought, since he'd known such delight in his heart? This was the new, *this was the new.* He lay her down onto the seat, gazed into her eyes that considered him as if they'd known each other always. She smiled, placed her hand alongside the back of his neck. "I love my sister very much," she said.

RICHARD came back to the hotel two hours later. Stephen was gone, the bed still made and pills on the table. This wasn't good, Richard thought. His brother needed to be in bed by eleven, it was a part of the routine, as was taking the pills at the appointed times. He left the hotel and returned to the car, began to back away when he saw his brother's profile in the restaurant.

He parked his car and got out, dashed across the street. When he came to the table his brother had his crossword puzzle in front of him, was eating the plate of french fries. He didn't look up when Richard sat down across from him, just kept eating. "You fuck her?" he said, finally.

"Now Stephen," Richard said.

"No," said his brother, his voice rising. Heads turned,

Stephen's eyes did their queer shake and Richard knew not to say a word. "You did. I know."

"Let's take those fries and go back to the room."

"I'll see you there," Stephen said. "You can leave me for the time being though."

"Just come with me."

"You can go to hell."

Richard left the table with the eyes of the patrons upon him, went back to the hotel room and lay on the bed. Until that moment he'd been filled with the happiness of being with Reese. But now the reality of what he'd done lay heavy. A decent man wouldn't have screwed this girl, would have taken into account his brother's affections and simply dropped her off. Or better yet, would have let her walk home because everyone knew everyone here, as Stephen had said. He remembered his first summer with Sandy, how he'd sat on the hot car seat and placed down the towel for himself, her sitting and burning her legs as he turned the ignition. *Goddamnit,* she'd told him as he rolled down the window. *Don't you ever give a shit about anyone?*

But he *did* give a shit. Driving with his brother across the country so he could simply know him, making up for all the wrong things he'd ever done, the bridges burned. He *was* a decent man, he knew deep in his heart this much was true. He was capable, he was better than this. He sat up and went to the window, found his brother gone.

■

RICHARD got into his car, drove up and down the street. But no Stephen. He became afraid, drove back to the hotel and only hoped since he'd been gone his brother had returned. Elaine, he thought, and he could picture her face as he told her he had lost Stephen somewhere in Ohio, the terrible disappointment of it as he'd let her down in this stupendous way. He got out of the car and went to the room—still, Stephen wasn't there—picked up the vials of medication. One more drive, he told himself. He would give himself one more drive all the way to the very end of the street, if he didn't see Stephen he would go to the hotel and call the police.

Richard drove slowly, peered out his windows side to side. "Please Stephen, *please,*" he said. The moon and stars peeked out over the tops of the trees, he found himself making prayers he hadn't made for so long. He imagined the paintings and sculptures of Jesus and Mary from the book on the Vatican, told them to spare his brother, that what he'd done with Reese was wrong, he could see this much and had learned his lesson. Richard drove all the way to the end of the street where Reese's porch light shined brightly, headed back for the hotel. The pills rolled on the seat and clicked against the plastic of their vials, the asphalt hummed beneath him as he sped along the road.

He steered into the parking lot and got out of his car, froze when he saw him. It was Stephen, up on the roof of the hotel, *the freaking roof* for God's sake, near the television antenna at its shingled peak. Stephen glared down at his brother, pulled his legs to his chest.

"Stephen," said Richard.

"Richard."

"Come down."

"I don't want to."

"You're going to get us in trouble. Come on. Down."

Stephen remained sitting.

"Just come on."

Richard scanned the building for the way up to the roof. He ran around to the backside, saw the aluminum ladder that was still in place. He scrambled up the rungs, carefully scaled his way toward the crest of the roof. When he reached his brother he slowly lowered himself down beside him, the shingles making their squeak and groan.

"We can talk about this back in the room."

Stephen said, "I like it here."

"That's good and fine," said Richard. "But unfortunately it's not our roof to sit on."

"I'm not going back in."

Richard slowly stretched out his legs, maintained his balance. "Look," he said. "I'm sorry about what I did. It was stupid. I didn't think was all."

"You didn't think," Stephen said. Then he stood and Richard felt his insides spin. Stephen raised his arms, pointed to the sky. "You didn't think," he said again, and he forced a laugh. He began to stumble, Richard reached out for his brother and Stephen pulled his arm, they were sliding down the roof and Richard tried to hold on. The antenna—when he grabbed it the rod bent and snapped, the metal came crashing down beside them. "We're going," Stephen said, and they were, right over the edge and into the air until there was just nothing, nothing at all.

THE AZALEA BUSHES broke their fall. Richard ended up with his head bleeding, Stephen with the broken arm. The owner of the hotel found them there, called the police, then the hospital, in that order as he told them later. They sat in the ambulance together, face-to-face while the attendants watched them closely. "How many fingers am I holding up?" said the attendant to Richard. "Count from ten backwards."

Once the doctors did their business, putting the bandage on Richard's head and the cast on Stephen's arm, Richard and Stephen met in the waiting room and called for a taxi. Back at the hotel, the owner sat on the bed in their room. He was a leather-necked man with gray hair combed back and bottom teeth that stuck out from his mouth, a seeming grimace. "You owe me for the antenna," he said. "And the broken shingles. And the bushes."

"It's not like we meant it," said Richard.

"You climbed my roof, you meant it."

Stephen excused himself for the bathroom, Richard pulled out his checkbook.

"No checks," said the owner. "Cash."

"But we still have to get to New York."

"Cash."

Richard opened his wallet and paid him for the damages, a

hefty amount that pretty much cleaned them out. At least he had his credit card, but unfortunately he was near his limit, having used it to pay for the countless expenses moving back home. He closed his wallet and stuck it back into his pocket, knew they would be lucky to make it to New York with the amount they had left between them. The owner pointed to the door. "Now if you will be so kind as to leave."

"Richard," Stephen said from the bathroom. "I need a hand. Literally."

"Excuse me," Richard said, dreading the request that was waiting. He opened and closed the door. "You can't do it?"

Stephen raised his casted arm. "You expect *me* to?"

Richard unbuttoned and pushed down his pants. "You need me to hold it too?"

"I can do that."

He pissed and Richard leaned into the towel bar, wondered what the hell he was doing here in the middle of Ohio, why he'd ever thought this trip would be a good thing to do. They had driven over two thousand miles and here was his brother with the broken arm who hated him, nearly flat broke with this bandage around his head so far from home.

"Okay," Stephen said.

Richard reached behind his brother and buttoned him up, washed his hands and handed Stephen the soap. When he came back out into the room the owner was dragging Stephen's suitcase across the floor. "Hey," Richard said. "I can do that."

"I'm sure you can," the owner said, grunting.

Richard took the suitcase and placed it in his car, went back to the hotel room and picked up his bag as Stephen came out from the bathroom. "We're going, I take it," Stephen said.

"By special escort."

Richard brought the bag out and put it in the backseat with the suitcase, got into the car with Stephen. "Say good-bye then," he said, and he pulled away from the hotel, kicked up the dust into the owner's face. "That's good," Stephen said, and they looked back to see the owner coughing and waving his hands.

"You've got to show them who's boss," said Richard.

"It's in the papers," Stephen said.

"We're the boss."

THEY DROVE PAST Reese's house and the porch light was still on, the woman oblivious to the drama that had ensued in her name. Richard figured she would hear, what with the restaurant being across the way. *These crazy brothers,* the hotel owner would tell her as he came in for his daily supper. And she would put it all together and wonder exactly which brother he was referring to, that maybe they'd both been mad when all was said and done.

Richard had forty-seven dollars. Stephen had twelve. The credit card had fifty-three dollars left after the accumulated debt. They talked about it, Richard eyed Stephen's cast, Stephen looked over Richard's bandaged head. "We've come this far," they said together. They slept in the car, bought their food in the various markets and tossed the wrappers into the back. Vagabonds, they called themselves, and when songs came on the radio that they recognized, they sang along like drunken children. Aspirin was liberally taken, Stephen ate ice cream with every meal.

"If I'm going to suffer," he said, "I may as well suffer splendidly."

Stephen learned to button up his own pants, took to wearing loose shorts to make the bathroom trips easier. He slept many hours because of the medication, would sometimes wake with the most scared expression. It was just past midnight when they passed into New Jersey and he woke screaming. Richard reached over and placed his hand on his brother's shoulder. "It's all right," he told him. "I'm right here."

Stephen wiped his eyes, blinked at the passing trees in the headlights. When their mother died, Stephen never cried. He'd considered Richard and Elaine with curiosity, said it was better to let go than to dwell on these things. And he seemed to believe it until their father died the two years later, and then something cracked as if everything he'd ever held inside had spilled out and knocked him down. "I can hear them," he'd said the morning of their father's funeral. "These voices that come into my head."

Stephen rolled down his window, glanced over at Richard. "Do you mind?" he said, and Richard said that he didn't, to go on ahead. Richard remembered when Stephen was a boy, how he'd told him he was an idiot, a fool, nobody's child. But the truth was he'd envied Stephen, been jealous of his decency and kindness. How Richard had so often wished he could be this way. To have such a clear view of right and wrong, to simply know deep inside and have this superior knowledge.

"It smells like grass," Stephen said.

"It does," said Richard.

Stephen wiped his eyes with his fist. "I'm a mess."

"You're not a mess."

"Yes I am."

Richard rolled down all the windows, let the wind come in. If he could only go back to the beginning, he thought. If he could only go back to the time before he'd tell his brother the bad things, before everything had gone so wrong. He put his hand out the window and opened his fingers, smelled the grass in the air. He pushed the gas, the paper wrappers in the back fluttered in circles.

THE HOUSE was higher up than Richard remembered it being, farther from the road as they steered onto the driveway. A mailbox that used to be the silver metal with their grandmother's name had been painted bright yellow, elm trees now surrounded the property. "Those trees are new," Richard said.

"Things grow," said Stephen.

The birds made their racket, the insects buzzed. The night before, Richard and Stephen had pulled over and slept on the side of the road. In the morning they'd bathed in the nearby creek, swam naked in the water. "Look at me," Stephen had said, his body pink and prickled with goose pimples as he held up his casted arm. "I'm just a bunch of tiny holes and hair."

They rolled down the driveway, the dust rising beneath

them. Richard had removed the bandage from his head, put on clean pants and a button-down shirt. Stephen too, had put on his jeans, a T-shirt, unworn. "I hope this works," Richard said, and the gravel crunched into the tires.

Stephen matted down his curly hair. "We'll make a good impression," he said.

The grass was mowed in patches, tall weeds sprouted up from the various bumps and indentations. In the middle of the field was a bowling ball, a truck with its engine taken out. And there even farther was a boat turned upside-down, its sails on the grass alongside the hull.

"Money," Stephen said.

"Not ours," said Richard.

And the money that should have been handed down never was, the grandmother losing all her savings and the house being used to settle the various debts. It had been a sore spot for their parents, the first injustice in the long line of many that followed. When all the money was finally divvied out and each child was given their fair share, a few thousand dollars was left for their father. Richard could still see him holding up the check and telling him, "This is a pocketful of sorrow."

The house looked magnificent, painted white with the green shutters and porch that took up its entire front side, the columns that supported its two stories. Like a house one would find in another age was how his father had often described it, this structure so large surrounded by these green hills and flowers.

They parked the car, got out. A woman stepped from the

house with a towel in her hand, and a man followed. The woman was older, probably on the shy side of sixty. She had dark hair that was going gray and her eyes were clear and watery. "Can I help you?" she said, walking down the steps of the porch.

"Well I hope you can," said Richard. "You see, our grand-mother used to live here."

"Your grandmother," the woman said. Her lips cracked a smile. "That would take you back twenty years or so."

"It would," said Richard.

Stephen nodded beside him. "It's been a while."

"What happened to your arm?" said the woman.

"We fell from a roof," Richard said. "It was an accident."

The man stepped down from the porch. "You fell from a roof?" he said. "The both of you? It sounds like a movie." He was much younger than the woman, likely her son. He was fair, fleshy-cheeked with brown hair that went red in the sunlight. He put out his hand to Richard and Stephen. "I'm John. And this is my mother."

"Tina," the woman said.

Richard and Stephen took John's hand, then Tina's.

"Well," said Tina. "Would you like to stay for lunch?"

"Actually," Richard said. "That would be nice." He stared past Tina and John toward the porch. "And if you could see to letting us stay until dark that would be perfect."

"Dark," Tina said, looking at her son.

"We used to sit out on the roof in the evening. But the porch would be just as good. If we could do that, then we could leave you on your own."

John gestured toward the house, Tina squeezed the towel. "Well I think we can allow that," she said. "I think we really can."

THE KITCHEN was different than it had been when they were children. Gone was the old white stove and the yellow walls, the tiny table with the shiny metal legs. The counter was tiled white and a light on the ceiling had a fan that made its breeze. "We fixed it up," said John.

Tina made the lunch, tuna fish sandwiches with salad on the side. She set the plates down before them with the glasses of lemonade, Stephen ravenously ate the sandwich with his good hand. Richard jabbed him with his elbow, told him to slow it down. "We ran out of money," he explained. "We've been pretty much living on soft drinks and ice cream for the last couple of days."

"I see," Tina said. "Well I can get you more if you'd like."

"Yes, please," said Stephen.

John crossed his arms and sat back in his chair. "So you drove all the way across the country to come here?"

"It was a journey," Richard said.

Stephen wiped his mouth. "A trip back to our youth."

"This house, you mean," Tina said. She drank the lemonade and nibbled from her sandwich. She had manners, Richard could see this much. He pictured her in a past time sitting in the boat that was now on the lawn, her hair darker and blowing in the wind as she sipped white wine from a tall glass. Her son had already finished one half of his sandwich, was working on the other. He seemed less schooled in the ways of etiquette as far as Richard could see. Perhaps he'd been appointed to take care of the place, the father leaving them with his money and connections to society.

She put the sandwich down onto her plate. "It's funny how you go to a place and it brings everything back. Me for instance, when I go to the farm where I grew up. It's in Pennsylvania and sad to say there's only a shopping mall there now. But I'll still go when I'm there. You know, to walk around."

"You can't explain it," Richard said, wondering how much of the life he'd imagined for this woman and son was true. Little to none, actually, as Tina proceeded with her sandwich and told them that her husband was away at work, that John had a job in the city as a stockbroker and had only come home for the visit. Funny how you could make up stories for people, thought Richard. But still, he told himself, regarding Tina. He could still see her on the boat. Drinking from her wine as the husband turned the sails.

Tina chewed her sandwich and John stood up from the table. Richard watched from the corner of his eye as Stephen took out the vials from his pockets and laid his pills out in front of him.

"You diabetic or something?" the son asked.

"Not exactly," said Stephen. "They're for my head, actually. You know. Psychological."

John looked across the table at his mother. "Okay," he said. He brought his plate to the sink, picked up Richard and Stephen's plates and brought them to the sink as well. Tina held the bread of her sandwich between her fingers, glanced warily at Stephen.

Richard rattled the ice in his glass. "It's no big deal," he said.

"This keeps things in check," said Stephen. He placed the pills in his hand then tossed them in his mouth, washed them down with the lemonade.

"Pills for everything now," Tina said.

Outside through the window Richard caught a glimpse of a deer as it casually made its way from the trees to the field. He pointed. "Look there," he said. "There's a deer right there walking across the grass."

Stephen shot up and his chair fell back to the floor.

"It's just a deer," John said.

"He likes them," said Richard.

Stephen scrambled to the window, then opened the back door and went outside. The deer froze in place as Stephen tiptoed from the porch to the grass. He stopped and looked back at the house, gave a smile, and the animal leapt away back into the trees.

"That's tough," John said.

"He almost had him."

"No. I mean, having a brother like that."

Stephen jumped back onto the porch.

"It's not tough," Richard said. "Not really."

"But sometimes it must be," said John. He put his finger up to his head and whirled it around. "You know?" he said, and he laughed. Stephen appeared in the door at this very moment, looked down at his brother. Richard felt the drop in his chest, wanted to shove John into the counter and push one of the plates into his face. But he only sat there, moved his glass across the table.

"I scared him," Stephen said, simply.

"Yeah," said Richard. "You got too close."

His brother stood in the doorway, let the screen close behind him.

"He was right there," Stephen said. "I could see his eyes."

"Yes you could," said Richard. "He was right there."

THEY HIKED around the area, checked out the various trails that had cropped up since they were children. A fruit stand had opened in its ramshackle building, they drank grape juice from cold glass bottles as they sat on the front bench outside and watched the cars pass. They saw a few rabbits, a woodchuck too. All in all, it was a nice afternoon, strolling beneath the trees, the soft breeze in their faces and the birds and frogs making their noise.

They'd left Tina and the son shortly after lunch, gathered their things and walked out across the field, past the property and onto the interstate road. "We'll come back in the evening," Richard had said. "Sit on the porch for maybe an hour and then we'll leave, easy as that."

"But dinner?" said Tina.

"No thanks," Richard said. "We'll be fine."

And they *were* fine, had picked up some apples and oranges at the stand, a loaf of bread. They brought the food along with them and ate it as they walked, ambled up the trail back to the house as darkness came on. When they finally cleared the brush there it was—the house bright and magnificent on its hill. "Come on," Richard said, and he moved ahead. They walked through the tall grass and onto the field, past the bowling ball and truck on the lawn.

Stephen peered under the truck's hood and laughed. "I can see the grass underneath." He trotted over to the bowling ball, bent over and picked it up with his good arm. "Bowling for dollars," he said, and he took several steps and lobbed the ball.

From the porch John watched them, came down and headed across the field with his hands in his pockets. "Glad to see you're making use of the playthings scattered about." He pointed to the truck. "It's my dad's," he said, kicking a clump of dirt past them. "He's here now."

Richard cast a glance up the hill, then at John.

"You're probably wondering about the bowling ball." John shrugged. "We found it there one morning. My mother calls it her good luck charm so here it stays." He walked around the truck, then to Stephen. "Look," he said. "I'm sorry if I hurt your feelings."

Stephen shook his head. "That's all right."

"My mother really tore me a new asshole for doing that."

"Really, it's okay."

John turned his eyes up to the sky and its first stars. "Well," he said. "It's getting dark."

They headed back to the house together. Tina came out to the porch as soon as they sat down on the chairs, stood behind them with the light pouring through the window. "John's fa-

ther is still finishing his dinner," she said, her figure the silhou-
ette. "I can get you something if you'd like. You're sure you
don't want anything?"

Stephen raised his casted arm. "We're fine."

The sun had gone down behind the mountains and the
moon was coming up, the birds chattered their last songs of the
day. "I suppose we can leave them here for now," Tina said, and
the screen door opened. It was the father. "How do you do?"
he said, putting out his hand. "So you used to live here?" he
asked, and Richard explained that it had been his grandmother
who'd lived here, that they used to come to the house as children during the summer.

The father looked the brothers over, then past them at the
field. "It's a beautiful evening," he said. He gestured to the
clouds passing over the mountains, their pinkness and orange.
He still wore his shirt from work, short-sleeved with buttons,
his shiny belt pulled tight. The father had a stately quality, his
cheekbones high and white hair combed neatly to the side. His
wedding band gleamed when he pointed to Stephen, asked,
"What's with the cast?"

Stephen held up his arm. "I fell from a roof."

"Uh huh," he said, one eyebrow rising. "So let me guess.
You must be the crazy one."

"*Edmond,*" said his wife, but it was too late, Stephen was
standing. When he looked at Richard it tore at his heart, these
same eyes like waking from the nightmare while they were
driving but even worse, this time clear without the sleepiness

and filled with boundless hurt. Stephen jumped from the porch, trampled onto the field.

"See here," the father said. "I didn't mean to hurt the boy."

"Of course not," said Richard, and he stood to face the family. *His brother,* he could have told them. His brother who'd looked at the world and seen how terrible it could be, stared into its very center and come back with the sadness of this knowledge. His brother, a man and not a boy, the very reason they were here and had come all this way.

He leapt down onto the grass. The fireflies were coming out now, their lights flashing then disappearing in an instant. Stephen marched ahead, his figure only a shadow. Back on the porch Tina stood with Edmond, John behind them. Here is where his grandmother would stand all those years ago with their mother and father, Elaine too. He remembered how as a boy he'd gaze at the house in this dark and pretend it was the earth below. *We're astronauts,* he'd tell Stephen as he wandered nearby. *We're astronauts just floating and floating.*

Richard tried to make Stephen out through squinted eyes, quickened his pace. A firefly zipped by, then another, when he tripped over the bowling ball and tumbled onto the grass. And there was his brother standing right before him, staring down and smiling. He pointed. "See there," he said, and the fireflies were suddenly everywhere. Richard got to his feet and Stephen took him under his arm. They walked across the field, the points of light like the stars in the darkness all around them.

Make Them Laugh

Father Harry had a car full of priests when he slammed into the California Highway Patrol car. He lost his tooth and parish in one fell swoop, kept the tooth in a jar to remind him what drinking seven glasses of whiskey could do. Every time he felt the urge to drink he picked up the jar and shook it, tinkling it like a tiny Communion bell.

He'd had it good. The lone priest to a well-moneyed congregation. A cook. His own car and big-screen television. Now he was low priest on the totem pole in the most financially destitute parish in Sacramento. He shared his car with two other priests. There was a tiny black-and-white television they huddled around like hoboes to a fire. They could only use the heaters in the evening. They had a *chore list*.

Father Glenn was a young priest who made it his job to shake everyone's hand while wishing them a good morning and good night. His hands were thin and cold, with two blue veins that reminded Father Harry of shoelaces. He started each day with a run around the neighborhood, a courageous act considering the poverty and crime in the area. But the man seemed oblivious. "If something happens," he'd say, "it happens."

"It will," Father Harry would tell him in a tone so ominous he'd have to laugh after saying it. Father Glenn laughed too, explained that being negative about things never got anyone anywhere. Like these were words of wisdom, Father Harry thought while agreeing.

Father Arthur, the other priest, was an older man with wild white hair who always looked as though he'd just woken up. "Please now," he began each sentence. "Please now let's hope for a good day. Please now I'm ready for dinner."

Harry didn't know how they could ever live this way, with nothing but the bare essentials. He was a spoiled creature, he was sure. This was the very reason he'd come to this regrettable point.

In his first sermon to the congregation, Father Harry talked about the importance of getting back on one's feet, how Jesus taught others even while hanging on the cross. He stared out into the faces of the parishioners, the fidgeting children and tragic widows. Father Arthur nervously ran his hands through his hair. It occurred to Harry that the other priests thought of him as a loose cannon. And why not? He'd been arrested, put on parole. What other priest could make such a claim? An elderly woman dozed in the side pew. He wondered whether it might be an appropriate moment to bring up his great crime, the subsequent punishments he'd endured. Perhaps the purpose of all this was to let people know that even priests could take wrong turns, make occasional mistakes. Jesus had lost his temper, Father Harry had had a few too many and almost killed three priests and a police officer. He cleared his throat, adjusted the microphone. "I've got a tooth I keep in a jar," he began.

THE BISHOP called Father Harry that night. "What's this about hanging your dirty laundry in the church?" he said.

This was ridiculous. Most everyone knew anyway. "I only wanted to make them see the power of realizing one's sins, of a humble heart," Harry said. He tried to remember the parishioners' faces during the sermon, whether or not anyone had seemed offended. There had been some tittering, but he assumed it had to do with the old woman in the far pew waking with a start, standing for a good minute before sitting again.

"An admirable effort," the bishop said. "But the problem is specifics. You needn't have mentioned the actual act that provoked such regret and penance." The bishop sighed. Father Harry figured he was praying to Jesus for patience at this very moment.

"I'm in an awkward position," he continued, "because I believe what you're doing is a step, a *step,* in the right direction."

He was a compassionate man, this bishop. Harry wondered how he'd come to be so peaceful and wise, if he'd ever kicked at his car or passed by the homeless person muttering under his breath.

"But it's not good for the parish I'm afraid," the bishop concluded.

"I only wanted them to feel comfortable with me," Harry said. "You know. Somebody from the kind of church that I came from."

"Of course. But there are less, well, revealing methods." The bishop paused. "Maybe it'd be a good idea if you didn't say mass for a little while. Serve Communion. Listen to confessions. But just stay away from the pulpit for a spell."

"Yes, Bishop." But what was a spell? A month? A year? Harry wanted to snap the telephone in two. Why was he being punished for trying to be truthful?

"Let's talk in a few weeks. Is that all right with you, Harry? A few weeks then?"

Harry hung up the telephone, pulled the keys from Father Arthur's sweater pocket and walked across the street to the church. He opened the big black doors that groaned and squeaked. His footsteps echoed as he made his way to the altar, the church was dark and he had to feel his way up to the podium. He stationed himself directly behind the pulpit, gripped its sides like the very steering wheel of the car he'd driven that infamous night.

When he was a child, he went to mass with his mother and father and felt the goodness of God course through him. He'd felt such goodness on the day he decided to become a priest, as if he could simply touch people and make them pulse with this boundless love. When he was seventeen, he'd taken his mother's hand over Sunday dinner. "Your son has heard the calling," he'd said. What had happened to this feeling? All he could do now was imagine the moment, and he remembered his mother squeezing his hand and asking again and again if he was sure. He pictured himself in church between his parents, his head bowed in ecstatic prayer. But now he felt removed from his own belief, his passion, as though it had only existed in a dream.

"Stupid me," Harry said, and the sound of his voice bouncing off the walls gave him a start. He said it again, and the words circled around him. Everything became very quiet and he listened for something besides his own breathing. A sign, perhaps. Where should he go from here?

Nothing.

What else needed to happen before he could truly feel retribution had run its course? His mother used to say that for every bad thing we did, a broken nail was waiting to happen. Everything had a reason in her book, she was a true believer in karma before most Americans even knew the word. The bishop could use some karma just about now—maybe a fall in the bathtub, or a stubbed toe before bedtime.

On the mantel in the common room was a picture of Jesus sitting on a rock surrounded by laughing children. Suffer the children, Father Harry thought. If they'd only known the fate that awaited this pleasant man. Did Jesus ever tell the story about losing his temper in the temple? And if he did, would an apostle pull him aside and tell him to stop? These adoring children, at least Jesus had these children. Father Harry made a fist.

All he had was a goddamned tattletale priest and an angry bishop. What did he have to offer? What did he *have*?

He slammed his fist into the podium. There was a crack and then the terrible pinpricks of pain before the darkness passing into white. *Heaven is my sign.* He could see the very words, hear them moving around him. *Heaven is my sign.* It was music.

TWO FINGERS were broken. He wasn't sure how he'd done it, must have caught the corner of the podium and passed out from the pain. Lucky for Harry that Father Glenn had decided to check things in the church before turning in. He'd found Harry on the floor of the altar, out like an island, as he'd put it, splashed some water—*unblessed if anyone asks,* he'd said on the way over—and Harry came to. Next thing he knew they were on their way to the hospital, his fingers all swollen and blue.

Father Glenn sat opposite him as the doctor bandaged the splint to his fingers. A little harder and he could have done some really serious damage, the doctor said. Father Harry nodded but had to ask himself what would have been more serious. Shattered knuckles?

"Live and learn," said Glenn, more for the doctor than Harry. He was playing priest, showing their shared acceptance of such misfortune. Harry wanted to give him a kick in the shin, hear him say that this was, perhaps, one of those things that served no purpose at all. That maybe he'd broken his fingers just because, and that was all there was to it.

"Keep still," the doctor said.

Father Glenn rubbed his hands together. "No piano for a while."

"You play piano?" the doctor said. He seemed to be genuinely pleased with such a revelation.

"It's a joke," Father Harry said. "I think."

The doctor turned to Father Glenn.

"I meant it to be funny." Glenn shifted in his seat. Father Harry liked seeing the young priest so uncomfortable. But then, he *was* young—his compassion still called attention to itself, unlike the bishop's. Harry wondered if the bishop had once been this awkward, if he'd ever made bad jokes and said the wrong things.

The doctor turned back to Father Harry. "I once had a patient who was a young pianist—twelve, maybe thirteen. He smashed his fingers on purpose. Can you imagine that?" The doctor held Harry's fingers in his hand, gently turned them. "His mother was doing all the crying. Had to send her out so I could look at the boy."

Father Glenn clucked his tongue.

"The boy hated the piano. Couldn't stand it. It was only after his mother left the room that he let himself cry and tell me these things." The doctor gently placed the hand on Father Harry's lap. The fingers pulsed. Sleeping would be difficult tonight. His dreams, if any, would be ominous—the dreams of the sick and drugged.

"I didn't know what to say," the doctor continued. "You guys though." He glanced at Glenn, then back to Harry. "You probably deal with that sort of thing every day."

Harry lifted his hand, felt the pain course through his fingers. "That'll hurt awhile," said the doctor. "I'll give you something for the pain before you go."

Father Glenn stood. "The boy was okay?"

"Huh?" The doctor had already forgotten. So many faces, so much pain. Harry wondered if he could even remember the boy's face, if it hadn't become some amalgam of different boys he'd seen over the years. It was probably much the same as with the faces of the dying. They all blurred together, fearful and exhausted.

"The boy is fine. I heard he plays guitar for one of these MTV bands. A star, if you can believe that." He gave Glenn a slap on the back, and Harry considered the fact that the doctor was a good soul. He was simply doing with Father Glenn what Father Harry had tried to do with the parish—make him see that he was okay, that they were in this mess together, human beings, mistakes and all. Harry wondered if he'd ever had some chief doctor tell him to cool it with the stories, that the real business was to cure and save. *Leave the stories for the writers,* he imagined the chief doctor saying.

"I'll get you some Tylenol and a little something to help you sleep." The doctor left the room and Glenn leaned over Harry on the examination table. "Looks better," he said.

"It still hurts."

"It probably will for a while at least." Glenn stepped back and crossed his arms. "I can't help wondering. What were you thinking?"

Here was the inevitable question that anyone with any

sense of tact would have saved for the morning. But here it was, the young priest with stars in his eyes asking like he had every right to know.

"I'd rather not talk about it right now."

"Of course." Father Glenn touched a hand to the back of his neck, as if mulling over a most difficult subject. "I know these past couple of months haven't been easy for you."

Father Harry could have knocked his block off. How could he know anything? All this priest had ever known besides cold seminary oatmeal was the life he now had. He had nothing to compare it to. How could he explain that he missed goose-down pillows, a VCR, real butter—the things no priest ever had a right to miss?

"I don't want to cross your boundaries," Father Glenn continued.

Boundaries?

"Just know that we're all here for you."

The doctor returned to the room with slips of paper. "Take these to the pharmacy." He handed the paper and a container to Father Glenn. "Tylenol for now, until the harder stuff comes." Glenn opened the container and placed two pills in Harry's good hand.

"Better make it three," the doctor said.

FATHER ARTHUR was sitting up close to the television when they returned. "Please now let's see what you've got," he said as they shut the door behind them.

Father Harry held out his hand.

"Dear God."

"Two fingers broken," Father Harry said. "God had nothing to do with it."

Father Arthur peered at the hand. "It hurts?"

"Extremely."

"The painkillers should help," Glenn said. He tugged at Harry's jacket. Harry held still while the priests pulled the jacket off, as if removing a robe from a leper.

HE SLEPT THICKLY, the sleep of drugs. There was piano music. The boy with the broken fingers sat at the piano, his hands wrapped in bandages, watching the piano keys move. Harry sat at the bench next to the boy and they watched the piano keys together. The music swirled and a girl he recognized from grade school hovered above them. It was Trena, the girl with the wonderful red and curly hair. Trena—when had he last seen her? Thought of her even? "Harry," she said, floating down and planting a kiss on his lips, marvelous and warm and filling him with joy. She floated back into the darkness, taking the boy with her. Harry stood on the bench, reached up. "Rain," came Trena's voice from all around. He waved his arms and the rain began to fall in tiny drops against his fingers. The music continued with the rain, becoming the very dream itself.

WHEN HE WOKE he realized it wasn't rain, but pain prickling his fingers. The sun shone against his face, and when he sat up the bed squeaked in a cacophony. He held his hand over his eyes and his fingers throbbed when he heard the rap on the door. "Everything all right?" It was Father Arthur.

Harry lay perfectly still and let the pain pass. "I'm okay."

The door cracked open and Father Arthur peeked in. "We were worried about you." He pointed to his watch. "It's lunchtime."

"Lunch?" How could this be? He'd only just lain down.

"We tried waking you but you didn't make a noise. Father Glenn checked on you this morning and you were soundly sleeping."

"How did it get so late?"

Father Arthur smiled, pleased with Harry's confusion. "Father Glenn said you looked like a child. Peaceful. Like a baby."

"It's the drugs." Harry kicked his legs over the edge of the bed and groaned. "I was out all night."

Father Arthur lingered in the doorway. "Is there anything more?"

What did he want? A rap on the head? Yes Harry knew he'd told the bishop. Yes he was angry and hurt by it all. But Father Arthur was an old man, it was to be expected. Father Glenn probably scared Father Arthur enough with his plan to save the world in twelve easy steps, starting with giving everyone the salute as he ran through the neighborhood. The priest with the police record probably scared the life out of Father Arthur. "Water under the bridge," Harry said, giving Father Arthur a wave with the splinted hand.

■

IN THE WEEK that followed, Father Harry regained slight use of his hand. He could put on his pants, eat and drink without spilling more than a drop or two onto his shirt. He'd been given light tasks around the rectory—dusting tabletops and watering the front lawn. Father Glenn seemed positively chipper, Harry's broken fingers giving him the permission to display his missionary tendencies. He set down a pillow at the table for the hand during mealtimes, told Harry to get plenty of liquids and rest. "Why don't you get me a wheelchair while you're at it," Harry said. And my own television. And garbage disposal. Not to mention a bed with springs.

TUESDAY MORNING while he was out watering the lawn, a girl holding a baby walked up to him. She wore sandals that slid and slapped the cement. "You're the priest," she said.

Harry nodded, adjusted his thumb over the hose end.

The girl wore a T-shirt that said *No Shit Sherlock,* she held the baby so close to her breast that Father Harry wondered if it were able to breathe. "I heard your sermon," she said. She laughed and her breasts jiggled into the baby's face. The baby stretched and began to cry.

"Shhh, baby." The girl suddenly became gentle, as if this were the way she was, really.

He set the hose down, the girl stared up from the baby. "You got a way with words."

Father Harry felt a surge of delight. The sermon had provided solace, served a purpose after all.

"I mean it." She smiled and drew a pacifier from her front pocket, put it in her mouth then circled it over the baby. "Buzz buzz, here comes the bee." The baby opened its mouth and laughed. She plopped the pacifier in.

"You know," she said. "You're a funny guy."

Harry felt the water soaking through his shoes. "Funny?"

"Yeah." The girl rocked the baby. "I especially liked the part about the tooth. Just thinking about it makes me laugh."

This was too much. He had the urge to pick up the hose and spray the girl in the face. "*There's* funny," he'd say. But he thought better of it, with the baby half-asleep rocking in her mother's arms like that. "I'm glad I made you laugh," he said. He bent for the hose. "I need to get back to my job."

"What happened to your fingers?"

"Nothing." He splayed the fingers and felt a tingle. "I'm going to put them in the jar with the tooth."

The girl laughed as Father Glenn ambled up, whistling and tossing his keys from hand to hand. "You're good," she told Harry. She looked down at her baby. "Hear that? He's going to put his fingers in a jar." The baby let out a whimper and she positioned it so that it could see Harry. "His fingers and a tooth," she said, and she let out a laugh, headed away down the sidewalk.

Glenn stuffed the keys in his pocket. "What was that all about?" He watched the girl with a squint.

"A fan," said Father Harry.

■

COMMUNION was out of the question since Harry needed his fingers to reach into the chalice for wafers. This left him with the task of hearing confession, a job Father Arthur and Father Glenn were only too happy to defer. Wednesday was confession night. He finished his dinner while Glenn explained to Father Arthur the virtue of pain. Glenn had gotten started on the idea after seeing Harry wince as he reached for the mashed potatoes.

"Courage," he'd said. "Soon this discomfort will pass."

"I'm not *dying*," said Harry.

Glenn got up from the table and went to the sink. "Imagine it," he said, and Father Arthur stood and handed Glenn his plate. "Never hurting at all. How empty life would seem." He was so young and glib in his righteousness. Harry wanted to shake his fingers in Glenn's face and say he'd take emptiness any day over this.

They began washing their plates and Harry realized he'd broken up a routine between these two, created a minor calamity just by being there. He figured the bishop had telephoned and briefed them on the situation, described Father Harry as a man simply in need of a lesson about humility. These two priests were probably groomed for such situations, indeed they were happy in their poverty. He remembered a sermon Father Glenn had given the day Harry arrived. It started with the thrill of putting on a freshly washed shirt and ended with the goodness of forgiving others for their sins. Harry wanted to scoff at the corniness, but found himself drawn in. There was a powerful charm to Father Glenn's similes—what would have been seen in his parish as laughably naive worked here. He found himself nodding along by sermon's end.

Glenn gave his plate to Father Arthur for drying. Harry wiped his mouth and stood. "I should head on over," he said. "Sins to absolve and all that."

Father Arthur and Father Glenn exchanged glances—it was like walking on glass around these two. "There might be a few upset parishioners," Glenn said. "Life is not exactly kind to many." He dried his hands on his pants. "You don't have to use the booth," he added.

"What's that?"

"The booth. You don't have to use it."

Harry leaned into the table and it groaned. Not use the booth? People had secrets, and secrets came out best in a dark place. He imagined Father Glenn sitting in a room, legs crossed, watching someone press a tissue to their eyes. The insensitivity of it made him shudder.

"I'd prefer the booth actually," Harry said.

Father Glenn crossed his arms. "You sure? We haven't used the booths in a while."

"I'd rather use the booth. I really would."

Glenn peered back at Father Arthur, who was pushing his towel in a circle onto the plate. "Maybe in the future. I think it's much more constructive to sit together as two human beings, as equals." He put his hand on Harry's shoulder, still warm and damp. "Consider it."

"I need the keys," Harry said.

71

∎

THE CONFESSION BOOTH was dusty. He could feel the dust on the tip of his splinted fingers as if it were ash. But this was better than the light. It was easier on both of them—confessor and hearer—keeping things from getting too uncomfortable and messy. The sermon had been just that. He'd thrown out his misfortunes only to have them come back at him in whatever way they would. From now on he'd play it careful and measured. No more laughing girls or angry bishops.

The door opened and there were footsteps. A nearby pew creaked. Father Harry waited a few minutes before peeking through the curtain and checking the green light above to make sure it was working. A man in a blue windbreaker glimpsed over warily. *Come on if you're going to,* Harry thought. He held out his splinted hand in the darkness, thought back to the mother circling the pacifier down to her baby.

The pew creaked some more. "Excuse me," came a voice through the curtain. "Are you hearing confession?"

"I am," Harry said.

"Because usually the other priest hears us in the back pew."

"I'm doing it this way." Father Harry leaned into the walls of the booth, felt the dust against the back of his neck. "If you like the way Father Glenn does it, I can get Father Glenn."

"No," the man said. "Your way is fine." He entered the booth and sneezed. "It's all dusty in here." He sneezed again.

"Sorry," said Harry.

The man laughed. "I'm the one who should be saying that."

Harry nodded, wondered if maybe the face-to-face confession wasn't such a bad idea when all was said and done. It's what they were used to. He was shaking things up, just like at the dinner table. He moved toward the screen, slid it open.

"This is kind of scary," the man said.

"I don't mean it to be."

"When I was a kid we'd draw straws to see who went first."

"Do you want me to call Father Glenn?"

"No. I'm only saying." The man coughed. "Jeez it's dusty in here."

Harry put his mouth to the screen. "Whenever you're ready."

"I was born ready."

These parishioners could be so crass. At his old church, the people would come into his booth and confess their sins in the most somber manner—there was a certain dignity to the proceedings, the conventions were always clear. Here, the people cracked jokes and made small talk as if they were coming in for a haircut.

"Begin," Father Harry said.

The man shifted and put his face close to the screen. "I don't know exactly how," he said.

"How to begin?"

"I've forgotten what I say, actually. The damnedest thing. Like when I was a kid. Just sitting in the dark my mind would go blank." He sneezed again, and Harry could feel the phlegm catch in the screen.

"Should I help you along?" Father Harry asked.

"Nah, give me a minute." The man blew his nose, presumably on the sleeve of his windbreaker. "I come here every two weeks. Do the same things each time. You'd think I learn but I don't. I drive Father what's-his-name crazy."

Harry imagined Father Glenn telling the man to say a rosary and do his very best not to repeat his sins. Count to ten backwards, he'd say. Get a puppy. He found himself liking this man for contradicting Glenn's idea that sin was like some grass stain, easily washed out.

"I want you to know I hate making the same mistakes," said the man.

"We're human," Father Harry said.

The man cleared his throat. "I heard your talk."

Father Harry braced himself for the part about the tooth in the jar, how much it made him laugh.

"It must have been tough," said the man.

"It was," Father Harry said, not sure if he was referring to the sermon or actually hitting a police car and being moved to the parish from hell. He thought of Trena from grade school, kissing her on the cheek and running with what could only be described as joy, through the rain. When he took his vows he'd had this same feeling. He'd considered it to be much like one's wedding day, when purpose and direction were so clear you could hear them ring.

"Bless me Father, for I have sinned," the man said. He laughed. "Funny how you remember. Just like riding a horse."

"A bicycle," Father Harry said. "You get back on a horse. You don't forget how to ride a bicycle."

The man laughed again, proceeded with the confession. There were the usual sins—lying to the wife, taking the Lord's name in vain. Then came something new. "My kids," he said. "I go over to their house and stick things down their drain."

"Go on."

"I visit my daughter on Thursdays and my son on Sundays. They hate it when I'm there, try to act like they're the busiest people anywhere." Father Harry could make out the moving hands through the screen. The man was describing this as if it were the most logical thing in the world. "So I plug up their plumbing."

"I presume this is ongoing," Father Harry said.

"'You bet it's ongoing. My kids treat me like crap I'm going to give it right back to them." He paused. "Not literally. I bring supplies. Balloons, newspapers. You'd be surprised what a mess it can make."

Harry tried to imagine what Father Glenn would say to this, pictured the priest nodding compassionately and suggesting talking it out. But this was exactly the sort of thing that couldn't be discussed—it didn't make sense to even try. Harry leaned toward the screen, remembered the phlegm before he drew back again. "Say a rosary and three Hail Marys."

"That's it?" the man said.

"That's it."

"I only thought there might be a little more."

"Pray," Father Harry said. "That's all I can tell you to do. You tell me your sins, I tell you how they get absolved." He could see the man bowing his head, as if already deep in prayer.

The man left the booth and Father Harry sat quietly, listening as he creaked into the seat to begin his prayers. Imagine having kids you loved so much you'd do something like that. It was a mess was all he knew, like his driving into the police car in the drunken haze. When he came to after the crash the first thing he'd said before spitting out his tooth was, "Are you happy now?" When one of the priests from the backseat said, "Not really," Father Harry told him to shut the hell up, that he wasn't talking to him.

He remembered after kissing Trena, coming back from his run around the schoolyard to find her in tears. He'd been so full of happiness while running, sure that the kiss had been absolutely right. It was too much like the priesthood, so full of promise and confusion.

Harry stepped from the booth and walked over to the man. "I smashed my fingers and I don't know why," he said, sitting down. He stuck out his hand.

The man nodded.

"Sometimes things turn out differently from what we expect and we get angry," Harry continued. "But the truth is we can't expect anything. It's when we expect things that we get hurt."

There was a look of mild alarm on the man's face as he watched Harry slide away down the pew.

"Okay?" Harry said, but the man didn't answer.

Back in the booth, Harry wondered how long it would be until word got to the bishop that he was scaring the parishioners. He ran his hand along the velvet curtain. When was the last time he'd seen Trena? It was right around when he'd told his parents about his decision to become a priest. She'd been sitting at the bus stop with two other girls, her legs crossed under her pleated skirt. It was after school, she'd been wearing her uniform.

"Harry?" she'd said.

He'd stopped and caught his breath, not used to pretty girls calling his name.

"Harry Mackey." Trena stood. "My sweet prince."

He'd dropped his books then, bent to pick them up from the gutter as the other girls laughed. Trena helped him with the books, took his hand. "I won't bite," she'd said.

"I know," he'd said, gathering the books to his chest. Then he'd run home the entire way. Why had she scared him so? Later, he would recall this moment and feel his stomach tingle. The touch of her hand. What he wouldn't give to feel it now.

He'd become a priest from love of God, but there had been more. He'd been afraid to ever commit himself to anything that required him to share more than the common courtesies. He liked things clean and simple. Like the tooth. What you could see and learn from and make the most common assumptions about. Whatever could be explained.

The curtain rustled. "Father?" The man stuck his face through. "Thanks," he said. "I appreciated that."

Harry told him it was no problem and heard the door open, the footsteps. When he raised the curtain he saw Father Glenn coming up from behind. Glenn glanced from Father Harry to the man. "Hello Ted," he said.

The man turned. "Father," he said. "I was just thanking Father—"

"Harry," said Glenn.

"Father Harry for being so understanding. He's great all right."

"We like to think so."

The man backed away. "Well then. So long."

"So long," said Father Harry.

"I thought you didn't like the idea of face-to-face," Glenn said. He raised the curtain, let in the light. "Sweet God. You look like a coal miner."

"It's only dust."

"Dust."

The church echoed as the doors closed. "That Ted," said Father Glenn. He pulled the curtain higher. "I hope you gave him a few good prayers to say."

"A rosary and three Hail Marys."

"Just one rosary?" Father Glenn shook his head, stared up at the ceiling.

Leave, Father Harry thought.

"Tell you what," said Father Glenn. "Why don't you call it a night and wash up?" He stepped back from the booth, pulled the curtain out. "Ted's the only one who usually comes on Wednesdays anyway."

"I think I should wait a little while."

"There's no point," Glenn said. "If you could only see yourself." He forced a laugh. "Coal Miner's Father."

The door from the rear of the church made its squeak and

groan. Father Glenn looked back, a smile frozen on his lips. Harry leaned out of the booth, saw the old woman, bent and gray, as the door closed behind her. She shuffled up the aisle, holding on to each pew for support.

Father Glenn let the curtain fall. "I'll light the candles."

The woman groaned as she made her way into the booth. "I'm old," she said as she situated herself on the kneepad. "Forgive me"

"Take your time."

"It's just that everything hurts."

"I understand," Father Harry said.

THE FOLLOWING SATURDAY there were people waiting outside the church when Harry came to open up. Each person wanted confession in the booth that he'd made it a point to thoroughly dust on Thursday morning. Some people wanted to hear about getting right back on the horse. A few wanted to hear about the tooth or fingers. Others just said their confessions and were on their way. The church was half full by late afternoon, according to one parishioner unlike any confession hour she'd ever seen.

"You've got quite a following," Father Glenn said when Harry returned to the rectory with a pink box of doughnuts. One of the parishioners had given it to him, told him *sweet pastries for a sweet man,* as she walked out from the confession booth and slipped the box through the curtain.

"Care for any?" he asked, opening the box.

"A charismatic," Father Arthur said.

"They like me," said Harry.

"They like you?" Glenn stared at Father Arthur, then back at Harry. "They *like* you? Well, thank you Sally Field."

"Is there a problem?"

"You bet there's a problem. These people think you're their friend. You can't be their friend. You're a priest."

This was more ridiculous than the bishop's telephone call.

"These people are seeking comfort and I'm giving it to them," Harry said, closing the box.

"Comfort?" Glenn threw up his arms and slumped against the fireplace mantel.

Father Arthur ran his hands through his wild hair. "I think we can iron this out. Please now we're rational human beings."

Harry shoved the doughnut box into Father Arthur's chest. "Take them," he said.

"Thank you, but no."

Glenn picked up the picture of Jesus from the mantel. "We're here to do our jobs," he said to the picture. "You can't expect to become one of them and do your job too."

Father Arthur set the box onto the nearby table. "There are lines."

"*Screw* the lines," Father Harry said. He went out to the back porch, slammed the door shut behind him. Beside the porch was the hose. He unrolled it, turned on the water as high as it would go. His broken fingers tingled, the water covered his face in a cool mist. He closed his eyes and let the water run over his head, into his mouth. It was fresh and clean and made his throat ache with its coldness.

"Hey there, funny man." It was the girl with the baby. But today she was alone. Her hair was tied back in a tight ponytail and she looked even younger than the last time he'd seen her. She wore a purple jersey with a tear in one of the elbows, dark blue jeans. "The cute one with the crazy hair said you were trouble."

Father Harry laughed. "I'm trouble now."

"Nothing wrong with that."

"There is when you're a priest."

She crossed her arms. "You're wet."

"You're observant."

The girl laughed. "Like I said. Funny."

Harry turned off the water and reached with his good hand for a handkerchief from his back pocket. It took some effort. "These damned fingers," he said, eventually pulling the hand-kerchief out. He gingerly touched the fingers, felt the pain shoot up his arm.

The girl held out her hand. "Let me see."

"There's not much *to* see." He ran the handkerchief over his face, stuffed it into his front pocket.

"Come on."

Harry gave her his hand and the blinds moved from the back window. Father Glenn and Father Arthur were watching. He might as well begin packing now.

"Say," he said to the girl. "How old are you?"

"Sixteen. But my grandma says I'm as wise as the trees."
The girl looked up, and Harry could see that her eyes were
puffy from crying. "I like to tell her you can know too much."

"And what do you know?" Father Harry let her run her
child fingers along his palm, feel the groove of his lifeline.

"I know that life's cheap," she said. "That we get hurt."

Harry gently took back his hand. "You know a lot," he said.

"Sometimes it's not the best thing *to* know." The girl produced a pack of cigarettes from her pocket, offered Harry one
and he waved it away. "My name's Katrine," she said, putting
the cigarette to her mouth and lighting it.

"Father Harry."

"I know that," the girl said, blowing out a lungful of blue
smoke.

Harry thought of the pacifier, the baby staring up at her
mother as though she were the sky itself. "Where's your baby?"

"Augustine?" Katrine took a pull from her cigarette. "With
my mom. A girl needs a break, you know?"

Father Harry nodded. "Tell me what's happened," he said.

"I'm all mixed up." Katrine flicked the ashes from her cigarette onto the sidewalk like a smoker who'd been at it for years.

"The baby's father, Spencer," she said. "He's an asshole if you
want to know the truth. They caught him over at Parkside Liquor
with a bottle of scotch under his jacket. Who knows how long
they'll keep him this time?" Her face crumpled and she let the
tears come. "Goddamn I hate him so much." After a minute she
stopped crying and wiped her eyes with the back of her hand. "I
came to ask a favor," she said. "Not to blubber like some kid."

But she *was* a kid, Harry told himself. He regarded her torn jersey, the cigarette in her hand. "What can I do?" he asked.

"Well," she said, and she looked past Harry to the rectory, wiped her eyes some more and sniffed her nose. She shifted from one foot to the other, stepped from the sidewalk onto the lawn. "The tooth," she told him, flicking the cigarette away. "I came to see the tooth."

THE OTHER PRIESTS tried to look busy, adjusting the pillows and moving the pictures along the mantel. Harry grabbed the tooth from the dresser drawer and made his way back out. Father Arthur gave a snort, peeking up as he fluffed a pillow, his lips red from a jelly doughnut. Father Glenn held the same picture of Jesus with the children, wiped its frame with a towel.

"Here it is," said Harry, coming out from the rectory and handing the jar to Katrine. This was absurd. No wonder people had laughed. Here was this stranger in the white collar, telling them the story of the tooth in the jar as if his life were a Bing Crosby singing–priest movie. "Go on and shake it," he said.

She held the jar up to the sky. "Augustine," she said. She shook the tooth. "Spencer." She began to laugh, and Harry began to laugh too. His eyelashes dripped water, cool against his cheek. He remembered his dream of the bandaged boy and the piano, the rain coming down and how he'd just stood and listened, reaching toward the very sweetest music he'd ever heard.

Sudden Mysteries

When Peter woke up Margaret was talking in the next room. The television blared down the hall, its music and laughter rose above her words. "Everything," he heard her say. Then, "They're right here." He pulled the pillow against his chest, stared at the cracks and lines in the ceiling. *A bad dream,* he thought. *That's all this was was a bad dream.* The television went quiet, there were footsteps and the bedroom door opening. Margaret stood there. "You're up," she said, and she came to the bed, sat down beside him. She wore a brown robe tied loosely at the waist, her breasts revealed themselves as she leaned over. "Sorry to have left you like that. Dumb business to tend to."

"It's fine," said Peter.

"You were sleeping pretty heavy."

"I guess I was tired."

She moved the pillow from his chest, placed her hand on his stomach. From the window Peter could see the late afternoon sun orange in the sky, the few clouds making their way across the horizon. Birds sang from nearby trees, their last songs of the day before heading away home.

Peter sat up. "I should go."

"Do you think that's a good idea?"

He got out of the bed, reached for his pants.

"Okay then," said Margaret. "But take these, at least." She stood and opened the dresser drawer, produced a pair of socks. They were brown and woolen, patterned along the heel. Peter imagined her picking out these socks for the husband, his stuffing them into the drawer and never wearing them at all. She'd described him this way, floating through his misdeeds, oblivious. She held out the socks and Peter raised his hand.

"I thought they'd help," she said.

"No thanks."

"These are as nice socks as you'll find."

"Really," Peter said. "I'll be okay."

Margaret let the socks fall back into the drawer, tightened the belt around her robe. "So you'll probably want to call the tow truck."

They walked out into the hallway, past the pictures on the wall above the piano, past the boy watching the television, the coatrack and all the coats and sweaters. Peter went to the telephone and dialed the number, Margaret handed him the piece of paper with her address. "I'll be changing," she told him, as the operator came on the line. He smoothed the piece of paper onto the wall, Margaret headed to the bedroom and picked up her pants and T-shirt from the floor.

IT WAS THE DAY before his wedding, so much to do and none of the time to do it. He'd gotten the haircut and stopped at the photographer's to make the payment, taken care of the business with the priest. On the way from the rectory, he'd dropped by his father's house, it being just the block away. "Dad," he said, as he came up from his car, and his father looked at him from the screen door as if he'd just heard the funniest joke in the world.

"The newlywed," he said.

"Not yet," said Peter.

They stood out on the porch, his father leaning into the post and asking him if he was ready to take the dive. "I mean this is it," he said. "No one else but you and your beloved, until death do you part, the real deal." He turned to face Peter. "You're absolutely sure?" he said.

Peter explained that he *was* absolutely sure, as he'd explained that he was absolutely sure so often. Ever since he'd announced his plans to marry Hannah, his father had razzed him. It was as if he'd wanted to undo any happiness his son might know, sabotage this marriage and all the good things it might bring.

His father pointed out the birds pulling the worms from the lawn, ignoring everything Peter had just told him. "They make some noise in the mornings with their chatter," he said, and Peter told him that's what birds did, they were birds after all, and they liked worms.

"Like the saying," he said.

"Oh yeah?" said his father, and he snatched a penny from his pocket, threw it onto the lawn. The birds scattered into the tree, he held up a dime and made his smile so that his gums showed all around his teeth, the fatty pinkness of them. Then he tossed the dime into the branches and the birds flew away toward the sky.

"Go on and get married then," he said.

PETER had been with many women before Hannah, almost too many to count. Rebecca when he was a freshman in high school, who'd invited him up to her roof where they could look over the houses and see the river. Lucinda not much later, who wore the Guatemalan skirts that folded above her knees and the ankle bracelet that jingled as she walked. The college years, girls from his dormitory and sometimes from other dormitories too. Adrianna, Shawn, Natalie, each face now a blur. And then later while teaching as an adjunct with a few of his students, even though he knew it was the most wrong thing he could do. These girls, who would come up to him after class wanting to hear more, as they had come up to him wanting to hear more since he'd begun his teaching. And he would tell them more all right, quote the Shakespeare from memory, watch as their eyes went soft and trusting.

He'd met Hannah in the supermarket. She'd dropped the eggplant onto the floor and it had rolled to his feet as she'd laughed. And it was her laugh, that was the first thing he'd noticed about her. Her laugh, deep and breathless, touching something deep inside him he didn't recognize. He'd picked up the eggplant, regarded her hair so curly and brown, the eyes that registered their humor. The first date she'd come over to his apartment after the coffee and he'd shown her the pictures of his family. His mother when she was young and beautiful holding him as a baby on the lawn. "She's gone now," he'd said, and he'd told her about the houseboat she'd bought from the alimony, how she hadn't come home since she'd left his father so many years ago.

Then he'd taken out the picture of his father, in his suit and tie standing in front of his desk at work. "Here is an unhappy man," he'd said, and Hannah had glanced from the photograph to Peter. They'd gone through the pictures a while longer, she'd looked at her watch and gotten up to leave. "Where are you going?" he'd asked, and she'd told him it was late, she had work in the morning. "So do I," he'd exclaimed, and she'd said then it made even more sense for her to be leaving. And that had been that, she'd slipped past him to the door and Peter had watched her make her way down the block, the streetlights illuminating her.

PETER had made his call to the tow truck service as Margaret dressed. The telephone operator told him it would be no more than an hour, but that there had been the unusual number of calls so it might be two. "Which is it?" Peter had asked, and she'd said she couldn't say, there was no need for him to be gruff. "I'm not being gruff," Peter had told her, explained that he only wanted to get home, that was all that he wanted.

He came out to the living room to find Margaret sitting on the couch next to her son as he stared at the television in his openmouthed way. Peter sat down in the rocking chair. Outside the sun was coming down behind the field, the clouds had melted into their golden traces. The clock on the wall made its ticking sound, rang with its bells that vibrated. "Soon it will be dark," Margaret said.

Peter rocked forward, the floor creaked and the boy looked over. "Yeah," he said. "I'll give it another ten or so minutes. Then I should probably call a cab."

"Nonsense. The tow truck will be here soon."

The show went on, something about a boy named Marvin who held the secret to time travel. From what Peter could make of the story that was all Marvin knew, falling from airplanes and stumbling into ravines, his companion dog helping him out of each and every mess. Of course there were the requisite bad men in pursuit, one fat and one thin, bumbling their way along and nearly catching the boy and the dog but never quite managing to get them.

He'd hit the tree squarely, hadn't seen it until it was right there before him. He'd been driving down the country road, not sure where he was going but only wanting to be out in the open air with these fields and trees all around him. He'd taken the turn, heard the skidding before everything had become the blur. The grass had rolled beneath his tires, he'd turned his wheel but the steering had left him, and then had come the tree in all its terrible noise.

Across the road had been a house. A long gravel driveway led back, bushes and trees hedged the lawn. "Okay," he said, and his voice sounded strange in his ears. He began to walk—the ground was shaky beneath his feet, quivery. At the foot of the driveway he saw her, the woman named Margaret on the porch, the boy next to her. "I'm okay," Peter said, waving.

Margaret came down from the porch and strode toward him, the boy alongside her. "We heard the crash from inside," she said, catching her breath. Her son moved aside as she put her hand on Peter's arm, a firm, steady grip that gave him some amount of comfort. "You could have been killed."

"I suppose," said Peter.

"I wouldn't suppose. You don't know."

The boy said, "You got blood."

Margaret grabbed a Kleenex from her pocket, handed it to Peter and pointed to the spot beneath his nose. She wore a small, black T-shirt and jeans that were faded, had blond hair that wasn't really blond from what Peter could see of the roots, more like a mousy brown. Her eyes were large and her eyebrows thin, giving her a slightly frantic air. She stepped close, took the Kleenex and rubbed it gently. "How's your teeth?"

Peter rubbed his tongue alongside his front teeth, then molars. "Okay, I think."

"Good," Margaret said, backing away. "Teeth are like gold. Better than gold, actually. People think money is the most important thing, but life without teeth, my husband Michael said there weren't too many worse things." She smiled and her lips stretched tight. "He's a bum," she added.

Peter peered back at the house, its porch with the empty wine and Coke bottles lined along its edges. The windows were caked with dust, a large wooden owl was bolted to the highest point of the roof. There were the cherry trees that surrounded the yard, the remnants of blossoms. "I think I'll be all right," he said.

"You seem a little shaky."

"Maybe a little."

"You want to sit down for a while?"

He considered the yellow chair on the porch, his dizziness. "Sure," he said. "But I have to get back to the city soon. I have to buy socks." Then he laughed despite himself, explained that he had to buy the socks for his wedding that was tomorrow, and wasn't this a fine situation to find himself in. Margaret took a step back, regarded him as if he had just put on a new coat that glowed.

"You don't say," she said.

"Yes."

She stared at her house, turned back to Peter. "Then what the hell are you doing out here?"

"I don't know," said Peter. "Some final alone time, I guess. Being out in nature and the wide open spaces."

"That's smart of you. In case you have any last minute change of heart."

"Oh, it's not like that," he said too quickly.

"Of course not."

They walked to the porch and Peter sat on the chair, it squeaked and the bottles reflected the sunlight from above.

"Do you want some water?" Margaret asked.

"That might be nice."

She went into the house leaving the boy to stare at Peter. Peter nodded to the boy, felt the dizzy of his head that he only hoped would subside in time for the wedding. He imagined the worst-case scenario, being wheeled up the aisle by his friend Ned, the best man. Ned was an insurance claims adjuster and Peter figured he would give him a call when he returned home. Ned would get quiet, tell him not to worry about a thing. No doubt the accident would end up as part of his best man speech the next day. *Contrary to popular rumor,* he would tell the wedding party. *It was a tree and not bachelor shenanigans that put old Peter in this chair.* He would wait for the laughter. *A tree,* he'd go on and the only sound would be the tinkle of silverware and ice cubes against glass. *A tree, a tree, a tree.*

THE BOY turned off the television when Peter heard the tires crunching into the gravel. He stood and ignored his dizziness, went to the window and saw the green pickup steering into the driveway with the face in the windshield he recognized from the pictures on the living room wall. The husband. Peter's chest sank. *This is where it ends,* he thought. The husband finding the suitor in the house and taking care of him before he could get out a word. And what word would he get out anyway? That he hadn't meant to sleep with the wife? That he was as stupid as the next man and the next man and the next man after that?

Margaret and the boy watched Peter from the couch, he remembered his father who always said this kind of thing would happen. The rain before the rainbow, the night before the day. He was constantly warning him that when he least expected it, that was when the ceiling caved in. Not that his father hadn't had his share of ceilings cave in on him during his time. Peter's mother said that his father built his own ready-made disasters, that their marriage had been the shining example.

Margaret came up behind Peter. "He said he would come later tonight," she said. "It's all right, there isn't a thing to worry about." But her voice betrayed her—the reediness of it—and Peter realized this was who she'd been talking to in the next room when he'd awakened in her bed. The boy got up from the couch, stood beside Peter.

"What happens now?" he asked.

"Nothing happens now," said Margaret. "Your father takes away his boxes."

The boy's face clouded. "All of them?" he said.

"All of them," said Margaret.

EARLIER on the porch after the crash, the boy had told Peter he must have been going pretty fast to smash the car against the tree as he had. "People drive crazy here," the boy said. "Once I counted eighteen skid marks around the corner." He pointed at the tree. "Some days I climb up and wait for the cars to come crashing into it. It never happens though."

"That's probably a good thing," said Peter.

"I guess," he said.

Margaret came back out of the house with her water, the boy sat down on the steps and watched her as she handed Peter the glass. "So you're getting married tomorrow, huh?" she said, and Peter nodded between gulps. "I'll say you're lucky you walked away from this one then."

Peter put down his empty glass and the boy picked it up, brought it into the house without his mother's asking.

"Michael got a nosebleed the day of our wedding," she said, eyeing Peter's nose that had stopped its slight bleeding. "Had to hold the ceremony up for a good two hours because it wouldn't quit. Finally he went to the hospital and they cauterized it. By the time he came back most everyone had left."

"Not a good beginning," said Peter.

"No it wasn't," she said, and Peter supposed this was the part about the nosebleed having been an omen for what was to come. But she didn't say anything more about it, talked instead about her job and her husband's job too. "I work as a housekeeper," she said. "That's how I met him. He was helping to build a swimming pool and there he was standing at the window with the shovel in his hand." She glimpsed away at the tree and road. "Three weeks later they were putting in the concrete. That's when he asked me to marry him."

Peter squeaked in his chair, checked his watch.

"So what's she do?" Margaret asked, sitting down beside

him. Peter smelled her perfume suddenly applied, the fragrant aroma. "Your wife-to-be?" she said, turning to him. "Wait, don't tell me, let me guess. A nurse. No, a lawyer." She smiled. "An exotic dancer."

"She studies stars," said Peter.

"Oh, an astronomer," she said. "So she looks at the various constellations."

Peter said that she did, explained that she taught astronomy to the high school kids as well. He didn't mention the other things. That she sometimes stared for hours through her telescope at the planets and their surfaces, wrote long papers on galaxies and the not-so-distant celestial spheres.

"Well that's interesting, I suppose," Margaret said. "Not as interesting as an exotic dancer, but interesting nonetheless." She considered her thumb, pulled on its cuticle and flicked the dead skin to the ground. "But you need to get back, Mister Get Me to the Church. Should we call you a tow truck?"

"I think we'll have to," Peter said.

She stared past Peter at the car. "I take it you got other transportation for tomorrow, the big day."

Luckily he did, Hannah's father had offered his Lincoln for the honeymoon, a trip driving across the country to Niagara Falls, to finally settle back in Sacramento. Once there, Peter planned to continue his job at the community college, Hannah teaching in the high school and studying her planets and stars. Then the house, the baby they had talked about, and Peter felt his heart leap at the possibilities.

The boy came back out with another glass of water, placed

it before Peter. He thanked the boy and took a sip from the water, noticed it was sweet.

The boy nodded. "I put sugar in it."

"Well maybe he didn't want sugar in it," said Margaret.

"That's all right," Peter said. "I like sugar."

"See?" said the boy.

Peter drank the water, tasted the tiny sugar granules scratch across his teeth and tongue. He realized there was something sour in this water too as he reached the glass bottom. He grimaced and wiped his mouth, put the glass down.

"I put salt in there too," said the boy.

"You *what?*" his mother said.

"Salt. To even it out."

She grabbed for the boy but he'd already run down the driveway. "You come back here right now."

The boy ran toward the car and tree.

"I *do* apologize," Margaret said. "He's been funny since his father left." She took the glass and shook its water, stared down into it. "I mean, eight years old and for that to happen."

Across the yard, the boy ran around the car, peeked into its inside. Then he wandered around to the hood and climbed up, walked across its surface. *Hey,* Peter thought, and then Margaret said it. "Hey," she yelled. "Get down from there right now." The boy ignored his mother, raised his hands and shouted to the sky. Margaret stood and he jumped off the hood of the car, proceeded to the other side of the tree and pulled himself up by its branches. In an instant he was gone from sight.

"He may be a pain but he *is* a good boy."

"I'm sure he is."

"Oh, he is," Margaret said. "He is. He really is."

PETER stood in the middle of the room with Margaret, listened as the husband opened and closed the door to the truck and scuffled up the driveway. The boy leaned into his mother and then pushed himself away, went to the living room window. The glass steamed before his face.

After the sweet and salty water, Margaret had asked Peter inside the house to make the telephone call to the tow truck company. The first thing he'd noticed was the piano, the pictures of the mother and child, the father too, on the living room wall. Then the old couch covered with blankets, a coatrack festooned with the coats and sweaters. "The telephone is over here," Margaret said, gesturing in the direction of the hallway. "Don't mind the mess."

Peter angled his way over the boxes in the middle of the floor, found the telephone on a small table.

"He's coming by some time tomorrow morning," Margaret said. She lifted a cowboy hat from the rack and put it on her head. "Picking up some of his stuff is all."

"I see," said Peter.

"Oh, don't you worry. It's been a month since he left here and moved into his apartment." She put the hat back on the rack. "He's just moving out," she said. "Slowly."

Peter picked up the telephone and dialed for the tow truck, Margaret stepped close beside him and wrote out her address onto a piece of paper. "Ask if Randy is there," she said. "Because if Randy is there he'll know exactly how to get here, his wife is my best girlfriend."

"Is Randy there?" Peter said, feeling a bit foolish.

"Who?"

"Randy."

And he realized that of course no Randy was there, that he was calling the central tow truck headquarters and for all he knew he was talking to someone in the middle of Nebraska with the way these things worked today. Margaret stood next to him, her perfume scent permeating as the voice on the line asked where it was he was calling from. His head rolled, and when he leaned into the wall the floor seemed to yank itself out like the carnival ride. He was falling, he thought, and what a thing, the carpet right there before him—thank God for the carpet—soft and plush as he tumbled and the piano thrummed as the plates on the nearby shelf rattled. His hands and feet tingled, he felt his chest go shallow. "Shit," he said, his voice sounding deep and buried, far away. Then, "What happened? How'd that happen?"

"You *fell* is what happened," said Margaret, and she pulled the telephone from his fingers, told the operator he would call back later and hung it up with the slam. Peter stared into her face, considered these eyes that had suddenly taken on some kind of tender quality.

"Now, are you okay honey?" she said.

He blinked, when he tried to sit up it was as if he couldn't find the muscles. "Okay. Now I'm okay."

"I would say you are not. You need to go to the couch and lay back until you feel better."

"It's only dizziness."

"Or maybe not."

"Really, I'm fine." Now he could sit up, and he did, but the spinning returned and when he lay back Margaret's hands were right there. She was close, her breath warm against his skin. He closed his eyes and could smell her flowery aroma, its thick fragrance.

"Come on then," she said, and she helped him to his feet and led him to the couch. He lay there with the blankets, sank down into the soft cushions. Margaret sat next to him, asked, "How are you now?" Her face was before him, close, as she held his gaze. "Tell me," she went on. "Better?" Then she kissed him, deep and hard, her tongue moving in his mouth as if searching for its very bottom. His head spun more and he wondered if it was from the crash or the kiss, he looked up to see the dust swirling around them and the sun high in the sky above the field. Margaret smiled, tipped her head back. "Better," she said.

WHEN MARGARET opened the front door the husband Michael stood before them. "Whose car?" he said in a heavy, guttural voice that reminded Peter of the cement the husband poured into the backyard holes. Margaret opened the screen door and held it open, he clumped into the house and rested his large hand on the doorknob. "Must be yours," he said.

Peter said that it was, stared past the husband to the road beyond the car and tree wanting to get out of there more than he'd wanted to get out of anywhere in his life. The boy stared up at his father, then Peter, tugged on his father's arm. "He's getting married tomorrow," said Margaret.

Michael's face went tight, he squinted. He had creases that ran along his mouth, severe lines. "Is that so?" he said.

"It is," said Peter, although then again, he had to wonder. Because if Hannah only knew—this secret that wouldn't be the secret the moment she looked into his eyes. He regarded the bedroom door moved ajar, the unkempt bed within sight, waited for the truth to out. And suddenly Michael's hand was outstretched before him. Peter took it in his, shook it up and down while the boy stood beside his father watching with his serious expression.

"A wedding is nearly always good news," Michael said. "But I suppose with the good news comes the bad." He took back his hand. "That car out there is bad," he went on as if explaining some math problem for a kindergartner. "But the marriage is good." He made a tiny smile and the boy pulled some more on his arm. "It all balances out."

"Balance is good," said Margaret, a bit too eagerly.

"So are you hurt?"

"He was dizzy," Margaret said. "But he seems better now."

"You be careful with that. It might be a concussion."

"I plan on getting it checked," Peter said.

The boy jerked away from his father and ran to the screen door, kicked it open. He jumped from the porch onto the lawn with a loud scream.

Michael reflected on the boy. "He's got some energy."

"Too much these days," said Margaret.

"Yeah. Well."

"You want to begin?"

Michael rubbed the back of his neck. "These are the boxes?"

"They are."

"I guess I could start then."

"You want help?" said Margaret.

He looked at his wife, ran his eyes over her small, black T-shirt and faded jeans. "How are *you* doing though?" he said.

"Great," she said.

"Yeah?"

Margaret glanced over at Peter and he wanted to shrink away from the world. *"Yeah."*

"Okay," said Michael. He reached down for the box. "I can do this on my own, really." He gestured with a nod to Peter. "But if you could do me the favor of going on ahead and letting down the door to my truck I'd appreciate it."

Peter said he would. Anything to get outside away from these two people, he thought, as he walked through the door to the porch, down the steps and onto the grass. The boy lay back on the lawn, now quiet, as if trying to read the empty sky. He stepped past the boy, made his way toward the truck as Margaret and Michael talked in their hushed tones.

IT WAS ON the third date that Peter said to Hannah when all else failed she could always tell the students their shit was simply bits and pieces of stars. "Stardust, all," he'd said, knowing that with his students the best way to explore the often grand and lofty ideas expressed in literature was to talk about its most base elements. Screwing and crapping, not to mention eating and sleeping, brought it back down to earth, allowed him to work his way up in the lecture. He explained this all to Hannah, she told him this may have worked fine with Shakespeare and Joyce but that stars were a different matter.

They were sitting in the restaurant. Hannah had finished her plate of fries, Peter drank his Coke. "It's not that I don't appreciate your suggestion," she said. "But it's more complicated than that." She adjusted herself in the vinyl seat, nearby the waitress scribbled out their bill. "Really," Hannah said, and the waitress placed the bill on the table. "No snow. Believe me, they see right through it."

"The all-seeing eyes of youth."

"I'm just saying they see through the bullshit." She took his glass of Coke and pulled on the straw. "Like with you," she said. "I see through your bullshit and I know that you sleep with your students and I can tell you that if you want to be with me that will all have to stop." She handed back the Coke, the blood rushed from Peter's head, a cold tingle.

"What students?" he said.

"Don't even try."

"I don't—"

"I said, *don't.*"

And that had been that, from then on he'd stopped, just as she'd asked. He'd taken it as his personal challenge to show Hannah he was more than a playboy, to prove he was capable of something resembling nobility. And in time she admitted that she loved Peter, even as she said she once thought she'd never know what love was. "I've been with more than a few people," she'd gone on to tell him, and Peter said that he had too. "Okay then," she'd said. "Let's count them." And they did. Right there as they drove back from Hannah's school. Peter told her about Lucinda with the Guatemalan skirt, Rebecca when he was the high school freshman, the rest of the history he could remember. She told him about Jeffrey the actor who played Jesus in *Jesus Christ Superstar,* Nick the stockbroker who drove the purple Saab. There were others, many others, and Peter found himself repulsed by these men, but strangely heartened by them as well. She laughed when he told her this, and he'd felt the deep stirrings in his chest. Here they were after so many adventures. They'd found each other, love had raised itself from the murk and given them the chance to see themselves anew.

MICHAEL came up to Peter with his box. "Well I hope you have insurance," he said, and Peter told him that he did, that his friend was a claims adjuster. Michael tossed the box into the truck. "Oh then, that's easy," he said. "Having him right there when things go wrong."

"I should consider myself lucky."

"I guess so," Michael said. "Although I'm not so sure I'd want any friend in a business like that."

Peter knew that he should have been mildly insulted but that Michael was testing him, putting in a few jabs because of what he suspected maybe, just perhaps, had happened. Although the wedding news surely pushed it to the back of his mind, Margaret announcing it as she had and the boy running out to the lawn must have left some funny impression.

"What about you?" Michael said. "What's your racket?"

"English," said Peter. "I teach it."

"High school?"

"College."

"Uh huh," Michael said. "So you read all about the human condition."

"You could say that."

Michael started back for the house, turned. "What if I asked you to mark the boxes with what they had inside? Plates. Tools. I'll tell you as I bring them up."

"I can do that," Peter said.

"Good then." He tossed Peter a marking pen. "The first one is shirts. Go ahead. Write that."

Peter wrote *SHIRTS* on the box and the boy was suddenly beside him. "What are you doing?" he said.

"Helping your daddy," said Peter.

The boy contemplated this, surely trying to put together

the idea of this man who'd just slept with his mother helping his father move out of the house. The boy had his father's hair, dark and bristly, his mother's jagged eyebrows and chubby lips. His teeth were large for his mouth, Peter supposed he would grow into them.

"What's your name?" he asked him.

"Silverware coming up," Michael yelled from the porch, and the boy ran away to the side of the house, jumped behind the bushes. Peter fingered the marker, peered over at the boy as Michael stepped beside him and set the box down onto the bed of the truck. "Say," he said. "What were you doing driving out here on the day before your big wedding anyway?"

"No special reason," Peter said. "Taking in the wide open spaces."

"Enjoying your final moments?"

Peter uncapped the marker. "Just thinking."

"Well think about this," Michael said. "Things change. That's all you have to be prepared for." He slid the box further, headed back for the house. "Silverware."

"Got it," said Peter.

He marked the box and rested against the truck's gate. There was the darkening sky, the imminent night. When he was a boy his father called this the coming time. What his father meant by this was never made clear, but Peter figured it had something to do with the evening changing to night, the time of day when it was plain to see the earth was moving in its own particular way. He scanned the sky, imagined the planets. There were the evenings he'd stand in the backyard with Hannah and her telescope as she did her studies, she'd ask him to look through the lens. "That one's Jupiter," she'd told him the first time he'd stood with her. "I think it's one of the most beautiful planets." He'd held the lens to his eye, marveled.

The screen door opened, Michael trotted across the lawn and set down another box. "Shoes," he said.

"Check," said Peter. He wrote out the word and Michael watched him.

"It's kind of ironic isn't it?" he said. "Helping me move out on the day before your wedding."

"I'm trying not to think about it," said Peter.

Michael kicked at the dirt, stuck his hands in his back pocket. "Women are funny," he said.

"This much is true."

"I mean you have to remember that."

"Sometimes it's hard to forget."

Michael pointed to the house, then nodded without meeting Peter's eyes. "The truth is I slept with her sister. She found out. It was a terrible mess."

Peter held the marker, turned its cap.

"Now that was wrong, I won't deny it wasn't. But then the sister calls Margaret and tells her, *tells her,* the very next day. She says she was plagued by guilt. Well I told her if she was plagued by guilt then she probably shouldn't have done it in the first place." He kicked some more at the dirt, creating a mild dust cloud. "I don't know," he said.

"It's hard," said Peter.

"Yeah?" he said. "You know about this?"

"No," Peter said, trying to keep his voice even and calm. "I can only imagine."

"Well that was more than a month ago now," Michael said. "And I thought it might blow over. You know, forgive and forget and all the rest." He shrugged. "But it didn't happen. It's like some big wall came up and the more I try to knock it down the higher it goes."

The bushes from the side of the house rattled and Peter imagined the boy was taking in everything his father was saying. *The poor boy,* he thought, and he knew that he'd have some words for him. That fathers were fathers, that they made the mistakes that never meant to hurt. The bushes went still, Peter gave the box of shoes a small push.

"Anyway," said Michael. He stared back at Peter's car. "Margaret said you called the tow truck people a good hour ago."

"More than that now. They said they were busy."

"Busy." He walked up the lawn to the house, stopped at the porch and turned. "Say," he said. "Did you talk to Randy?"

Peter explained that he had telephoned the central tow truck headquarters, their offices in faraway places. "Satellites and all," he said.

"So you didn't talk to Randy," said Michael.

"I didn't talk to Randy."

Peter sat back against the truck's gate and folded his arms. The sun hung low, its light fading. Soon the day would leave, the sky black as ink with the stars smeared across the sky, the coming time over and just the darkness. He thought of his father and felt a terrible pang, remembered how earlier that day he'd tossed the money at the birds. His father, who'd left Peter's mother to be with the secretary. His father, living in the house with the termites in the walls and television always on, because as he'd told Peter earlier that very same afternoon, he needed to hear the voices to fill the quiet, it was so terrible with everyone gone.

Michael walked back from the house with a stack of boxes, hesitated for a moment and lost his balance. The boxes tumbled and magazines spilled out and scattered across the lawn. "You stay there I can do this," he said to Peter with his finger, pointed. He bent over and gingerly picked up the magazines. *Popular Mechanics. Sports Illustrated.* He stuffed them into the boxes and stood, went back to the house.

The boy came up to Peter from behind the bushes. "He's got a lot of magazines," he said.

"He does."

"He likes to save them and read them later."

Michael kicked the screen door open and trampled down the steps, across the grass. The boy ran back to the bushes. Peter went out to the lawn and picked up one of the boxes of magazines with Michael, walked with him to the truck and placed it into the bed. Michael set down his box beside it, Peter became suddenly aware of the odor of the man's sweat, its bitterness. Michael leaned against the truck and crossed his arms.

"So you're getting married tomorrow."

Peter said that he was.

Michael looked Peter up and down. "Margaret is singing in the kitchen," he said. He uncrossed his arms, let his hands fall.

There were the lines in his face, as if the weight of all his sorrow had been manifested in these very wrinkles. His brow knotted, two folds of skin pinched together. "Margaret never sings and now she is singing."

Peter heard the bushes shake, glanced over at the boy as he stood and trudged out to the driveway. This was it, Michael finally knew, there was no doubt in Peter's mind as he watched him look from the boy to him with his appraising eyes. He wondered if he should give the boy a message before his father slammed him to the ground, to tell Hannah that he was sorry for what he'd done, that he only wished he could have been a different person.

"It's unusual," Michael said. "I mean, people don't just start singing out of nowhere like that."

But sometimes they did, thought Peter. There was the blind man who could suddenly, miraculously see, the young girl waking from the coma. All these, events beyond explanation. What was singing in the kitchen, when compared to such things, these sudden mysteries?

A pair of headlights flashed across the yard, Michael glanced past Peter and held up his hands. "The tow truck," he said. Then, "It's too bad, with the conversation we were having."

Conversation, *right,* thought Peter, and he slipped past Michael, walked onto the lawn, did his very best not to break into the run. The driver of the tow truck met him just beyond the roots of the tree, his T-shirt stained with grease and jeans hung low. "How you doing?" he said, tipping his hat and putting out his hand, stiff and fleshy. "Randy at your service."

■

THE BOY came over and watched Randy move the car, Michael and Margaret followed close behind. Randy shined his back lights onto the tree and pulled the car with the chain he attached to its rear bumper. The fender made its sound as the front of the car unwrapped itself from the trunk. The tree shuddered and groaned. Leaves and a few twigs and branches fell, the tow truck accelerated and dragged the car away.

Randy stepped out of the cab of his truck and came up to Peter. "So that wasn't as bad as I thought it might be." He rubbed his hand on a towel he extracted from his back pocket. "I've seen jobs that wrapped around trees like they were part of the trunk." He rolled the towel into a ball with his greasy fingers. "I mean," he said, "some of these were real doozies."

The boy circled the tree, climbed its side. He stood on the lowest branch and smiled down at his father and mother, Peter too. "You all look different from here," he said. "Like you're smaller now."

Michael stomped away from Margaret and ran his fingers alongside the tree's bark where the car had hit it, made the green dent. He shook his head, looked at Margaret. "He ruined it," he said. "Like he took an ax and hacked it. It's ruined."

"Hey now Michael," said Randy. "Just thank the Lord he's all right."

"*Thank the Lord,*" Michael said.

The boy sat on the branch and dangled his feet. His father gave each foot a swat as if he'd made the decision to prove to himself that none of this really mattered anyway. "Okay then," he said. "I think I'm going to have to come up there and teach someone a lesson."

"You can't," the boy said.

"I *can,*" said Michael. And he pulled himself into the branches.

"There's something new," Margaret said under her breath.

"He's pretty good," said Peter.

"Oh, he's only a boy." She sighed. "A boy in a man's body." She pushed her heel into the ground, patted down her stray hairs. "I guess you'll be heading back now."

"It's that time."

"You'll have a happy life, I'm sure."

"Right," said Peter.

"You will."

Peter regarded the car and its crumpled body. The grille, its intricate plastic that was smashed to bits, the radiator inside bent and sheared. He thought of where he'd be tomorrow, taking Hannah's hand and looking into her eyes. Her eyes, like the most beautiful planet, as he'd told her so often. Her eyes, like Jupiter, from that very first night he'd stood with her and looked up into the sky. His head gave a tiny spin. Only this time he didn't fall, he simply leaned into Margaret and breathed in the air that tasted like the grass. "Whenever you're ready," Randy said as he stuffed the towel into his back pocket. He went to the truck and got in, sat behind the wheel and wrote onto his clipboard with his tiny yellow pencil.

"Well this is it," Margaret said, and Peter said that it was.

Randy placed the clipboard beside him onto the seat, draped his hands over the steering wheel. The sun came down behind the hills, the first stars glimmered in the sky. There was the boy and his laughter, then the father's laughter too, deep and determined. Margaret stared up at them, her face took on a smile. The leaves, they came down in their green shower, a cascade, turning, just turning.

The Gift

Manuel Garcia knew the man who shot the boy. His name was Henry Sanders and he would bring his car into Manuel's auto repair shop. It was the usual, sad story. Henry had shot the boy in his yard because he thought it was a thief stealing wood from his porch. Now the boy was in critical condition in the Sacramento hospital with a big hole in his stomach. The terrible part wasn't only that it was a twelve-year-old child, but that it was Henry's nephew who had come by to drop off his father's sprinkler.

Rosa was the boy's nurse. She worked in the critical care unit at the hospital and monitored his progress. Each evening she would stop by Manuel's garage after work, sit down in the chair across from his desk and tell him the stories. But tonight it was too late for the stories, Rosa just off her late shift and still in the uniform as she was. She was tired, as she'd let Manuel know when she'd walked through his door, the long day and then having to make the drive from Sacramento to Winters, these forty minutes of headlights in the dark. She leaned forward in the chair, rested her elbow on Manuel's desk. "So then," she said. "How about you? Maybe you could tell me. Do *you* have any stories?"

Manuel stared up at the ceiling. Outside the crickets scratched their legs together in the rhythm, the motorcycle roared its engine in the far distance. Manuel shuffled his feet onto the floor, opened his desk drawer. "Well," he said, peering down at the pencils and pens, the paper clips and change. "An old woman and her Studebaker."

"A Studebaker," said Rosa. "You like Studebakers."

"When they run," Manuel said. "But this one. The truth is it should have been tossed but the old woman would never let that happen." He went on to tell Rosa the year and make of the car, the fact that it practically needed a new engine, too many small parts to mention. He shook his head. "But she still wants it. The car is falling to pieces and she still wants it."

"*Viuda?*" said Rosa.

"One would guess."

"The car holds memories."

Manuel looked at Rosa and her eyes registered their typical concern that he knew so many of her patients had seen. He'd heard the stories of Henry's nephew from her, the relatives coming by, Henry too. There was the day after the shooting, the boy's mother and father sitting at the bed and Henry walking in.

"I thought the father was going to kill his brother right there," Rosa had told Manuel. "But the father just cried. Then the brother cried, so sad like they were, all gathered around the boy." Rosa stood. "Are you coming?" she said.

Manuel opened his desk drawer farther. "You go ahead."

"It's already late."

"I need to finish a few things."

"You're sure?"

"I'm sure."

Rosa went to the door, gave him the wave. "All right," she said, and she walked outside. Manuel got up from his desk, watched from the window. She pulled out the keys from the pocket of her skirt, glanced back at Manuel and he raised his hand. The dog began to bark from next door, the Doberman named Charlie, and Rosa got into her car and started the engine. She drove to the curb and pulled away from the station, made her way down the street and around the corner.

HENRY stopped at the garage the next day. He looked terrible, his chin even more drooping than Manuel remembered it being, his gray hair unwashed and matted. He stepped over the parts scattered across the floor, went to the Studebaker and leaned into its side. "This was probably once some clean car," he said.

"*Once,*" said Manuel. He had to wonder what Henry was doing here, only a few days after the shooting and the hurt in his face so painful to see. His car had sounded fine as he'd parked it outside the garage, the oil changed in the last couple of months, the tires rotated.

Henry said, "It would be something to make this car run again like old times."

"It would," said Manuel.

Henry peered through the passenger side window of the car, cupped his hand to the glass. The Studebaker was a 1954 Starlight Coupe, had surely been a beauty in its day. It was a light blue, a Champion two-door. The first thing it needed was new brakes, which was no small deal since most mechanics no longer had the special drum puller required for such a job. He knew the cooling system would need work as well, had heard the rumbling, chirpy sound as it pulled into the garage. All in all, it would be a big job but not too big, just the kind of work he liked to do taking a car on the edge of the rust heap and fixing it up so that it could run again.

"You have a gift," Henry said.

"What's that?"

"A gift. Being able to bring an old car back like that."

"Not really."

Henry turned to face Manuel. "Yes, really," he said.

Outside a clatter of tools echoed from behind the garage, the sound of Hector and Johnson as they struggled with an old Malibu station wagon. Earlier in the day Johnson had told Hector that if it had been *his* kid that had been shot he would have gone after Henry and taken care of the business himself. Manuel had walked by with his cart of tools and when Johnson asked him what he thought of all this, he said a person didn't know what he'd do until he was put in such a position.

Henry tugged at the antenna of the Studebaker. "You know a few things," he said. "I mean, like about family, the importance of it." He let the antenna go so that it wobbled back and forth in its springy way. *"La familia,"* he continued. "I guess I just wanted to talk to somebody who might be able to understand my circumstances."

Manuel's eyes froze on the antenna, he couldn't look up at Henry for fear of what the man would say next. The truth was it had been almost a year since his son Octavio had died in the crash, the vehicle losing control on the old Winters road. And it wasn't only Octavio who'd died, there were the other children. Gabriela Navarro from up the street, Victor Reyes from Vacaville. Octavio had taken a turn much too quickly. Then came the tree, and all three of the children had been thrown from the truck, not wearing their seat belts at all. They found them on the porch of a nearby house laid out together, almost like sleeping except for the terrible blood all around.

The parents of the children who died didn't talk to Manuel anymore. They ignored him at the market, said things that would circle back, eventually. And each time he'd hear the lies they'd say—that he let Octavio drink and this was why it had happened, that he was a drinker too and what could they have expected from the child of someone like that.

Henry moved away from the car, folded his arms together. "When you lost him," he said, as if reading from the script Manuel knew only too well, "I bet that it hurt you something terrible." He leaned close and said in a hushed tone, "But there *were* extenuating circumstances."

"You mean my boy was drunk."

"Well," Henry said. "Yeah."

"Now listen here," Manuel said, his face growing hot. "My boy didn't mean to kill anyone. He didn't take a gun and shoot it at somebody moving in the dark without saying a word." Manuel could feel his heart beating, the hard rhythm of it. *La familia,* what the hell nerve did he have coming in here and telling him something like that? "You can leave right now," he said.

Henry backed away, held up his hands. "Look here," he said. "I thought we could talk."

"Well you thought wrong," said Manuel.

"It's just that so much has happened." Then he began to cry. Manuel stared down at his feet, outside Hector and Johnson banged their tools against the Malibu's engine and he was only glad they weren't here to see this. Manuel offered Henry his rag, he took it and wiped his face. There was the grease mark alongside his nose when he handed back the rag. "All right then," he said, and he shuffled from the garage.

MANUEL finished the Studebaker five days later. When the woman came by to pick it up she clasped her hands together, walked from one end of the car to the other. It had been as big a job as he'd expected. He'd replaced the brake lines and re-aligned the front end, flushed the cooling system and cleaned the carburetor and transmission. He had put in new hoses. Then too, the valve seals and spark plugs, the shift tube as well.

Her name was Mrs. Hamlin and she peered at Manuel behind his desk. In the back of the shop Hector and Johnson worked on their cars, sticking their bright lights over and under the engines, swinging their extension cords from side to side. "I wasn't sure you'd be able to fix it," she said.

"It wasn't that hard," said Manuel.

Mrs. Hamlin stepped close. "Nonsense," she said. "I've taken this car to other shops and they haven't been able to do a thing." She opened her purse, asked Manuel how much it would be. Manuel punched the numbers on the calculator, Mrs. Hamlin spread her hands onto his desk. Her fingernails were bitten short, she had a gold ring with a blue diamond that glinted.

"I was married in that car," she said.

"Is that right?" said Manuel.

"Well not married, but we drove it to Nevada to elope."

He waited for the part about the husband dying but it didn't come. "We're going to celebrate our fortieth wedding anniversary this Saturday and I wanted to surprise him," she said. "You know, catch him off-guard."

Manuel considered Mrs. Hamlin, the wrinkles that folded under her eyes, the lines in her forehead trailing downward like a frown. He pictured the face before these lines, Mrs. Hamlin sitting beside the young husband as they drove the Studebaker past the tumbleweeds and desert of the Nevada highway.

"Well?" she said. "What's the damage?"

He told her the amount and she examined the slip on the desk. "That's all?" she said. "I mean, I don't think I've ever asked any mechanic that." She shook her head. "You said it would be much more, I can't believe I'm telling you this."

"It was the brakes and a few other things," Manuel said. He shrugged. "Most folks don't have the proper tools."

His father owned a Studebaker, had bought it used on the brink of collapse. Manuel had learned to fix these cars tinkering through its innards. Coating the edges of the core plugs with zinc chromate primer was one thing he'd learned from his father, creating the special tools to get to the engine's valves and put in the new seals was another. Working on Mrs. Hamlin's Studebaker had reminded him of his father, and then his son Octavio, the boy's pickup and how they would work on it in the garage. Actually, Manuel would work on the pickup—the boy would sit on the stool as Manuel pointed out the various parts and tell him the best ways to keep the engine running. "Yeah, sure," Octavio would say, in his indifferent way. He'd lean back into the wall with his baseball cap pulled low over his eyes, drink his sodas and stack the empty cans onto the desk like the castle. "You're going to rot your teeth drinking those things like that," Manuel would tell him. "Yeah, sure," he'd say again.

Mrs. Hamlin gave Manuel her credit card. "So you like Studebakers?" she said.

"I know them pretty well."

"My husband used to call it the Shitbaker. Said that it was a junkyard relic."

Manuel pushed the card under the carbon slip, slid the machine over it to make the impression. *Mrs. Lorna Hamlin,* said the card.

"He can be a real pain sometimes," she continued. "Stubborn. Crotchety." She took the carbon and signed it, pulled the receipt in half. "He smells too."

"Sounds like the perfect combination," Manuel said.

"That's a good one."

He gave Mrs. Hamlin her keys.

"People ask our secret."

"It sounds like you know," said Manuel.

Mrs. Hamlin smiled, jingled her keys. "Well," she said, and Manuel figured she would tell him about stopping to smell the roses, taking the time to see the small things. The ordinary bullshit advice, not taking into account the real world and all of its lousy problems.

"It's really quite simple," Mrs. Hamlin said.

"These things usually are," said Manuel, and he waited for her to talk about the flowers.

"The secret," she said, "is everything."

"Everything."

"You know, looking at the big picture." She turned away from Manuel and went to the car, ran her hand over the roof and its paint slivered and flaked. "The truth being that my husband can be a son-of-a-bitch, but that he can be the sweetest man." She clapped the dust and made the blue cloud. "Like I said, everything," she said.

Manuel proceeded away from his desk, folded the carbon

receipt so that its gummy underside stuck to his fingers. *Of course everything,* he thought, the secret being no secret to anyone. Mrs. Hamlin got into the car, Manuel closed the door behind her and it squeaked and groaned. "I mean that," she said, looking up at him. "He can be a real sweetheart."

She turned the key in the ignition, pressed the accelerator and the engine roared. Manuel listened to the timing and felt good knowing he'd fixed things as he had, although for how long was anyone's guess. But right now the car was running fine, one would say it was running almost perfectly. "Music," said Mrs. Hamlin, and Manuel remembered Henry Sanders telling him that he had a gift for being able to bring an old car back like that. Henry Sanders, with the nerve to come by the garage as he had, Henry Sanders who could mention his nephew and Octavio in the same breath. How Manuel wanted to take this Studebaker and drive it up over the man's lawn, to turn deep circles into the grass. *There's your gift you stupid fool,* he would tell Henry when he walked out from the house. *There's your gift with all the ribbons.*

Mrs. Hamlin steered from the garage and onto the street, Johnson ducked out from under the hood of his car and the light swung by its orange cord. He smiled and shook his head, his gray hair shined with the Brylcreem. He'd met his wife working in Manuel's garage, had walked up to her and said he may not have been the president of the United States, but that didn't mean he couldn't pretend he was. "Which gives me the liberty to ask you out," he'd told her, as if this had made any sense. Hector, who was nearly ten years younger than Johnson, had a much quieter demeanor. He'd been hired after O'Reilly—Manuel's partner who'd helped him open the shop so many years ago—had moved across the country. Hector had sideburns that gave him a menacing quality, but he really wasn't menacing at all. He was married to a woman who was a waitress at the local coffee shop, had a gut from all the hash browns and pancakes he'd eaten at her table. He poked with his wrench under a Range Rover, pulled out a bolt, then another.

"It takes all kinds," Johnson said.

Manuel rang the cash register and stuffed in the credit card receipt. Johnson gave Hector a glance and nodded, pushed back the blue sleeves of his work shirt. "I don't know what the hell she's going to do with that car anyway," he said.

"She got married in it," said Manuel.

"So?"

"So it's got sentimental value."

"My left nut has sentimental value too," Johnson said. "But you don't see me spending *my* life's fortune on it."

Hector laughed.

"Not that you didn't give her the break."

Manuel stepped from behind the cash register and picked up a metal bucket, set it next to the Cadillac in the far corner of the garage. He lifted the hood of the car and peered down at its monstrous engine, reached in and dug out some hardened grease from the carburetor. He knew what Johnson was thinking, that he'd been too kind to this woman. As he'd been to Henry, just that day Johnson telling Hector the man should have been locked up in jail for what he'd done—Henry Sanders had shot a boy and this was the indisputable truth, never mind the U.S. Constitution. Manuel could have told Johnson there was more to the story than the boy and the gun, that there were complications he could never begin to know. But he'd kept quiet, as he kept quiet now, taking out the carburetor's filter and dropping it into the bucket. Johnson peeked up from his car at Manuel, Hector buried his head under the hood.

MANUEL drove to Rosa's house the next day after work. She lived outside Davis, the town halfway between Winters and Sacramento, had moved there because it was so much easier for her to get to the hospital living there. He waited on her porch. An hour passed, then another. Neighbors walked by and he waved, they looked at him twice surely wondering who this stranger was. Of course being dark like he was didn't help matters any. He knew this neighborhood—that the only Mexicans seen here besides Rosa were the gardeners and nannies. Go to hell, he thought as they stared. *Ándale pues.*

That morning he'd awakened with a sadness that reminded him of the deepest sea. He'd gotten out of bed, squinted at the calendar and wondered how it could be that Octavio had been dead a year. He'd driven to work, the sun had been like some cruel joke and he'd remembered the day of Octavio's funeral and that it had been this same way, having to put on his sunglasses and questioning how it could be anything but night.

When Rosa finally pulled into her driveway, he stepped down from the porch and came up to her car. "I wanted to see you," he said, and she seemed surprised he was there. She hesitated, then put out her arms. There was the smell of the hospital in her hair, its disinfectant and soap from her constant washing of the hands. "Let's go inside then," she said.

Rosa opened the door to her house and led Manuel in, they went to her bedroom and she lay back on the bed. "It's been a terrible day," she said, and she told him about the old man cracking his skull on the toilet, the little girl who'd lost her fingers in the lawnmower. "But here we are now," she said with a heavy sigh. Manuel lay next to Rosa, her body warm against his, her breath soft. She pulled him closer, the room spun and he couldn't even remember the reason he was there.

HE WAS BETWEEN sleep and dreams when he thought of Henry Sanders' nephew, the boy lying in the hospital bed with the tubes stuck into his body. Then he thought of Octavio, the fact that he'd never even *had* the opportunity to lie on a hospital bed, the death coming so quickly. He remembered after his wife Elena had left them, how he would sit on the edge of Octavio's bed and read him the stories from the books she'd left behind, some in Spanish, others in English. Sometimes in the middle of the stories he would start making things up, Charlotte the Spider might become Elena and Wilbur the Pig would accidentally sit on her. Or Willy Wonka might name Elena as one of the five lucky ticket holders, and she'd ride the glass elevator up into the sky before he pushed her out the door to watch her fall to the ground. When Elena called that first

Christmas, Manuel was cordial and polite as he asked about her new life, and Octavio sat on the chair and stared at his father with his concerned, disturbed eyes.

"I should go," Manuel said.

Rosa turned on the light, propped herself up on her pillow and considered him. "Oh Manuel," she said. "Can't you just stay?"

He got out of the bed and put on his shirt, his pants, his shoes. She asked him what was wrong and he didn't answer, simply gathered the keys and went to his car. He drove back to Winters and up and down the town's roads, past the mailboxes and fences and under the bats that flew above the headlights. Then the fields where his father had worked, toiled, under the blistering sun for so many years. He rolled down the window and smelled the alfalfa, remembered when he was a boy and running along this same road beside these fields with his father—laughing, actually laughing, from sheer happiness. What had happened to this feeling? Manuel thought. When had he lost the capacity for such joy? Had it been the day his father died from the cancer Manuel could only guess had come from working with the pesticides? Or when his mother had moved back to the Mexican town where her family still lived, where she'd met his father all those years ago? The night before the accident, Manuel had sat at the kitchen table opposite his son and said a joke, something about the pope and a horse, heaven and hell, dirty but not obscene. Octavio had brooded over the joke and forced a smile, and it occurred to Manuel in that moment that the boy had never been happy, not really, and what a terrible thing.

He pulled over onto the side of the road and stared out at

the darkness of the moonless sky, listened to the breeze move through the field. There were the birds calling to each other from far away, the crickets too. A star shone through the clouds, when he put his head out the window he could see there were even more.

THE NEXT MORNING Manuel went to the shop early. He worked on a Volkswagen and moved on to a Caprice, each a fairly easy job. When the sunup came through the window, Hector and Johnson wandered in, coffee mugs in hand. "You already moving?" Johnson said, his hair shining with its cream. His face was clean and smooth, by afternoon would be blue in its whiskered darkness.

"I wanted to get a head start," Manuel said. He pointed to the Volkswagen and Caprice. "These are finished. We can get going on the others."

The first customer of the day was a teenage boy with yellow hair and the largest Adam's apple Manuel had ever seen. His car was a Honda Civic that he said was making a terrible noise, likely the fan belt. Next came a young woman with a Toyota Camry she explained was losing its power steering. It was already shaping up to be a busy day, and Manuel was glad he'd come in when he had, the owner of the Volkswagen arriving with the baby in her arms telling him in Spanish that she had to get her daughter to day care.

"*Aquí están,*" said Manuel, giving her the keys.

Then came Rosa. She steered into the front of the shop, sat

in her car. He walked toward her and Charlie from next door barked as he told the dog to shut the hell up, to hush. Rosa stared ahead and rolled her window down. "I wanted to see how you were," she said, and her voice sounded distant, as if she were talking to one of her patients before the inoculation.

"I'm fine," Manuel said. "Please, don't worry."

Rosa regarded him. "Manny," she said. "You can talk to me. You know that."

"I know," said Manuel. "I have things on my mind is all."

"Like Octavio," said Rosa.

He slowly nodded.

"Well," Rosa said, and she put her car into gear. "You can talk to me is all I'm saying." She put out her hand and Manuel took it, squeezed and let go. Then she rolled up her window and drove off the lot and onto the street, her back signal blinking as she drove away and turned the far corner.

MANUEL had gone to high school with Rosa. They had talked once while he'd been a student there, although he didn't even remember until Rosa had reminded him of the incident. Even then, he wasn't so sure it had happened. But she insisted that it had, Rosa a freshman and Manuel a senior—he'd walked past her with his group of friends and looked her up and down, told her she would be pretty when she was all grown up. "I *am* grown up," she'd said, and Manuel had laughed. And that had been it, he'd left her standing there.

It was nearly thirty years later when Rosa showed up in his

garage to tell him she'd heard about Octavio dying in the crash. "Yeah, I guess most everyone has heard about it by now," he'd said, and she'd reached into her bag, placed the sweet bread into his hands.

"Lo siento," she said.

He'd thanked her, glanced from her eyes to her feet, then back up again. "Say," he'd said, and she'd broken into the smile. "Who are you anyway?"

Her story was not much different than Manuel's, being married and then not being married, the husband moving away and finding another person not long after. "Everything went wrong," she'd told Manuel the first time they'd gone out. They'd sat in his car staring out across Old Man Mason's cornfield—the same Old Man Mason his father had worked for so many years ago—with the sun coming down. Rosa squinted in the light, grabbed for the windshield visor and it slipped in its usual way. "It's broken," Manuel had said, and he'd explained how he'd met his wife in the accounting class at the junior college, that she'd left him for his business partner named O'Reilly—*O'Reilly*—he'd said with the sneer. "And now there she is—*pocha*—living in the middle of Idaho or Wisconsin or wherever it is they ended up." Rosa nodded and leaned back into the seat, the occasional car passed behind them and the sun set onto the field. Then came the soft blue of the early night, the eventual purple, then black, a slow bruise forming before them.

∎

HENRY SANDERS came by again the next day holding the paper bag against his chest. The bag was worn at the edges with the illustration of the Christmas tree, the words *Season's Greetings* in the red and green letters. "Hey Manuel," he said. "I only wanted to apologize for stopping by like I did." He handed the bag over, filled with oranges. "They're from my backyard," he said. "Nice and sweet."

Manuel took the bag and set it down on the floor.

"I just thought I'd bring them here," said Henry.

Hector and Johnson moved around their vehicles, watching Henry as they tried their best to look busy. Henry stood in the middle of the shop. His chin seemed to hang even farther, he still had the trace of grease alongside his nose. "You know I haven't slept since it happened," he said.

Manuel moved the bag with his foot, stared up at Henry. "You can expect that," he said. "The memory of the event coming back like it does."

"So you know?" said Henry. His eyes were opened wide, his hands outstretched. Manuel knew that all the man wanted was for him to tell him it was going to be all right, but of course it *wasn't* going to be all right, this much he could explain. The pain lessened, but the emptiness grew. And nothing would ever fill it.

"What I really wish is that I could go back to that night," Henry said. "I wish I could go back to that night and make it never happen is what I wish more than anything." He closed his hands. "You know?"

Manuel stepped back from the bag.

"Do you?"

Johnson marched by and yanked a pencil from behind his ear. *Please don't say a word,* thought Manuel, thinking back to what he'd said about locking Henry away in the jail. He paused before them, and Manuel could only imagine what he had stored in his accusing mind. *Go away,* he wanted to tell him. *Leave.* But Johnson didn't move, he just stood there and scratched his chin, glimpsed into the bag. "Somebody brought oranges," he said, sticking the pencil into his pocket. "From your tree?"

Henry nodded.

"Uh huh," Johnson said, and Manuel braced for what was coming, the terrible wrath of words. But before he could say anything Henry lifted the bag from the floor, held it out. "They're for all of you," he said placing the bag in Johnson's arms. "You, Manuel, Hector. Everyone."

Johnson gave a hard smile and glared down into the bag.

"I should be going then," Henry said, and he pointed to the door. He told Manuel good-bye and shuffled out of the garage, got into his car. Johnson held the bag in his arms, then dropped it to the floor so that the oranges spilled out. "Fucking criminal," he said, walking away.

THE ANSWERING MACHINE was flashing its red light when Manuel came home and he knew it was Rosa. He went to the kitchen and set the bag of oranges on the table, boiled some water for noodles. Then he clicked on the television and sat down at the table, watched the news but didn't really watch it, kept thinking about Henry Sanders telling him about the night and wanting to change it.

The water boiled and he put the noodles in, the telephone rang. *Not now,* he said to himself, and Rosa's voice came over the machine. "Manuel," she said. "Manuel, if you're there please pick up."

He stared at the boiling water.

"Just know that I'm here."

He had the picture of Henry in his mind, could not shake it, the man standing there before him wanting Manuel to come up with the words. *Words,* he thought, and he remembered Octavio as a baby in his arms and the boy's eyes opening for the first time, trying to think of the words for this moment as well and not being able to come close. He figured he might be able to tell Rosa this, how it was that he couldn't make sense of his son dying like he did, and he considered what she'd once told him about her marriage. "I get a shooting pain sometimes," she'd said. "Thinking of what could have been, the possibilities."

He reached for the telephone but she'd already hung up. The answering machine rewound and clicked, he turned over the idea of calling her back, but then didn't know what he would say. On the television were the images of people in boats, roofs blown off houses, and the anchor talked in his somber tone about the terrible flooding from the monsoons in the Indian town. "Mother Nature's anger," he said, and Manuel switched the television off, went to the table. The bag of oranges. He pulled one out and peeled off its skin, put the wedge into his mouth. The sweet juice ran over his chin, splattered onto the table, he chewed the pulp and tasted its sourness as it rolled down his throat. He unpeeled another piece of the orange, the water boiled on the stove and its steam rose in the air.

MR. HAMLIN, the husband of the woman who'd brought in the Studebaker, came by the garage the next day. His wife dropped him off and rounded the corner, driving the Mercedes that was silver. The husband walked from the car with some great effort. "She'll be right back," he said to Manuel, who met him at the door. "She needs to drop off her dress at the dry cleaner's and the chemicals they use make me itchy."

Mr. Hamlin used a cane and his head shook as he spoke, giving the words a tremor. "I'm not sure what they use," he went on, "but just driving by the shop can make me break out in hives." He pinched the bridge of his nose between his thumb and forefinger, let his hand fall down beside him. "You ever have that happen?"

Manuel said that he hadn't, went to his desk and sat down.

"My son tells me I'm a hypochondriac," said Mr. Hamlin. "I tell him to stuff it in his ear." He glimpsed around the shop, then back at Manuel. "I heard that you fixed my car," he said. "Did you fix my car?"

"I did," said Manuel, wondering what this business was all about.

"Well," Mr. Hamlin said, and he wiped his brow with a handkerchief from his sleeve. "Why the hell'd you do that?"

"Come again?" said Manuel.

"You fixed my car. There was no reason for you to fix my car. And now it's running again and I have to drive it."

Manuel got up from his desk. "Now listen, mister," he said. "I'm not crazy."

"I didn't say you were."

Mr. Hamlin leaned forward on his cane, Manuel watched the man's hands go pink, the blue veins purple and thicken. He looked up at Manuel, his eyes brown and clear. "We got married in it," he said.

"I heard the story."

Mr. Hamlin smiled and Manuel saw the man's teeth, chipped and brown from too many years. A funk emanated from his coat—stale like old bread—and he remembered Mrs. Hamlin telling him about the smell. He raised his cane and knocked it against Manuel's leg. "She told me what you charged. You could have asked her to pay double."

"I grew up fixing these cars," said Manuel. "It was easy."

"Regardless," Mr. Hamlin said, bumping the rubber end of the cane onto the floor. "You charged a bargain is all I'm saying. But we're too old to have to deal with a car falling apart every other Tuesday. Especially now with our children gone and far away, hearing from them once or twice a year with their too-busy lives." The man stuck his handkerchief back into his sleeve. "The truth is I'm going to give the car to my grandson."

"He'd like that."

"Of course he wouldn't like that. But what else am I going to do?"

Mr. Hamlin coughed, went breathless and coughed again. "Could I please have some water?" he asked, and Manuel went to the water cooler and got him a glass. He took a long drink and wiped his mouth. "November, 1953," he said, and he gave the glass back to Manuel. "That particular spell was for every cigarette I smoked during the month of November, 1953, and what do I have to show for it now?" He pointed to his temple. "Memories. Memories. But *what* memories, if I could only play you the movie."

Hector and Johnson watched from the far corner of the garage. They each held different parts of the same car, a bumper and front grille they'd removed to get at whatever problem they were working on. Manuel put the glass down onto the hood of the nearby Pontiac, knew there'd be no end to their wisecracks about this old man and his banter the instant he walked out the door.

"So then," Mr. Hamlin said, shaking his head, scrunching his eyes. He reached into his jacket pocket and presented a wrench. "My wife is the one who found this in the backseat. She figured it must be yours, so here I am." He handed the wrench to Manuel.

"You came all the way here to give me this?"

"I don't know, I guess I just wanted to see you. The miracle worker."

"I'm a mechanic."

"No," Mr. Hamlin said, raising his cane at his wife as her Mercedes pulled up in the driveway. "You're something more than that. My wife said it and I suppose I can see it too." He moved around Manuel. "And I like to see these kinds of things, however rare." He walked outside and Manuel followed. When they got to the car Mrs. Hamlin peeked up at Manuel from behind her dark sunglasses. Next door the dog Charlie growled.

"He was surprised," she said.

"I'm glad."

"But it's too much trouble and we're giving it to the grandson."

"So I hear."

"You got the wrench?"

Manuel held it up in the air. "Thanks," he said.

Mr. Hamlin got into the car, Charlie yelped from behind his fence, scrambled along its base and scratched at the wood with his nails. "All right then," Mrs. Hamlin said, and she backed the car from the driveway. Hector and Johnson came out from the garage up to Manuel and stood beside him.

"Quite the pair," Hector said.

"Made for each other," said Johnson.

Manuel stuck the wrench into his back pocket, headed back for the shop. When he got to his desk he looked through the window to see Mr. Hamlin give a wave to Hector and Johnson from the Mercedes before it turned onto the street. Hector and Johnson glanced at each other, shrugged, and raised their hands.

■

ROSA called him the next evening with the news that Henry Sanders' nephew had died. Her voice was calm and steady, and Manuel could tell she was doing her best to hold herself together. "But that's not why I'm calling," she said, and Manuel leaned into the kitchen table and waited for what was coming next, that she'd had enough of him and that these last couple of days had simply made clear what she'd already known. That he was a selfish *pendejo*. An idiot good-for-nothing.

"It's Henry," she said.

It turned out the reason Rosa had called Manuel was to tell him that Henry was in the boy's hospital room, and that he wouldn't leave until he could see Manuel and talk to him face-to-face. "Can you believe it?" she said.

"He's sitting in there?" said Manuel.

Rosa sighed. "The boy is gone. Now it's just Henry."

"He's sitting in there right now?"

"Look," she said. "I give you half an hour to get here. Then my supervisor is going to call the cops and have them take him away."

"Just like that."

"What else can he do?"

Manuel washed his hands and put on his clean shoes, walked out to his car feeling the pain of his heart, the emptiness that came from deep inside. Like the stirrings during those first nights after Octavio had died, waking in the middle of the night filled with the dread that he was absolutely, utterly alone. *Mi hijo,* he'd only wanted to tell him now that he was gone. *I am sorry for whatever it is that made you so sad. Your mother's leaving, what I can only guess I should have done to make things better.*

He found Rosa waiting for him outside the hospital, smoking a cigarette and pacing along the walkway. Her hair was tied back into a tight ponytail, the uniform almost too white against her brown neck and arms. He could tell she'd been crying, her eyes were puffy and red. She took a deep pull off her cigarette, tossed it onto the ground. "He won't leave," she said. "He's crazy as far as I can see."

"He's not crazy," Manuel said.

"*Estás bromeando.*"

"He's just upset. He's the one who did it is all."

They stood outside the hospital and an old man pushed his wife in a wheelchair past them. Manuel could feel the fear in his stomach from knowing Henry was up in that room waiting for him. All he wanted was to run away and get back into his car—drive and drive down the freeway until the night was over. To Santa Cruz, to Los Angeles, maybe even all the way to his mother's in Mexico. He imagined pulling up in front of her house, knocking on the door and giving her the surprise. But when Rosa pointed up to the second floor window of the hospital he knew he would do no such thing. "Well," she said, and she stared at him, wiped her eyes. "He's up there. He's up there and he's waiting for you."

HENRY sat on the bed in the dark, hunched over and rocking. Manuel came into the room and stood across from him, said, "I'm here." Henry didn't seem to take one bit of notice. His

breathing clicked in his throat, heavy and congested—outside
an ambulance pulled in below and its red lights flashed onto the
wall. Manuel went to the bed and sat beside Henry. He held his
hands faceup in his lap, the palms red from the light of the ambulance.

"I can't talk," Henry said.

"I know," said Manuel.

"I don't know what to do."

"I know."

The traffic moved on the street below, he listened to the
murmur of the people going inside and outside the building. A
siren whooped, went quiet. A bell rang from the desk outside.
Manuel stood and walked to the window, tapped on its glass
and the streetlight from the walkway shined inside. "I almost
got back into my car," he said. "So I wouldn't have to come
up."

Henry glanced up from his hands. "So what made you?"

"I couldn't say."

"You got something inside. I always knew you were
strong."

"I'm not strong," Manuel said, thinking of how many times
he'd almost never even gotten out of bed during those first days
after the accident. In fact, there had been the days when he
hadn't gotten out of bed, watching the room brighten and go
dark with the blankets pulled up around him. Henry got up,
came over to the window and stood next to Manuel. In the
light he looked even worse than when Manuel had last seen

him. There were the circles under his eyes that had become pouches, the sallow paleness of his skin. He turned to Manuel, then back to the window. "Which one is your car?" he asked.

Manuel said it was the Chrysler parked on the curb.

"So it is," Henry said. "I always wondered what you drove."

"It's nothing."

"*Nothing,*" said Henry. Then, "Did you get the Studebaker running?"

"I did."

"Good as new?"

"Almost," Manuel said, thinking of Mr. Hamlin and his cane, the smell of him and how he'd placed the wrench in his hand. "The owners don't want it though. They say it's too much trouble to keep so they're going to give it to the grandson."

Henry smiled, just barely. "That's gratitude."

"I suppose. But I guess I can understand it too."

"Can you?" said Henry.

"It was an anniversary present, the wife giving it to him when he hadn't even asked. I could tell he appreciated it. But then what? I mean, he got the Studebaker but it was going to start falling apart again, eventually. Her idea was a good one, but sometimes I think it's the thought behind the gesture that's the most important thing."

There was a knock on the door, then another, more forceful. The door creaked open with its light that poured inside, Rosa peeked in. "I'm sorry, Manuel," she said.

"What is it?"

"He's here."

"Who's here?"

"The police. I mean the security. They want the room."

"You said half an hour."

"That was an hour ago."

The door closed and Henry turned to the window.

"Well," Manuel said. "The time has come."

Henry nodded, his congested breathing fogged the glass. Then slowly, the bottom of his shoes squeaking against the dry, linoleum floor, he stepped back from the window and walked across the room. He stopped at the door, opened it the tiny crack. "I'm glad you fixed the Studebaker," he said.

ROSA came into the room after Henry left. She stood before Manuel and crossed her arms, leaned into the empty chair. Outside another ambulance pulled into the building, its red light reflected up through the window and gave the room the illusion of moving. "Grief makes you do funny things," Rosa said. She looked down at her feet, the white sneakers. "You know?"

Manuel turned and stared out the window. The sky was dark with the night, its patches of stars shining. And he could see it now, that Henry Sanders' nephew's death was simply a part of things. Like Octavio's birth, holding him in his arms as his eyes opened for the first time. Like the alfalfa field, running beside it with his father and laughing for no reason that he could ever name. And when he reached out and took Rosa's hand he knew that life could be terrible and sweet, that all there was really, were these small moments. The room swam, Rosa's breathing filled the silence, marked the glass. "That's me," she said, and he said that it was, ran his finger along the cloud. Down, then up, into the circle. The cars passed in the steady hum, their headlights bounced up toward the darkness of the sky, the stars above.

The Sun in the Sky

S ummer evenings were the best time. Alma sat on the lawn and stared up at the trees that rose around her house, the stars coming out in their clusters. She listened to the tones of her mother and father on the porch as they argued but didn't argue, talked about whatever it was they'd talked about so often. Her father stepped down from the porch, there was the glow of her mother's cigarette that crackled, the cloud of smoke that swirled up before disappearing. Her father walked across the lawn, placed his hand onto Alma's head. "Quite a night," he said.

"Yes," said Alma.

Her brother Daniel sat on Mr. Taylor's lawn at the end of the street. It's where he went whenever the fights started. One moment he'd been sitting there next to Alma and the next he was walking away. She looked over at him, wondered what Mr.

Taylor thought about her brother sitting on his lawn like that. She liked Mr. Taylor. He would sit on his porch and ask her the state capitals as she passed him on the sidewalk, toss her a golf ball whenever she named one correctly.

"Underneath this ground are more bones than we know," said her father. He held his hand steady on Alma's head, as if to see what she might say to something like that. Then he lifted his hand, strolled from the lawn to the car and reached into its open window. He glanced back at Alma and gave her a smile. There were the crickets screaking in the near distance, the hum of the freeway. *Bones,* thought Alma, *the grass coming up from the skeletons all around.*

Her father leaned back from the car. "Here we are," he said, and he held the car's cigarette lighter between his thumb and forefinger, orange with its light. "Go and tell your brother," he said. "Run back to me by the time it goes out or that will be the end of me. *Capiche?*"

"No *capiche,*" said her mother from the porch.

"What's the matter?"

"They're children."

"Exactly."

Alma shot up, immediately understood the rules of the game—her father had done this so often—it was a ritual as he'd explained to Alma and her brother. She ran to Daniel, told him their father would die if they didn't reach him by the time the lighter faded. And he understood too, this ritual, after all. They ran, their bare feet slapped the concrete, its cement still warm from the heat of the day. The cool air pressed into Alma's face, made its whistling sound past her ears. The orange, the orange, it was a tiny mark ahead jittering in the movement of her running. Daniel ran ahead, reached their father before Alma. But their father was already falling. "It's too late," he said. "You didn't quite make it in time." Alma bent over him, her breath hot and sticky in her throat. He closed his eyes, let the lighter fall.

Their mother smoked her cigarette. "And the award goes to," she said.

Nothing from their father.

"Okay then," she said, coming down from the porch onto the lawn. "We'll see about that." Alma and Daniel parted, their mother knelt beside their father, brought the cigarette to his lips. "Breathe," she said.

Their father kept his eyes closed, didn't move a muscle.

"I said *breathe.*"

A small intake, a sudden glow.

"That's it."

Then deep and bright, like the warmest fire. Their mother looked up at Daniel and Alma, her eyes radiant. She turned to their father, took back the cigarette and bent down close to his face. She kissed him then, long and hard. Their father's eyes fluttered, she stepped back and smiled. "You're a son of a bitch," she said.

THEIR FATHER LEFT the next week, Alma came home from the swimming pool and he was gone. He'd written a note to each of them, typed on the stationery with the letterhead of the Sacramento university where he taught. But when they all compared the letters they saw that nothing was different, really, all that separated each was their names. The letters were short, telling them he was so sorry, that he only wished things had turned out differently. *Please know that I will always love you,* he ended each letter.

Alma got through the sixth grade thinking about her father most every day. It was funny, she'd long expected him to leave after so many of the arguments and the fact that he'd spent less and less time at home. But his absence left her bewildered, stunned. "It will get easier," her mother said, but it didn't. Alma would walk home from school and imagine him coming up to her with his arms out, telling her that he knew there was no way he could ever come back but that he thought he would give it a try anyway.

He officially left his teaching position at the university and moved to Portland with one of his students. Her name was Lynn and she was getting her degree in anthropology, could "write like nobody's business about Hegel," as he'd explained to Alma's mother and she'd gone on to tell Daniel and Alma. "You should know this only proves how much of a prick your father is," she would end the story each time, her voice always breaking. "A coward afraid to grow old."

She quit her low-paying job at the adult school where she taught ceramics, took work at a law firm while telling Alma and Daniel sometimes one had to work for the devil to get his or her wings. One weekend she put everything their father had left behind into boxes, gave it away to the Salvation Army. Alma could have no doubt, she thought, that her mother was getting over her father.

Then one night she woke to hear music quietly playing. She got out of bed and padded down the hallway, opened the living room door without a sound. And there was her mother, staring out the window with the cigarette in her hand, wearing her father's bathrobe pulled tightly around her waist as the radio played its almost familiar song.

SUMMER FINALLY came again, the world slowed down and the air grew heavier with the unrelenting sun. Mr. Taylor tossed the golf balls without asking Alma any questions at all, told her that her father's leaving was how things could sometimes be, and what a shame she had to be so young to find out about it like that. At night Alma lay out on the lawn gazing at the sky while her mother sat on the porch reading her book and smoking her cigarette, Daniel watching the television with the volume turned up much too loudly.

It was the middle of July when Alma fell asleep on the lawn, the roots below her pushing against her thin shoulders, the dirt clumped beneath the grass here and there. *Bones,* she thought, and she had the dream that had come and gone, a flash of her father holding her mother and the stars falling down. Alma opened her eyes and her mother sat on the porch behind her, the television blared. She knew in that instant that her father was gone forever, and for the first time it didn't give her the pang she'd expected but a tiny sense of peace. The stars moved although she couldn't see the movement, her father moved too. She imagined him far away in Portland, his house surrounded by the trees she'd seen in the pictures of the city from magazines. She could see him sitting on the couch, the book on his lap with his large, thin hand flat across the page. *Alma,* she imagined him thinking as she spread her arms wide. *Alma,* the very name.

SHE BEGAN high school, wrote for the school newspaper and was told by her teachers she had talent to burn. She wrote articles on the homeless, followed them around and spent a night underneath the freeway, much to her mother's dismay. The faculty held her up as a shining example of the good one person could do, while the students gave her the cold shoulder, called her the Ragamuffin with the heart of gold. She had a few friends, mostly girls who were quiet and strange. There was Chloe, who smoked cigarettes behind the school's field and read her poetry aloud, Francine, who smelled like insect repellent and always wore orange socks. Alma found that she could feel comfortable with these girls, be herself while offering her hand through friendship, a small gesture of kindness.

Graduation loomed and she made plans to leave Sacramento, to move to San Francisco and get her degree in journalism at the state university there. Daniel had already moved out, gotten married to a woman with a six-year-old child. Her mother told Alma to go ahead and leave too if she wanted, that it was time she found out about the world and all its secrets. Some good, some not so good.

Like death, which was no secret at all, but sometimes felt like it the way people acted so surprised whenever it came. Mr. Taylor had the stroke in December, was gone six months later. For the first couple of months after the stroke he sat on the porch wrapped in the blanket not even recognizing her. Then he stopped coming out. Three weeks later he was dead. The house was emptied not long after, a new family moved in and painted the house a new color, cut down all the bushes and planted new ones. Mr. Taylor was gone, and Alma still had the golf balls in a drawer that he used to throw her way, and all she could think was how sad it was that a person could disappear forever and these golf balls could still be here like that.

ALMA signed up for a book-making class during the summer to pass the time. A boy named Kent who worked in a printing press taught the class. She brought in her various articles on the homeless, he helped her make it into the book that he tied together with string. He took the book in his hands and flipped through the pages, held the string down when she tied the knot.

A week later she was sitting in Kent's car as he drove along the river road. The moon was over the water, the tall grass brushed along the sides of the car and when she put out her hand she came back with a clump of the green stems. Kent drove for miles and miles, finally pulled the car over. "This is where I like to go sometimes," he said.

"It's nice."

They sat and listened to the crickets and the owl that hooted in the distance, the nearby gurgle of the water. Alma stuck her head out and stared up at the stars in the sky, breathed in a mouthful of the sweet river air. "My father would call this a night good enough to eat," she said.

"Yeah?"

"Yeah."

"He left me when I was a kid," Alma said. "He was a son of a bitch."

"But not always, I bet."

"No," Alma said. "Not always."

She ran her fingers along the vinyl dashboard and pushed in the cigarette lighter. "There was this game he played," she said, and she went on about the way he held out the lighter and told her he would die if she didn't reach him by the time it faded. "It was the best feeling running toward him like that," she said.

Kent opened his door. "Come on."

"Where?"

He walked out to the side of the road. "Right here," he said, and he disappeared behind the tall grass.

Alma got out of the car and stumbled through the dark, found him sitting on the ground. "This is crazy," she said.

He patted the ground next to him.

"But it's the middle of nowhere."

"I cleared this area myself," he said. "It's really nice once you sit down and put your head back."

Alma looked at the car, the empty road black as grease.

"Come on," he said.

And this was how Alma spent her summer, going out to the road each night to lie back on the grass that pricked into her arms and shoulders. Sometimes he would kiss her as they lay there and her chest would go warm just below the breastbone, as if being filled by the warmest liquid. *Heavy,* she would think. *Love was heavy.* And sometimes he would just hold her hand and this same warmth would overcome her, and she would squeeze his hand back as he said it into her ear, softly, then more loudly. The leaves would move in the breeze, the birds and insects make their sounds. "Just us and everything around," he would say.

ALMA stayed in Sacramento if for no other reason than to be with Kent, took a job at the bookstore and worked in the children's section. She felt a restlessness during these days that made her want to jump, like the world was just opening up, these truths laid out before her in succession with each passing day. She read and read, taking home countless books from the bookstore. She would go into work with her eyes wider open than they had ever been, each sound and sight taking on some greater significance. *I know why this is happening,* she wanted to tell each and every customer. *I know why you are sad and why this world turns and what it is that makes the dog cry for its master.* She filled her head with these books, grew anxious with the possibility of what tomorrow might hold.

It was the end of the week when she came home to find Kent lying in bed in his boxers, just as she had come home to find him lying in bed in his boxers every day, it seemed, since she'd moved into his apartment. Alma sat at the dresser and removed her earrings, set them down into the tiny wooden chest. "Don't you ever get tired of the same thing?" she asked, watching him in the mirror.

"I like it," he said.

She shook her head. "No bird soars too high who soars with his own wings."

"I hear a book talking."

"William Blake."

"Of course William Blake," Kent said. He leaned onto his elbow and considered her. His eyes shone from beneath his long lashes, when he put out his hand there was the black of the ink that lined his palm. "Listen," he said. "Change is the gas we put in our cars to drive us away from each other." He nodded. "I made that up right now. You can quote me."

"*Please,*" said Alma.

"Why don't you just come here?"

She kicked off her shoes and sighed, got up from the dresser and sat down next to him. He reached over her lap and pulled her close, gazed into her face with a smile. His front teeth protruded slightly, giving him a slightly goofy air. "See, this isn't so bad," he said before he kissed her. He pulled the sheets over them and his breath was warm against her cheek. "See," he said, moving even closer. "This isn't so bad at all."

■

SHE MOVED to San Francisco the next month. It was foggy and cold, as expensive as Kent told her it would be. She took a job in a health food store working afternoons and weekends, found a tiny studio out near the ocean where the rent was something she could afford. Besides the daily work, she volunteered as an English tutor at the university that she planned to transfer to in the fall. She made salad in the evenings with the fruits and vegetables from the store, arranged her studio with used furniture from yard sales in the neighborhood. A Russian man named Vladimir lived below her. He would come up occasionally and see how she was doing, point with his hat around the studio and tell her that someday she would look back at this time and wonder how she had ever lived this way. "Not that you have anything bad here," he'd say. "But a rug or painting would help warm it up."

New Year's Day she invited Vladimir over for dinner, said this would be their new start to a fantastic year. She served him a salad but he declined, said he couldn't digest greens and that salad dressing gave him heartburn. He eventually settled on bread and butter, drank the red wine and began to talk about Russia and how much he would give to go back once more and have things be the way they were. "Things were not so good," he said. "But it was home. And home is home no matter what." He finished the bottle of wine and asked for another, Alma told him that was all that she had. "Oh?" he said, and he shook his head and began to sing a song from his childhood. Then he covered his eyes and grabbed his hat, staggered out of the studio. From that day on when she saw him in the hallway he would give her an embarrassed face and move past her as though they had never shared this time.

THERE WAS A BOY named Duncan who came in for tutoring at the university. He needed some brushing up on the fundamentals, as he put it with his odd accent that she later found out was Canadian. One day he asked her out and she agreed, figured she'd lived in the city for nearly a month and wasn't it time to have some fun. They went out for a burrito on a rainy night, he told her about his major which was business administration, how his father owned a hardware store and that he eventually wanted Duncan to take it over. "But maybe I don't want that," he said, gesturing to the poster in the taquería of the busty woman riding on her horse. "Maybe I want something more."

Afterward they ended up at his nearby apartment where his three housemates were gone, *likely for the evening,* as he'd unnecessarily explained. He lived above a restaurant where belly-dancing accompanied the meal, they sat on the couch in the living room and listened to the swirling music from the musicians below. People clapped and the music stopped, Duncan raised his hand. Next came the finger cymbals, guitar and bongos as the music began once again. "She's going for her encore now," Duncan said, opening a bottle of beer for Alma, then one for himself, placing them on the nearby table.

"Is she pretty?" Alma asked. She'd caught a glimpse of the woman through the restaurant window on the way up, had seen her long flowing hair but little else. Surely she was pretty, but she wanted to hear what Duncan had to say about it.

"Maybe," he said, and she guessed that he'd probably watched her dance too many evenings to count, that he was in love with her but would never tell. He put out his hand, pulled her close. *Kent,* she thought, and suddenly felt a sadness she tried to push away with all her might.

"Not yet," she said.

"That's fine." He reached for his bottle of beer and took a drink. "You like the neighborhood?" he said.

She nodded.

"I've got to say it takes some adjusting," he said. "Where I come from the only thing going on this time of year is the snow. Maybe a car wreck here and there." He stood, looked out his window. "Why right now there is a man pushing his shopping cart across the sidewalk through the rain, and I can only imagine the stories he has to tell."

Alma recalled her articles on the homeless, knew what the homeless man would have to tell all right. That life was a bitch and that a car wreck in the middle of Saskatchewan, or across the street for that matter, didn't matter a hill of beans. Duncan was a romantic, she had no doubt about that. She figured he'd probably come from a nice family, that they stayed up nights worrying about their only son as he sent home postcards describing in vivid detail the various calamities outside his window. He faced Alma, gave her a collegiate smile. He had thick, dark eyebrows, hard, blue eyes. His complexion was smooth like an egg, untroubled and clear, his nose broad and slightly upturned.

"The rain is really coming down," he said.

"Like cats and dogs," said Alma.

"I never understood that. I mean, why cats and dogs?"

Alma said, "It's the racket."

Duncan came back to the couch and sat next to her. He put his hand on her thigh. The music from downstairs got louder, its rhythm increased. *Perfect,* thought Alma. *Like the soundtrack to this moment that was meant to happen.* Duncan came in for the kiss and she reciprocated, considered how funny it was that here was another pair of lips pressing against hers, tingling in this exciting new way. His tongue slithered inside her mouth, she rubbed her tongue back against his and tasted him. The clapping came from downstairs, the encore. Alma pictured the woman onstage spinning her head from side to side, her belly doing its intricate moves. Duncan reached under her shirt, slid his hand up under her bra and onto her breast.

THE NEXT MORNING there were the clouds in the sky, threatening more rain. Alma walked along Valencia and then up Sixteenth, the coffee shops were just opening and the buses rolled along the street making their blue sparks from the electrical cables. She passed the Mission Dolores church when the clouds opened, the rain began to sprinkle down. Older women wearing plastic head coverings, gray-haired men in dark blue raincoats, young parents holding their children's hands, and grandparents holding their grandchildren's hands too—all of them skittered from their cars and buses, streamed into the church past its magnificently huge, wooden doors. Alma stepped onto the curb and the rain became suddenly fiery. She circled back toward the steps of the church, hesitated for the moment, then went inside.

There she found the familiar, warm dimness she remembered from her childhood. She dipped her finger into the bowl and placed the cool water on her forehead, ducked into the pew and felt the comfort of the place. The candles made their waxy, oily smell, the light shined through the stained-glass windows, each color a jewel. The priest walked up the aisle, the song rose from the congregation. When the song ended the priest made the sign of the cross, raised his arms. The rain pinged onto the roof and drummed against the windows. "Welcome to mass on this very wet day," the priest said.

He read from the large red Bible held in front of him by the altar boy. Alma listened but didn't listen, these words she'd heard so many times. She recited the prayer, sat down and closed her eyes, felt their stickiness from the lack of sleep. And it occurred to her where she'd been, how funny it was that she could spend the night with a boy she barely knew and come here like this. It gave her a tiny thrill knowing what she'd done, that this was a part of moving on. But with the moving on came a profound sadness, a sacrifice she could not quite name. She remembered Kent in his boxers, his goofy smile and the way he'd told her that change was the gas we put in our cars, how he'd pulled her close and thrown the sheets over their bodies. He'd kissed her mouth, her neck, her breasts. They'd moved from one side of the bed to the other, she'd rolled from top to bottom. And when he'd finally made his sound there'd been the warmth that started from her heart, then spread. She'd held him, wanting him to be a part of her—fused together as one—even while she'd felt the tears beginning, this moment passing, this conclusion.

The mass went on and the priest's deep voice rang out and echoed. Alma stood, then sat back down. Her head was light and she had the very distinct impression that she was fainting. But she didn't faint, she simply held her hands together. And when the priest raised the Communion wafer over his head she imagined lifting above him, the golden bells ringing as she floated up into the ceiling's arches, above the heads of the parishioners, around and around, just circling as the rain came down.

ALMA kept on seeing Duncan, although she didn't feel for him in any special way. He discussed with her his various theories about right and wrong, slowly came around to the idea that perhaps nothing was as clear as he wished it to be. *A man piss-ing in the street was wrong,* he would tell her. *But what if the man had nowhere to piss?* Alma would ask. *Then the man should have considered that before drinking the six-pack,* he would respond as she named something called addiction. And this was how it went, Duncan slowly realizing that maybe the world was a more complicated place than he thought it was, Alma taking some small pleasure in his learning.

She continued to tutor at the university, moved up as an as-sistant to the director of the center when the prior assistant left without warning. The director gave her his class one evening, watched from the back as Alma made the marks on the chalkboard and diagrammed the various parts of the sentence. Duncan watched with the director, smiled proudly as she wrapped up the talk and tossed the chalk from hand to hand. "You were like some weathercaster," he said afterward, giving her a kiss on the cheek.

KENT called Alma from work the morning after her classroom lecture. They talked for a few minutes about the insignificant matters, she told him about the tutoring and health food store, how things were opening up for her in San Francisco. She listened to the sound of her own voice, how far away it seemed.

"That all seems nice," he said.

"It is. It really is."

"But Alma," he said. "When are you coming back?"

"Back?"

"Yeah, back. As in here. As in Sacramento."

Alma wrapped the telephone cord tightly around her finger, looked out her window and watched as Vladimir crossed the street, stepped onto the curb at the bus stop. He took out his leather change purse, counted his change and snapped it shut as the bus pulled up. "I told you before," she said slowly. "There's nothing for me there."

"Of course there is."

"There isn't."

Alma could hear the hum and clank of the printing press in

the background and she thought back to Kent's long, pointed finger pushing down the knot of her book all that time ago, how she'd neatly tied it. Her chest tugged, when next came the memory of their sitting on the bed as she'd tried to explain she wanted more from life than this, the end of the road already within sight—growing old with this boy who would become the man happy with so little, staying in Sacramento until the end of his days. "Kent," Alma said, and she could hear his breathing, slow and steady, like his heart so measured and sure. "I need to go," she said finally, before hanging up.

AT THE STORE she washed the carrots and the celery while she tried not to think of Kent. Hearing his voice had left her agitated, stirred up. She moved on to the cabbage when Duncan suddenly came through the door and sidled next to her, gave her his hug. "What's the matter?" he said in his breathless, Canadian way. "I can tell there's something the matter."

She said it was nothing, that she had a lot on her mind, stuff he could never really know.

"Well tell me then," he said.

Alma ran her hands over the cabbage. "I'd rather not."

He put on his earnest face, crossed his arms. "You can talk to me," he said.

Talk, thought Alma, and she let out a tiny, mean laugh that she didn't recognize. She'd used him, it was plain to see, and she could feel her mouth go sour from the thought of it. Nearby a customer rolled her cart toward the cantaloupes, picked one up and put it to her nose. Another opened a plastic bag and dropped in several oranges. Alma turned to Duncan, said in a lowered voice, "You think I teach like a weathercaster?"

Duncan smiled. "What?"

"Like I said. A weathercaster?"

"Is that it? That I compared you to that?"

"Do you?"

He held his smile, obviously trying to come up with the right answer. "A weathercaster has all those charts and graphs."

Alma tended to the cabbage, grabbed a head from the pile.

"What's the big deal?" said Duncan.

She plucked the head's leaves, tore at the brown edges.

"*What?*"

"The big deal is that weathercasters are dopes. Nerds. Geeks. They stand around and tell us what's coming as if they even know." She pushed the head back into the pile, rolled it on top of the others. "Guesswork is all it is, even with all those *charts and graphs,* and still they can't get it right."

"So I used the wrong analogy."

"Oh, Duncan," Alma said. "The problem is that's all you ever do."

"Oh yeah?" Duncan said, his voice suddenly booming.

Heads in the store turned, the manager peeked out from the office.

"Cool it," said Alma.

"Cool it? *Cool it?*" He picked up a cabbage and stuck it under his arm. "Okay then," he said. "This is your head. How's *that* for an analogy?" He tossed the cabbage back and stormed out, slammed the door behind him so that the wind chimes used for bells clattered. The manager came out from his office, rubbed his gray beard and squinted his eyes.

"That wasn't good," he said, carefully.

Alma stared at the cabbage. "No it wasn't."

"We have a policy about bringing your outside life to the store."

"I know," said Alma.

"Maybe you could go home to think about it."

"I'll be fine."

"No," he said. "I think you should go." He raised his hand and quivered his fingers. "As in good-bye."

"You're letting me go?" Alma said.

The manager shrugged, grinned tightly at the few customers taking it in. "Let's just call it a leave of absence."

"Perfect," Alma said. "Perfect, perfect, perfect." Then she walked across the aisle, grabbed an apple and gave it a tremendous bite before tossing it onto the floor. She smashed it into a pulp under her shoe, left the door open on the way out with the chimes ringing in the wind.

WEEKS WENT BY. Alma spent her time walking in the park and reading books from the library. She applied for jobs at the bookstores but was told there were no openings, finally tried for a position at the café up the street from her apartment and they asked her to start that day. The work was hard, she made the coffee and steamed the milk, washed all the cups. At the end of the shift she cleaned the rubber mats and washed down the counter, mopped the floor and wiped the windows. It was difficult work she told herself with each new appointed task, but work nonetheless. And this work was a gift, albeit a small one, that left her more tired when she left the café than she could ever remember being.

VLADIMIR knocked on her studio door one Saturday afternoon. He stood in the doorway smiling, holding a painting. "I saw this in the store," he said, holding it up. There were the trees orange with autumn, a creek running to the side. It left a serene impression, and when he handed it over Alma could only think he was trying to make up for the terrible New Year's dinner. "It's Russian," he said. "Do you like?"

Alma said that she did, although she thought it was a touch sad, this portrait of quiet and passing. The fading sun speckled in the water, leaves covered the forest floor.

"I found it in Goodwill," Vladimir said.

"The leaves are very pretty."

Vladimir nodded. "It's the best time," he said. "The air is not too cold and not too warm." He closed his eyes. "The smell."

"It's nice?"

"It's better than nice. It's wonderful."

He tipped his hat and left her with the painting. She

placed it against the wall and sat down on her couch that was covered with the blanket because of the springs that popped out. She was supposed to be at work in ten minutes, and it was going to be a particularly busy day in that it was the weekend. She looked out the window and the sky was white with its usual fog, a few patches of blue. She turned back to the painting.

Ten minutes passed. Then twenty. The telephone rang and she covered it with a pillow, went back to the painting and sat down next to it. She ran her fingers over the brushes of paint, the tiny dots of light rippling in the water. Like Monet, she thought. Or the light itself. The telephone rang again and she moved closer to the painting, imagined herself deep inside it. Gone from this place with only the trees all around, the creek burbling beside her. Now then, a falling leaf that circles down, listening, just listening.

SHE GOT A reprimand from work for being late, was told if it happened again there wouldn't be a next time. "It won't," she said, even as she told herself she should be so lucky. She stayed late that evening cleaning the refrigerator as well as the counters and rubber mats and windows, came home even more exhausted than on her first night. It wasn't until the next morning that she saw the letter from her mother in the mailbox. *I heard from your father,* the letter began. The writing was careful, as if her mother had contemplated for days how to say it. *He wants to spend Easter Sunday with his family,* it said, *because it has been such a long time.* She ended the paragraph with a large break, then a star she had drawn for no apparent reason, jagged and colored in with the blue ink. *All of us together,* the letter concluded below the star. *Daniel too.*

Alma resisted the temptation to immediately call her mother and ask if she had lost her mind. Here was her father coming home with some kind of romantic idea that he could make everything as it was before. *The goddamned fool* was all she could think, even as she dialed her mother to tell her to stop, to turn him away, to say no. But then her voice came on the line, asking first thing if she had gotten the letter, telling Alma that her father had cried to her on the telephone and only asked her forgiveness, saying he wanted nothing more.

Nothing more but his own peace of heart, thought Alma. She put the letter back into its envelope, set it down on the table and remembered her mother calling their father a prick and coward, her voice always breaking. And she knew that her mother still loved her father, even after all these years, that to come home would be the smallest favor she could offer. *I will be there,* she said in her head, then to her mother when she finally asked. *I will be there,* she said aloud.

HER FATHER looked older, but of course he did, it had been nearly ten years since they'd last seen each other. His hair was cut short as ever, his face wrinkled with lines that gave his eyes the illusion of sinking. She had taken the bus in, caught a taxi from the station. When she pulled up to the house there he'd been, sitting on the porch with her mother. Alma had gotten out of the taxi and walked across the lawn, her father stepped down from the porch. "You're back," she'd said as she stared at him with her hands in her pockets.

Daniel had called Alma the night before and explained he was ready to bury the hatchet, but when he said that he loved their father almost as much as he hated him, Alma could see he wasn't ready to bury it too far. Things hadn't turned out so well for Daniel. He spent most of his time at his house when he wasn't at the job stuffing boxes with files that would be silverfish in twenty years anyway, as he put it. There were the inestimable nights of pasta and bad television, and the fact that his wife was living with an auto mechanic who owned a blue boat that sparkled. He told her all this and seemed to take some kind of sick pride in the wrong inflicted upon him. "What have I done to deserve this?" he'd asked, ironically and not ironically too.

When Daniel came up to the house it was with great hesitation, refusing eye contact with their father while he nudged ahead the daughter that wasn't his. Her name was Shannon, and she was seven years old, pretty despite her thin lips and too large forehead. She wore a blue dress that tied in the back, white espadrilles and a sun hat. Daniel hugged their mother, then Alma, shook his father's hand when there was nothing else he could do.

DINNER WENT as well as could be expected, which wasn't so good but not so bad either, now that Alma considered her father

at this table. After all, there could have been yelling and screaming, broken plates and glasses as they all made the point about
what a thing it had been for him to leave them as he had. But
here they were, carrying on in the conversations that explained
their lives from the time he'd left, this talk of her father's teaching at the Portland university and Daniel's paper-pushing at the
company he hated, their mother's work in the law firm. Alma
told her father about her tutoring and how she had even taught
a class while the director looked on. She explained that the students in the class had taken notes, how funny it was to glance out
and see them writing down every word she told them. "I even
wrote on the chalkboard," she said. "Like a weathercaster," she
added. "As some dumb boy once put it."

"There are a few of those," her father said. "Dumb boys, that is."

Come now, thought Alma, *don't try to ingratiate yourself.* She
took a long drink of her water, put the glass down.

"Right?" he continued, and Alma glared at the water in the
glass, the ice and its slivered, blue lines.

Her father wiped his mouth, nodded to himself. "So you're
in San Francisco then," he said, and he told her that he'd been
to San Francisco during Christmas, that if he'd known she'd
lived there he would have called. "If that would have been okay
with you," he added.

Alma took another drink from her glass.

"I was there for a convention. The Modern Language Association." He laughed hoarsely, an empty sound. "What a boring
load of stiffs."

"Boring," said Daniel.

Alma pointed out that she'd read somewhere San Francisco was the most popular place to have a convention, that it was the favorite place for conventioneers to go to for such things. Daniel shook his head, put down his knife and fork. "The Modern Language Association?" he said.

"That's what it was."

"Uh huh."

He stared around at the table, rested his deadpan eyes on their father. "And were there any Hegel scholars at the event?"

"Hegel?"

"Yeah Hegel. Boring stiff Hegel scholars."

"I'm sure there were a few."

"Yeah I'm sure there were," said Daniel. "What about your one particular scholar? The one you left us for?"

"Daniel," said their mother.

"I'm asking."

"That's okay to ask," said their father. "She's gone, a long time now, went and married a boy her age." He leaned back in his chair, pushed his thumbs together. "It was all for the best. I'm convinced it's all for the best. All of this. Everything in this life of mistakes that we learn from."

"You've got to be kidding," said Daniel.

"No," their father said, and he offered a meek smile. "I'm not."

After dinner Daniel and Shannon left the kitchen, Alma went to the telephone in the guest room. She wanted to call Kent, tell him that here was her father trying to make things okay that would never in a million years be okay, to change what couldn't be changed, the terrible damage done. She wanted to say these things to him into the telephone, hang up and sit back in the chair. She wanted to drift off into a deep sleep and wake, look at the window and see Kent standing there. She would go to the window and open it wide. "Hello then," he would say. He'd put out his hand, the sky would turn its colors from blue to black.

But Kent didn't answer his telephone, the machine picked up. She waited for the beep, not sure if she really wanted to leave a message. "I'm in Sacramento," she said, after a long pause. "I was hoping you could come by and we could talk about things." When she came back to the kitchen she found her mother and father sitting at the table, quiet and gazing off at different walls. The birds squawked outside the window, the poplar tree swayed in the gentle breeze. Alma leaned against the door. There was the dust that swirled above her mother and father like tiny planets, the quality of the fading light as the day neared its end.

HER MOTHER and father cleaned up the table while Daniel watched the television with the volume turned high in its usual way. Shannon sat on the couch next to Alma and looked through the pictures of Daniel as the child, marveled that her stepfather could have once been so young. Inside the kitchen their mother was speaking loudly, her voice in the waver.

"The plate goes *there*," she said. "Not there, but *there*."

Daniel's eyes met Alma's.

"I'm putting it there," said their father. "No problem."

171

The sound of plate against plate, the dishwasher door slamming.

"Okay?"

"Maybe this wasn't such a good idea," their mother said.

"It's not so bad."

"No?" their mother said. "Easy for you to say."

"Oh, Elizabeth."

"Oh, Elizabeth *what?*"

"Here we go," Daniel said. "Just like old times."

Alma stood and reached out for Shannon. "How about we go for a walk?"

Shannon flicked back the hair from her eyes and regarded Alma. The girl's large forehead seemed to carry the weight of all her thoughts as she considered the question. "Well?" Alma said, and from the kitchen came the metallic clatter of the silverware being dumped into the sink. "What do you say girlfriend? Outside? Me and you?"

"A walk?" Daniel said. "Now?"

"Why not?"

"I don't know. It's getting kind of dark."

"So it's getting kind of dark. It'll be nice."

The air was sweet with the grassy smell, the sun gone with its remnant of light still lingering. Alma closed the door behind her and they stood out on the driveway, the streetlights blinked on, one by one, illuminating the sidewalk and all the houses. "Look at that," Alma said.

Shannon took in the flickering lights, hiked her dress above her knees and let it fall. "Neat," she said.

They walked up the sidewalk to the Taylor lawn, sat down after Alma saw that the house was dark and the new occupants—who weren't really the new occupants anymore—were gone. Alma stretched her legs and took off her shoes, Shannon took off her shoes too. "You know the man who lived in this house used to toss me golf balls," Alma said. "He would ask me the state capitals, and later when my father left he would just toss them without asking anything at all."

Shannon looked down at Alma's hand. "I like your fingernails," she said.

"Thank you," said Alma. She'd painted them silver for the trip home, bought the polish in a store that sold wigs and candles.

"I ask Daniel if I can paint my nails but he tells me I can't."

"What does your mother say?"

Shannon brought her palm close to her face. "I don't know," she said.

"You ever talk?"

"Not for a while."

"See her?"

Shannon moved the hand, spread her fingers and peered through them. The sky was a dark and stately blue, its light giving the girl's skin a luminescent quality. The first star had come out with its brightness, the night coming on now. "Daniel watches her on the boat."

"Boat?"

"He goes to the levee and watches my mom and the boyfriend on the boat in the river, takes me along and he sits in the chair."

"He takes you?" Alma said, as calmly as she could manage.

"He cries," said Shannon.

A car sputtered by and when Alma saw it was Kent she caught her breath, got to her feet. Kent drove past Alma and Shannon and parked across the street, got out of his car and stood there with his white T-shirt glowing blue from the light of the sky. Alma marched across the lawn toward him. "Kent," she said in her steadiest voice. When he held her she wanted to fold up inside him, lose herself in his arms. But something was wrong, she could feel his awkwardness. She stepped back, looked him over. He was still the same Kent, his hair long and unkempt, blown this way and that from the ride over with the open windows. "What is it?" she said.

He stared down at his feet, the tennis shoes with the holes.

"What?" she said, even though she knew, and she could feel the downward swerve of emptiness, the pain that could be located. Alma's legs quivered, her fingers did some kind of tingle. "You're seeing someone new?" she managed to say.

"I never figured you'd come back. Especially after the last phone call."

"The last phone call," Alma said.

"Hanging up like you did."

Alma crossed her arms over her chest and could feel the tears coming but held them back. *Please,* she thought. *Don't happen. Don't happen now.* Her head went light and she remembered the mass from that wet morning, the sound of the rain coming down with the windows shining their colors so brightly. Kent put out his hand. There were the black lines from the ink that ran along his palm, cracked and intricate like a map indicating the trajectory of the wind and all its patterns.

ALMA'S father stood with Daniel on the driveway. He had his suitcase in one hand, looked out at the street. Her mother had put on her sweater and was holding Shannon's sun hat, shuffling toward Alma's father's car. "At least he made it through dinner," Alma said. Her father waved and pointed to his watch as if this explained anything.

"Your father?" Kent said.

"It was."

Shannon shuffled down the sidewalk with the espadrilles in her hand.

"Girlfriend," said Alma.

The girl turned, made a half-smile with her thin lips.

"We'll see you again."

"Okay."

"You be good."

"I will," Shannon said, and she broke into the run. Alma's father knelt when Shannon reached them, hugged the girl for a good, long while. Daniel gaped down at his keys as if they were new and unexpected, her mother twiddled the sun hat in her fingers and glanced both ways down the street.

"God," Alma said. "I can't think of a worse Easter."

"I guess so," said Kent.

Alma looked up at the clusters of stars now dotting the sky, the yellow moon that rose slowly over the horizon. *My family,* she thought. Her father coming home with these ridiculous, false hopes for redemption, her brother taking the little girl to the levee and crying. Alma shoved her hands into her pockets, the breeze moved through the trees and the dampness from the lawn came up around them. She could just make out her father's deep voice from the driveway, her mother telling him it was probably time to get going.

Kent trotted from the lawn to the sidewalk.

"You're leaving?"

"No," he said, going to his car. "I'll be right back."

Alma stared back at the sky, its stars that glimmered. *Drive away if you want to,* she said to herself. It would be the perfect ending to this night that could only get better. She turned away from Kent, buried her toes in the grass and felt its scraggly blades push up between them.

"Here comes the moon."

It was Kent, and in his hand was the cigarette lighter from his car.

Alma stepped back. "Jesus Christ," she said. "*Kent.*"

He smiled.

"It's a surprise is all."

He gave her the lighter. It glowed bright orange and the heat from its metal burned against her fingers, its cigarette smell reminding her of so many years past. Kent crossed his arms and Alma remembered driving with him in the car at night and putting out her hand for the stems of grass, how they would lie on the ground as he whispered into her ear as if she were the only person he had ever really known.

"Well," Kent said. "Go on."

Alma walked to the middle of the street and held the lighter out. "Hey," she said, then more loudly, "*Hey!*" Daniel froze, looked in her direction. Her father put down his suitcase while her mother clapped, Shannon came out from the car. Alma centered herself in the street, raised the lighter. *I'm alone,* she thought, even as she felt her heart move, its warmth spread outward with the heaviness that filled her. Because here was her family, all that she had, her home and no home, these people. And suddenly they were running—her father, mother, brother, and Shannon—a mad, stomping rush down the middle of the street, the streetlights illuminating them between the patches of darkness. Alma raised the lighter higher above her head. When she closed her eyes they were almost there, pushing and stumbling, their faces right before her.

A Dream, Not Alone

R odney drove to the hospital with Viviane slipping in and
out of her fevered sleep. She was in pain, that much was
evident. The treatment had likely run its course, the illness now
doing what it had originally set out to do. This past month or so
had simply been the stopgap, the temporary solution, they'd
been told as much by each and every person. But still, Rodney
had wanted to believe it might turn into something more last-
ing—he thought of the tomatoes spilling out onto the table and
looking up at Viviane and being certain of it in that moment.

He let a red pickup pass from behind and glanced over at
Viviane, her eyes crinkled tight. When she'd had Lydia, the
baby had slipped out pink and wet—the doctor had called it
the textbook delivery. It had been different with the next pregnancy, and Rodney knew this was why she'd fretted over Lydia
so as her time got closer. Viviane had lost the second baby, two

months into the pregnancy for no apparent reason. Rodney still remembered the morning he'd awakened with her crying his name from the bathroom, coming in and not being able to do anything but hold her.

The September morning was brilliant, the frost having burned off and the trees along the roadside still wet with dew. Occasional patches of water reflected the sky, there were the cows in the fields that stared out from the fences. He pulled onto the road to the city. The buildings shone in the near distance, and then just as suddenly the sign for the hospital appeared. Rodney pushed the gas to cross the bridge. There was the river below and its ripples of white, the water that skimmed over the rocks and moved past the columns.

THEY'D GOTTEN INTO the car first thing that morning to see their grandchild. But she'd begun to feel the pain just as Rodney had backed out from the driveway, said this was the worst it had been. Even then, as she'd twisted her head to the window and breathed out loudly, she'd told Rodney, "I'm going to see the baby."

He steered into the parking lot, parked in the empty space for the emergency that he supposed this was. He turned off the engine, gently squeezed Viviane's arm. "Okay now," he said into her ear, and when she opened her eyes they were yellow and it was as if she wasn't seeing anything at all. She licked her lips, reached out and scratched his cheek with her nail. "I want to see my grandson."

"You will."

"I want to see my grandson and hold him."

He helped her across the parking lot, the emergency room door swished open and the nurse met them there. Rodney set Viviane down onto the chair, the doctor walked over with the stethoscope swinging from his neck. "What do we have here?" he said in his too cheerful way, and Rodney could see he was little more than the kid. His hair was thick and messy, his smile crooked as he put his stethoscope to Viviane's chest. He asked her to cough, then asked Rodney, "When did this happen?"

"On the way here," Rodney said. He explained about their daughter Lydia having her child the night before, driving the distance to see it. The doctor listened patiently and finally interrupted, none of this having anything to do with Viviane and the condition she was in. "Who is her physician?" he said.

Rodney named the oncologist, a doctor who worked in this very hospital.

"Dr. Williams," the young doctor said. "Well, I'm going to call him. In the meantime, let's get your wife situated."

The nurse and Rodney lifted Viviane into a nearby wheelchair, placed a blanket over her lap. "I don't like this," Viviane said, throwing the blanket onto the floor. "There's no baby here." She glowered at Rodney. "You tricked me." Rodney picked up the blanket from the floor, the doctor returned.

"He said to bring her up," he said, fingering his stethoscope.

"To Dr. Williams?" said the nurse.

"The third floor."

The nurse faced the wheelchair toward the elevator. "Here we go," she said as though talking to the child. The doors opened and she wheeled Viviane in, Rodney followed. The nurse pushed the button to the third floor, the elevator lurched and Viviane looked around, reached out for Rodney's hand. He squeezed it and watched the numbers light up above them. "It's slow," the nurse said.

Viviane had had her good spells. In just the past week she'd picked the tomatoes from the garden and brought them into the house emptying them onto the table. Her cheeks had been flushed, the complexion ruddy. But that may as well have been years ago with the way things were going now. The elevator came to its halt and they stepped out, the nurse pushing the chair.

Another nurse met them at the desk, was apprised of the situation. Viviane peered up, suddenly cognizant. "My grandson is in this same hospital," she said to the nurse. "Just upstairs and I haven't yet seen him." Viviane told the story of the baby being on the seventh floor and their being on the third, how ridiculous it all was. The nurse, a black woman whose gentle, sure-handed manner almost set Rodney's heart at ease, nodded. She had almond eyes and a sharp, pointed nose, braids that clicked as she shook her head. "Believe it or not," she said, taking the blanket from Rodney and placing it on the desk, "I've seen crazier things." She gave the wheelchair a push, they went into the room where she pulled back the sheets from the bed and came to Viviane. "Last week a man was here for a cut across his finger. Well it turns out the woman in the next room was his ex-wife and she was in for a fracture to her ankle." The nurse braced the wheelchair as Rodney held onto the handles. "You work here long enough baby, you see *everything*."

But this *wasn't* everything, Rodney wanted to tell her. This was his wife and she was very sick and he'd never seen her as bad as this. The nurse guided Viviane to the screen, Rodney handed her the gown and she slowly walked back with her bare feet padding onto the green tile. He helped the nurse lift her into the bed, Viviane heavier than she looked, meatier and more solid than her appearance suggested. "This one's tricky," said the nurse. "She looks like a little bird."

The nurse left them, and Dr. Williams came into the room. "Viviane," he said, talking loudly as if through a darkened cave, the way he always did. Rodney knew he was a good doctor, had been told by more than a few that he was one of the best. But he didn't care so much for the man's bedside manner, the arm's-length approach he took with his wife. He put down his clipboard and took Viviane's wrist in his hand.

"We just had our grandchild," Viviane said.

"So I heard."

"He was a boy."

"Congratulations."

Dr. Williams wrote a few words down onto the clipboard and stepped back. "We're where we expected," he said. "Not where we wanted to be, but then we always knew this would eventually happen." He went on to talk about the medicine likely doing as much as it could, having to run the necessary tests to determine the next course of action. Rodney nodded even while he understood that at this point the courses of action were few and far between, knew that all he wanted to do right now was to go up to the seventh floor with his wife and hold the baby, push it into Viviane's arms and let it slobber down upon her arm.

LYDIA came up to the room with her husband Andrew, despite the doctors' and nurses' wishes that she stay in her bed. Andrew pushed her in the wheelchair, they came in with their long faces. Lydia looked exhausted, the circles under her eyes bluish in the bright light. Her brown hair was pulled back into a tail, the hospital gown dropped slightly revealing her freckled shoulder.

"Mom," she said, and her voice wavered.

But Viviane had made herself over as soon as the first tests were finished, colored her cheeks with the rouge and put on the lipstick. "I had a spell was all," she told them, even though Rodney knew it had been no such thing. "The truth is I only wanted to be closer to my grandchild."

Lydia stared up at Rodney, puzzled.

"This is a hell of a way to get closer," said Andrew. His concern showed itself more like an annoyance, but Rodney knew this was how he was. Earlier that morning Andrew had called Rodney in his businesslike way with the news of the baby. "It's a boy," he'd said. Then, "His name is Timothy, after Viviane's father, we decided." And there it was, Andrew in the nutshell—as sensitive and kind as they came, but only in the tiny glimpses.

Rodney had seen the way he'd put his hand onto Lydia's back whenever she was upset, how he talked gently into her ear. This was a good boy, of this Rodney was sure.

Lydia said, "They won't let us bring the baby down here yet. It's regulations."

"Is that so?" said Viviane. "Well, I guess I'll just have to go up there to see him myself."

Lydia squinted and Rodney could see she was close to breaking into tears, the exhaustion and stress of the last day or so—*having a child* for Christ's sake—culminating in this unfortunate moment. "Get better," she said, before Andrew wheeled her out. "Please."

It was decided that Viviane's organs were failing which explained the yellow eyes, that they could try to stave things off but that there really wasn't much point any longer. "She's beginning to go," Dr. Williams said, his voice going soft for the first time since Rodney had known him. Viviane took the news as if being given the weather, nodded thoughtfully.

"Just bring me the baby," she said.

Dr. Williams glanced from Viviane to Rodney. "The grandchild."

"Yes," said Rodney.

"Well now, we'll see what we can do." He wrote a long note onto the clipboard. "For the moment, let's do everything we can to make sure you're comfortable."

"I'm fine," said Viviane.

Dr. Williams went to the door and gestured to Rodney, asked him to follow. He stood off to the side beside the tray of sheets and towels, crossed his arms. "Of course we can't bring the baby down here," he said. "At least not right away. I mean, the child was born not more than twelve hours ago, and there are the regulations."

"She needs to see it," said Rodney. He knew that if one thing had ever been certain in the world it was that his wife see their grandchild.

"She will. Only not today," the doctor said. He turned his head both ways as if about to reveal top government secrets. "Dr. Lee delivered your daughter's baby and she's a good friend. I'll see into bringing it down tomorrow morning."

Rodney stuck his hands into his pocket, suddenly taken with this doctor for thinking to go through such trouble. His bedside manner may have left much to be desired, but it was clear that he *did* care. "Okay," Rodney said. "I appreciate your looking into it like that."

"It's a special case," said Dr. Williams.

Then he put out his hand and Rodney took it in his. The palms were smooth, the fingers spindly, and he thought here was a life devoid of any hard labor. "Okay then," Dr. Williams said, and Rodney watched the doctor walk away, imagined him as the boy reading the book while the other children played, his diligence paying off as he went away to the big university. Rodney really hadn't had the time to read much when he was a child, being raised on the farm and spending his early years waking so early to take care of the assorted duties. Then had come the Korean War, he'd gone away to fight and returned home to find the farm gone to pot, the field hard and untended, the horses and cows wandering in the yard. It turned out that his father had lost his foot in a tractor accident, that his mother had done what she could to hold things together. Rodney had stood in the living room as they'd told him this and his mother had cried. It had been the most awful thing to see his father hold up the stump that had been his foot and say, "There, that's what happened all right."

Of course, there were the better memories. Walking into Randle's General Store and seeing Viviane for the first time, her short brown hair and sad, dark eyes. "You're the soldier," she'd said when he'd placed the Tootsie Roll onto the counter. He'd looked her over, the blue dress and pointed, white elbows, the moles that made the triangle from thumb to forefinger to wrist to thumb. "Is that what they fed you on the front lines, *Tootsie Rolls?*" He'd said he was enough of a soldier to like his candy, she'd laughed and he'd asked who she was. "Randle's niece. He's my dad's brother. I've been working here for almost a year and you're the first man I've ever sold a Tootsie Roll to."

He tried to remember this Viviane when he came back into the room and to her bed, sat down in the nearby chair. "Hey Viv," he said, and she smiled. He could see her now, just a girl, the long legs in the blue dress as she'd stepped around the counter. The hand, he held it in his and there were the moles. Thumb to forefinger to wrist to thumb.

RODNEY went up to the seventh floor to see Timothy. The baby was beautiful, his eyes blue and cloudy. "But what about these red splotches along his arm?" Rodney asked, and Lydia said the doctor had assured her they would clear up in the next week or so. Timothy let out a whimper—Andrew and Lydia watched as Rodney pulled the baby to his chest. He couldn't believe this baby would grow into the boy, then the man, so tall. "He's so little," Rodney said.

Lydia laughed. "Of course he's little. He's a baby."

Rodney thought back to Viviane holding Lydia just after she was born, how she'd cried. Viviane had put her lips to her daughter's cheek. "Here's what we call a kiss," she'd said, and Lydia had gone quiet. Of course Lydia would never remember this, and Rodney considered just how much it was we didn't know, these bits and pieces of our lives known to others, as he handed the baby to Andrew. He stepped back into the wall, Andrew adjusted Timothy in his arms. "Dr. Williams tells me Viviane can see Timothy in the morning," he said.

"The morning," said Lydia.

"It's the best he can do."

"It's a bunch of crap if you ask me. He's her grandchild, after all. And there she is, right downstairs."

"You're talking to the choir," Rodney said.

Timothy fussed and cried as his father held him. "It's okay," he said, and he rocked the baby, then patted his back.

"Let me try," Lydia said.

Andrew carried the baby to Lydia, sat down on the bed and placed him in her arms. "There now," she said into the baby's face. "It's okay, everything is going to be fine."

Rodney regarded his daughter as she took to this motherhood. She was a natural, and should it have been any surprise? Viviane had been much the same, raising her daughter as though she'd raised a hundred others. He thought of her kiss to the forehead, Lydia going quiet and falling asleep in her mother's arms. Rodney went to the door, leaned into the jamb. They didn't even notice as he slipped out of the room.

VIVIANE was asleep, the thick tubes had been placed in her arms and the machines were all around her. He went to the side of the bed and stood there, watched her breathe. The red line on the screen moved with its beep to each beat of her heart, the machine hummed and vibrated. He pulled the blanket over her shoulder and settled into the chair, watched her chest move up and down.

When he came back to Lydia's room she was asleep as well. Andrew and the baby were gone, Rodney decided to go out to the courtyard for some fresh air, to watch the people. It was the middle of the afternoon, the weather was unseasonably warm for September. He rolled up his sleeves and sat down on the bench, the priest sitting next to him raised his hand in greeting.

"A fine day," he said, and Rodney said that it was.

"Not that a hospital is the best place to notice these things."

Rodney wished the priest away. He was not a particularly religious man, had shied away from churches his entire life. He remembered the war, the priest asking his denomination before he headed away to the field. "None," he'd said, and the priest had looked at him with no small amount of pity. But Rodney saw it as plainly as he figured he could, that a man lived and died, what came in between was the only part that really mattered. His father had said heaven was for fools, hell was for idiots, and that dying was easy. What his father had meant by this was never made clear, but Rodney supposed it had something to do with doing good for good's sake, not thinking of the eternal consequences for each and every deed. *Good deeds go unnoticed,* his father would always tell him. *But that's what makes them good in the first place.*

The priest leaned back into the bench. He was a gangly man, younger, probably in his mid-thirties at best. He had reddish hair and a chin that slightly receded. Rodney imagined he'd probably had the difficult day, the sigh offering the indication. "You from around here?" asked the priest.

Rodney said he was, that he lived about an hour away in the country.

"The country," said the priest. "That must be a nice place to get away to."

"Or to live," Rodney corrected in his mild way.

A woman and her daughter walked by, the son trailing behind. The son held a balloon and stared at the priest and Rodney. The priest smiled and gave a wave, the boy waved back and the balloon loosened itself from his hand. "Shit," said the priest.

"Joseph," the mother yelled.

The boy started to cry.

"Take it easy," said the priest. He jumped up onto the bench, grabbed a branch from a nearby tree. "Cover me," he said to Rodney, and Rodney simply nodded. The balloon slowly climbed, the priest was right alongside it as he reached out from the branch and pulled it in. The boy clapped, the priest came down from the tree and handed him the balloon.

"That wasn't necessary, Father," said the mother.

"It was nothing." He was breathless, his face red.

"But it was."

"And I said it wasn't."

The mother hesitated, pulled her son's wrist with a yank.

"Christ," said the priest. "I wish everything was that easy." He wiped his brow with a handkerchief, shook his head. "You know?" he said.

RODNEY told the priest about Viviane, the baby, how so much had happened in the past twelve or so hours. The priest listened and squeezed the handkerchief between his fingers, stood and walked around the bench. He stared up at the hospital. "Which floor is your daughter on?" he asked.

Rodney told the priest she was on the seventh floor.

"And your wife?"

"The third," he said, not sure what difference it made.

The priest stuck the handkerchief back into his pocket. "She got to see the baby?" he said.

"She did not. And there she is, four floors down and they won't let her. Or they won't let her until the doctor says she can."

"Why can't she?"

"Regulations," said Rodney, with the sneer.

"Of course, regulations."

"They say the baby isn't equipped to deal with the germs on the third floor that might come into his system."

"I see."

"That if we were to bring him down then it could do some kind of damage."

"Well," said the priest. "That's not good."

"But she only wants to see the baby."

The priest returned to the bench, sat down. "So how long does she have to wait until they let her see him?"

Rodney said, "The doctor is trying to pull a few strings."

"Which doctor?"

Rodney told him the name of the doctor, the priest rubbed his inward chin and glanced up at the woman who'd appeared in the courtyard. Rodney watched as she stepped over the sprinkler head in her blue tennis shoes, marched straight toward them. She wore a dark gray dress, a white sweater. Her head was almost perfectly round, her short, cropped hair accentuating the green of her eyes. "Father," she said, and she stood before the two of them holding her hands. "The Chelsea family. They're looking for you."

"Sister Angela."

"They say that it's urgent."

The priest got up from the bench and cleared his throat, gazed down at Rodney. "Well then," he said. "I suppose that's my cue to leave."

"It would seem so."

Sister Angela turned and walked ahead, stopped at the edge

of the courtyard and looked back. The priest took a step, held his mouth open as if he'd had a thought that he'd suddenly forgotten. He nodded, then pointed to the building. "Just make sure she sees that baby," he said.

LYDIA was awake when Rodney passed by her room, sitting up against her pillow. Andrew was still gone—at home retrieving the change of clothes, taking the nap. "What's going to happen?" she said, as he settled into the brown vinyl chair beside her bed. "I mean, is she going to be all right?"

"Now Lydia," said Rodney, and he took his daughter's hand. The hand was firm and solid, Lydia having the same physical makeup as her mother. Even when she'd been a child he'd sometimes found it the challenge to carry her. He'd come home from the days working in the field, she'd ask to be held and it would be harder than carrying the feed from the truck to the trough. He imagined the woman as the girl, remembered how as she'd gotten older she would help him with the duties. Feeding and milking, the work in the garden too. He could still see her walking out to meet him in the field, holding the metal pails with her blond hair messy and the face still creased from sleep. She'd go straight to the cow and put down the stool, pet her side and tell her to get going.

"I'm just asking."

"And I'm saying I don't know."

Outside the window was the view of the city, its trees and houses. The setting sun made its shadows, Rodney watched a car circle through the parking lot. Lydia loosened her hand, sat up farther and moved her legs over the bed's side. "You okay to do that honey?" he asked, and she said that she was. They stared out the window together.

"It's so much at once," she said.

"Yes it is."

She rustled loose from the sheets. "I want to go see her."

"She's sleeping."

"Still," she said. "Can't I?"

"Better to wait until she's awake," said Rodney, recognizing that to see Viviane so helpless with the thick tubes sticking inside her, the machines humming and beeping, would simply be too much. He wanted Lydia to think of more than her sick mother when she recalled Timothy's birth, to know some of the joy this time was supposed to bring. He forced a smile. "Let's talk about this baby of yours," he said.

Lydia got back into the bed and pulled the sheets over her legs. "He *is* beautiful, isn't he?"

"He is."

"I'd say he takes a little bit after everyone. Of course it's hard to tell right now."

"His eyes are blue."

"That's from Andrew's father. But a baby's eyes can change color." Lydia leaned into her pillow. "What color were *my* eyes?"

Rodney remembered Lydia as the baby, but not her eyes. "Blue," he said.

"And see. Now they're brown. Just like Mom's."

A nurse walked by and took a peek in, doubled back. "Hey

now, you're up here too?" It was the nurse from downstairs who'd helped Viviane into the bed. Rodney stood, she stepped into the room and put out her hand. "And you must be the daughter. Congratulations. Your mother, all she talks about is your lovely baby boy. I'm sorry, I can't recollect his name."

"Timothy," said Lydia.

"My name is Nadine. I don't have to tell you she's something. Your mother, that is."

"Thank you."

Nadine took back her hand and nodded to Rodney. "Well now, you never know who you're going to run into. I was actually saying earlier you see the craziest things in this place." She headed for the door, rested her hand on its handle. "Mothers on one floor and daughters on the other. I suppose I'll remember this."

"I suppose so too," said Rodney.

"Do you want it closed?"

"Please."

Lydia pulled the blanket up to her chin. "I'm glad she's with Mom," she said, and Rodney told her that he was too, sat down in the chair. He reached for the lamp on the table and asked Lydia if she would mind. She shook her head. "All right then," he said, and he clicked off the light, leaned back and closed his eyes.

HE DIDN'T EXPECT the dream but there she was, Viviane standing near the tree as young as the first day he'd met her. He walked up to her and she handed him the metal cup, he drank from it and the water was silvery cool. "See?" she said, "I told you it's the very best water you'll find." He wiped his mouth and agreed that it was, they went to the stream and he drank more. Rodney fell into a deeper sleep, knowing this wasn't any dream but a memory, and Viviane was suddenly naked and lovely as the most beautiful song. She lay down on the bed, told him to come over. But he was stuck, his feet may as well have been nailed to the ground.

"You're going to die," he said.

"Bullshit," she said, "I'm right here. Come to me."

"But I can't."

"Lift your feet from your shoes."

And he did as she commanded, the shoes stuck in place but his feet moving across the floor. Then he was in the bed and the walls were gone, there was the tree beside them with the leaves moving in the gentle breeze. She opened her arms and he rolled on top of her. "That's it," she said. "Yes, just like *that.*" And when he woke he was shocked to find himself wetted, his underwear sticky against his leg. "Jesus," he said, and Lydia stirred. Outside it was dark, an ambulance pulled out from the driveway and its lights bounced against her face and the walls.

"Daddy?" she said. "What's the matter? Dad?"

"Nothing," he said. "Go back to sleep." He got up and knocked the flowers from the vase.

"Are you all right?"

He set the vase upright, headed for the door. "Fine," he said. "Sleep. Sleep."

When he opened the door Andrew was coming down the hallway, his hair standing up and eyes bleary as though he'd just awakened too. "Rodney," Andrew said, holding out the paper bag filled with the change of clothes. "You were in there with Lydia?"

"I was," said Rodney. A nurse passed them with an armful of towels, a man pushed a cart filled with empty plates. "We both fell asleep." He looked down at his pants, only hoped he'd make it to the bathroom before the wet showed through. "I guess we slept through dinner."

"That's good."

"We were both tired. And you too, you went home and got to rest for a spell?"

"I did," said Andrew. He pushed back his hair, rubbed his eyes. "How's Viv?"

"The last I saw her she was sleeping."

"You want that."

"I suppose."

They both stood in the middle of the hallway. Andrew moved the paper bag from one hand to the other and Rodney glanced toward the elevator. He'd always been a touch awkward with the boy, having as much to do with Andrew's coming from money as anything. His family owned land throughout the county, built offices and homes. After Andrew had graduated from college, his father had given him a job at the company. He'd met Lydia there—she'd worked at the office as the secretary. They'd gone on to get married, bought the house in the middle of the city. And yes it was true, he *was* a good boy. But sheltered, and Rodney only hoped he'd be able to take the tumbles life would throw. He'd been keeping an eye on him throughout the day, was pleased with what he'd seen so far. He shook his leg.

"Well I should get back to Viviane."

"Yeah." Andrew nodded toward the door. "Lydia still sleeping?" Rodney said she was.

"I'll be quiet."

He slipped in through the door and Rodney gingerly proceeded toward the elevator. Everything was so bright, the telephones ringing with the doctors and nurses squeaking in their shoes. He pressed the button, noted with no small amount of irritation the stain in his pants that was beginning to show through. The elevator arrived, he stepped in as soon as the doors opened.

NADINE was waiting at the elevator on the third floor. "Oh, Lord," she said, and the elevator closed behind Rodney with its noisy clatter. She stretched out her hand. "Come here with me," she said, and when he saw the door to Viviane's room wide open he knew everything was wrong.

"Now I only just got here from my break," Nadine said. "And she was already going." She put her hand to Rodney's shoulder but he couldn't feel anything, his whole body going numb, *this isn't happening, this isn't happening,* all he could think. "Her heart decided to stop. But the doctors tried. You'll want to know that she asked for you, and that she asked for Lydia too. But the name she kept saying again and again was Timothy. Timothy was the last thing she said."

"I wasn't here."

"Rodney," said Nadine. "She wouldn't have known if you were."

He shook his head because he knew she was only saying what she thought would help him get through this. He looked past Nadine to Dr. Williams and his clipboard, walked away from her. "You said she'd be able to see the baby," he said, popping the clipboard from his hand. "What happened to that? A fine thing to say."

The clipboard clattered to the floor, one of the assistant doctors picked it up while another told Rodney to cool it, this wasn't the time. But Dr. Williams said that it was okay, to leave him be, he could understand the man's anger. Rodney faced the doctor. "Yeah?" he said, and Nadine was suddenly taking his arm and guiding him to Viviane's door.

"Go on," she said.

Rodney went into the room and she was there on the bed, the tubes unplugged and machines quiet, her gown hastily drawn over her chest. The door closed, he sat next to the bed and when he took Viviane's hand it was already going cold, her eyes sinking and mouth slightly open. "Sweet girl," he said, and he couldn't believe he'd been gone when it happened, this stupid sleep and dream where he'd shot his wad for God's sake in the very moment she was leaving. *Alone,* he thought, *she was all alone.* He put his head down onto her chest and pulled her arm over his head, remembered how she'd stood under the tree and handed him the cup filled with water, the green leaves above them as he'd held her there.

THE PRIEST was waiting for Rodney when he came out from the room. "You, again?" Rodney said, as he lurched past him. "Don't you ever leave this place?" He didn't want to talk to any priests, he didn't want to talk to anyone at all. He made his way along the hallway toward the bathroom and Nadine stepped in front of the door. She put out her hand as the priest sidled up beside her.

"I assume you want to tell your daughter yourself," she said.

He blinked hard, Nadine seemed far away even though she was right before him. "I guess that's something I should do."

"So I told the doctor we'd leave that up to you."

"She never got to see the baby," he said.

Nadine shook her head and the braids clicked. "It happened so quickly, we couldn't have known."

"Yeah, sure," said Rodney "The nature of the universe."

The priest said, "It might be hard to believe."

"Now don't you start."

"I'm not starting anything. I'm only saying that it might look terrible now."

"It doesn't look terrible. It *is* terrible. There's a difference. And I don't want to hear the answers from you about how even in this there's a reason, because frankly I don't *believe* there's a reason." He turned to the bathroom door. "Now if you don't mind I have some spunk I need to wash from my leg."

Rodney went into the bathroom and pulled out the paper towels, doused them under the faucet. In the stall he pushed down his pants, then his underwear, cleaned the ejaculate. And that's when he got the idea. He wiped his thigh and felt the chill from the water that dripped to his knee, rubbed the towel in circles. "Viviane," he said aloud, and he knew it was the only thing he could do.

THE PRIEST was still waiting outside when Rodney came out from the bathroom. "I thought you'd still be here," he said. The priest bowed slightly, gestured to the hallway. "Look. You want to help and I suppose I can understand. But I need you to help me, I mean, *really* help me." Rodney clicked the heels of his boots onto the floor. "Would you be able to do that?"

"I'll do whatever I can."

"It might be somewhat of a sacrifice."

The priest shrugged, stretched out his long arms.

"You're sure?"

"I'm sure."

Rodney stood in the middle of the hallway. There was the wet of his pants, the cool dampness of the fabric against his skin. He stepped close to the priest, the doctors and nurses watched him from the corners of their eyes. "What I need," he said. "What I want you to do." He moved closer, the priest backed against the wall. "I need you to help me get my daughter's baby."

HE BROKE the news and Lydia sobbed, he held her and then Andrew held her too. But Rodney was somewhere else now, he'd strangely lifted above the grief to the purpose at hand. He'd talked to the priest and made the plan. In the early morning the priest would slip into the maternity ward and lift the baby, tell the attendant he was taking the boy to his mother and that she'd asked to see it. Everyone knew the priest here, there would be no questions as he carried the baby away.

"It just can't be," Lydia said.

He glimpsed out the window. The night sky was filled with the multitude of stars, and Rodney found it hard to believe it had been only weeks earlier that Viviane had asked him out to the back porch to look up above their house and the trees. It had been nearly midnight, she'd pointed to the stars and told him it was funny to think she hadn't really looked at them for so long. "There they've been," she'd said, "every night for all these years." And he'd known she was thinking of her days coming to their end, the pain had been increasing, she'd taken to getting up as late as noon to avoid the many hours of discomfort. But then the lull had come, and she'd been out in the garden with the tomatoes. And now this. It had been the roller coaster, that much was certain.

"I'm going to sit in the hallway for a while," Rodney said, even though he had no intention of sitting in any hallway at all. He was going to meet the priest in the chapel, it was very nearly time. "I'll be back in a while," he said. Then, "Everything will be just fine."

■

A Dream, Not Alone

THE LIGHTS were dimmed, the smell of the oil and candles permeated. Rodney stepped in and one of the pews cracked— it was the priest, sitting in the darkness. He stared ahead at the tiny wooden altar, his thin, pink hands neatly folded on his lap. "Sit down for a minute," he said, and Rodney took the pew. The priest rubbed his face, breathed deeply.

"Now you know that I normally wouldn't help somebody out like this."

"I know," said Rodney, and he knew that it was true. This was a priest, and going outside the boundaries was not something the higher-ups looked kindly upon. Rodney had taken a gamble in asking such a thing, but he'd nowhere else to turn. "I suppose you're going to tell me now that you can't do anything."

"It's an unusual situation."

"Yes it is," said Rodney. "But aren't they all?"

The priest stared at him. "I don't know is what I'm saying."

"She died alone," said Rodney. "I need to make it up to her."

"We all die alone."

"Father." It was the first time he'd addressed the man with the particular title.

"I'm only talking in a literal sense." He turned back to the altar. "Let's say I agree to do this," he said. "We take the baby and you get your moment, we return him to your daughter unharmed and all is forgiven. But what about me? I still have to answer to people. I still have to pay for what we've done."

"That's true," Rodney said. "But if you don't you'll be passing up the chance to actually do something to help."

The priest shook his head. "I help people every day."

"You talk. Here you'll *do*."

"Praying is doing."

Rodney threw up his hands. "If you say so."

The chapel was quiet, the stained glass somber in the absence of light.

"Can I tell you something?" the priest said.

"Go ahead."

"I hate this place. I didn't always hate it. It's just that after a while you see so much that is terrible. Today. Today I watched a boy die in his father's arms. He was in pain. Had been in pain since the day he was born. And then he comes here and dies and I'm standing there offering my condolences wondering, *What in the hell am I doing here?*"

"I couldn't imagine," said Rodney.

"Yeah, I bet you couldn't. So when you came up and asked me to help you steal a baby, I said to myself, okay, I'll lend a hand because there's not much else I'm able to do around here. So what you're saying about *doing* something—and don't you assume for one minute I'm not *trying* to do something every day that I'm here—is hitting me right where it hurts. And I'm saying okay, why not? I'll help the poor sap out."

"I'm not a poor sap," Rodney offered in his defense. "I'm a bereaved poor sap."

The priest squeezed his hands together, smiled, then laughed, and Rodney laughed too.

"I can't believe I'm laughing," he said.

"It comes when you least expect it," said the priest. "Look

at me. *I'm* laughing. A child dies, I'm there to see it." He
crossed his arms and sat back in the pew so that it let out another crack, then pop. He sighed. "So where are you parked?
Right out front like you told me?"

Rodney nodded.

"I'm going to walk into the ward and they're going to ask
what I'm doing. Since it's Thursday it will be Nurse Bloom-
field and not Nurse Ratched. I'll tell her that I'm bringing it to
your daughter, go on about her mother's passing and that will
be enough to throw the woman off. Then it will be straight to
the elevator, out to you, and away we go."

"You got it, Father," said Rodney.

"Well then," he said, making the sign of the cross and standing. "Let's go and get this over with."

RODNEY went out to the car and waited. It was cold, the sky
was beginning to lighten. He imagined his house now in the
field beyond, so quiet with all of Viviane's medicine bottles and
her pillow up just so, the pain always too much to lie straight
back anyway, the shape of her body in the bed.

He stared up at the hospital and the room that was likely
Lydia's. He'd left a note in an envelope with the night nurse,
asked her to give it to his daughter in the morning when she
awakened. The note read simply, *Not to worry, me and a priest took
the baby, will bring him back safely. Love, Dad.*

A security guard passed and Rodney ducked into his seat.
The guard paced along the front lawn with his flashlight,

around the building and to its far side. *Come on,* thought Rodney. What the hell could be taking this priest so long anyway? One could only make so much small talk. Grab the baby, explain the mother's grief and needing to hold the infant, then shoot down. It couldn't be so complicated.

The guard walked into the hospital and ten seconds later the priest came out holding the white blanket. Rodney started the engine, turned on the lights. The priest threw the door open and got into the car. "That was perfect," he said, buckling his seat belt over the infant and himself as best he could manage. "Frank the cop asked me where I was going at this hour with a baby."

"The security guard?"

"Just drive."

Rodney put the car into gear and slowly accelerated from the lot. "What'd you say?"

"That I was stealing it, what do you think I said?"

"I don't know."

"I told him that it wouldn't stop crying and that I'd agreed to take it out for some fresh air." The priest rubbed his thumb over Timothy's cheek, kissed his head, Rodney resisted the urge to pull over and take the baby to his chest, to hold it. "We can only thank the powers that be that old Frank isn't all that bright, that by the time he puts together something was wrong we'll likely be there and back."

"And Lydia will most hopefully still be sleeping."

"Let's hope."

They drove and the baby slept, the sun began to rise over

the river. It was a beautiful sight, the stars slowly fading. The first ray of the sun stretched up into the sky, then another, and soon the entire river was bathed in the golden light. "Now *that* is something," said the priest.

Rodney peeked over at Timothy, his pink face and wrinkled eyes, the hair black and matted in tiny bunches. He appeared to be even smaller now, the priest held him like the delicate china. "You hold kids before?" he asked, and the priest gave him a look as if it were the world's stupidest question.

"Have I held kids? I'm a priest."

"So?"

"*So?*" He glared at Timothy. "Haven't you spent any time in a church?"

Rodney shrugged and stared into his mirror at the headlights that happened to be square, knew the chances of it being the police were little to none but slowed down anyway. The car passed—an Oldsmobile sedan—and he steered back into the lane behind it, resumed his regular speed.

"Paranoid, aren't we?" said the priest.

"Careful."

"So are we getting close? I mean, we're pretty much in the country." He pointed to the window. "Just ahead is the mountain."

"Twenty minutes or so," Rodney said, and he could already notice the sky going clearer, the clouds taking on their definite shapes. *Soon,* he said to himself, and he would step from the car and there would be the sharpness of the air and wetness of the ground, the shadow of the mountain and his house so far below.

The baby began to stir and cry. "Oh no," said the priest.

"What do you mean, *oh no?* I thought you said you held kids."

"Sure I held them. I didn't say I nursed them."

"Should we get milk?" It hadn't occurred to Rodney that the baby might need something, he hadn't gone that far ahead in his plan. Timothy moved and wriggled, kicked out his tiny foot from the blanket. *This isn't good,* thought Rodney, and he pressed on the gas. The priest patted the baby's back and Rodney shook his head.

"Sing," he said.

"What do you mean sing?"

"Sing. Lydia always liked it when I sang."

Rodney drove along the road and the river disappeared as he climbed, the trees came up beside them. The priest sang, then hummed, and the baby eventually went quiet, fell back asleep. Rodney slowed as the road changed into its curves and he took the exit that would take him to his house. The morning sun shone from below, Rodney gestured to the snow on the highest ridges and the priest smiled. "So that's where you met her?" he said.

"Not met," said Rodney. "She showed me a stream. It was the best water I ever tasted."

"It's very beautiful," said the priest. "All of it."

"It's home," said Rodney.

They drove past the house. The fence he'd put in not long after he and Viviane had gotten married, the stumps from the trees he'd cut down. In the middle of the yard was the rusted pickup that he'd junked but never managed to tow away, the engine on the ground. Beside the garage was the sewing machine that had quit working long ago, Viviane having given up the sewing when the machine had become the clunker, only using the needle and thread when she'd absolutely had to.

They climbed up the side of the mountain, there was the dented guardrail and bushes that spilled over onto the side of the road. When they rounded the corner the entire county came into view, the priest tucked the baby into his chest and let out a sigh. The car whined, they climbed one more hill and Rodney slowed, pulled over. "Here we are," he said, and he turned off the engine.

"Here?" said the priest.

"Yes."

Rodney got out of the car and walked around to the passenger side, the priest opened his door and lifted Timothy up. "Go see your grandfather," he said.

"Hello baby," said Rodney.

"I'll go up the road and see what I can find."

Rodney proceeded toward the tree, taking small steps and being careful with this baby in his arms. The tree was still green, the remnant of summer yet holding. He went to its trunk and pulled Timothy close, sat on the ground beneath the branches. The baby stirred and opened his eyes, the stream made its flowing sound in the distance. Rodney considered the stream, thought of Viviane and wondered if this was enough bringing Timothy here and he knew that it was. Here was her grandchild, the baby, in this place that was theirs. He held Timothy to his chest, remembered coming here all those years ago, how Viviane had handed him the silver cup and its cold water.

The priest walked down the trail, stopped to examine something underneath a bush. He picked up the object and it shone in the light—a green bottle that he stuffed into his back pocket as he continued along. Rodney pulled Timothy close, the baby let out a sputter and closed its eyes. The breeze moved through the leaves. He stared at the sky and its traces of clouds along the far horizon, the sun that rose before them.

The Clear Blue Water

I was thirty miles from Mexico when the Buick finally decided to give out. As if it was any kind of surprise, the car acting up since Bakersfield, spewing out the black exhaust all along this desert highway. The radiator light flickered in its red buzzing, I pulled over and got out and nearly fell from the heat. The steam, it rose in a cloud. I popped open the hood and walked around the car once, twice, and I should have known better than to push it like this, I really should have known.

I began to walk—there was the heat that waved, the sun that burned down. Crows flew above me, shiny and black, the mountains in the distance jutted up over the miles and miles of sand. My head went light, I stumbled along the side of the road. A nearby cactus made its shadow, sagebrush spread itself out in the random patterns. And then, what looked like the building but could never be. Because this was Bumfuck, Nowhere. Because this was where the only people were those who passed in the cars.

I continued along, the building took on its distinct shape and I could hardly believe it was there. There were the gas pumps side by side, the Cadillac parked near the fence. "What the hell is *your* problem?" came a voice from the shadow and I glanced over to see the man who sat in the chair. I stepped up to the station, he stared at me and shook his head. He had brown, leathery skin, whiskers on his cheeks sprouting in patches. His eyes were pinched and black, like tiny seeds that went even smaller as he told me he'd seen the steam from the car. He stood from his chair. His pants were smudged with grease stains and the shoelaces to his boots were in tatters. "You gotta make sure you put in the water," he said.

I agreed, even though I knew the water wouldn't have helped anything. I glimpsed back at my car in the road, the dilapidated Buick with its cloud still rising. *This was the end of the world nowhere,* I wanted to tell him. *What the hell was he doing here anyway?* Just then a car passed and the dust kicked up from the road, we both watched as it disappeared on its way toward the border.

"I suppose you're thirsty," the man said.

I nodded.

He went inside, closed the door and the blinds rattled. I looked around. The outside of the shop was covered with dust, its white paint peeling in curls. Tumbleweed was everywhere, gathered along the porch, the fence, beside the pumps. And these pumps, that appeared to be as old as the man with their faded metal and numbers on rollers. Past the pumps was the empty road, the crows dancing along the shoulder.

"Better here than on the other side," the man said when he returned with the bottle of Coke. "That your car would break down," he added as he handed me the bottle. I drank the Coke in three swallows, set the bottle on the ledge. That's when I noticed the HELP WANTED scrawled onto the frayed yellow paper in the window. The man noticed me considering the sign. "Interested?" he said.

I peered out at the empty road and the mountains in the distance, then my car, and only wished I could tell him that I wasn't. A shudder moved through me as I mulled the possibility of being trapped here, the man regarded me with his squint. "Here's the deal," he said. "I own this place but live down the road. A place just before the border called Calexico."

Of course Calexico, I thought, I'd seen it on the map so many times. And here's the scene I'd imagined—stopping there in the air-conditioned bar for my bottle of beer before driving on into Mexico. I'd stand there and the men would glance at me from beneath their cowboy hats, the señorita would sidle up alongside and ask how far I'd come and had to go. I could have told the man this, but thought better of it as he spit into the dirt and rubbed it in with the heel of his boot. "I've got a room in the back," he said.

"Okay," I said, knowing what came next.

"So. Come on."

He walked me around the station with my stomach going tight. It was a room all right, just barely. So tiny with the bed the size of the matchbox, the dusty-glassed window and the view of the sand dunes. It was hot and airless, the man seemed to read my mind as he went to the window and opened it wide. "So what do you say cowboy?"

"I'm not a cowboy," I said, and he laughed.

"Well?"

I didn't have much choice. My car was broken and I had no money, I was at this man's mercy—it was plain to see. So I told him I would take this job even as I told myself, *Only long enough to fix my car and get the hell away from here,* and he smiled for the first time since I'd arrived. "Okay then," he said, reaching into the closet and placing a clean, white T-shirt into my hands. "My name is Justin and this is my gas station."

I CLEANED my face in the sink with the water that was warm and brown, the broken mirror above reflected my tired eyes. I splashed more water into my face and went to the bed, lay down. The mattress was lumpy and squeaked with my breathing, I closed my eyes and felt the world going away when I heard the knock against the door. "Customer!"

When I came out a rusted pickup had just driven into the station. The pickup was filled with men wearing baseball caps talking loudly in their Spanish, I tucked in my T-shirt and made my way to the pump. "See, I *told* you we got customers," Justin said as if I'd said otherwise. He clapped his hands together, sat down in his chair. "There's a reason we're here."

Reason, I thought, and I considered the humor of suddenly

missing my cab. Or San Francisco—I wasn't sure which. Because I had driven the cab in San Francisco, which was as far from this wasteland as the stars. There was the freedom of making my own hours, driving all over the city, passing one fare and picking up another. And the fares. I never knew what to expect, and I suppose this was the attraction. I'd met more than a few women driving my cab, made my small talk and watched them in my mirror. They'd tell me their stories, laugh and sometimes cry. I learned as much about women driving my cab as from any book or song, probably even more.

I turned on the pump and put in the gas, the numbers clicked as I washed the windshield down. "Make it fast, *hombre,*" said the driver, and the men in the truck sized me up. I dried the glass, one of the men gave a laugh. He had longish hair and red pimply skin, a troublemaker from the get-go. "The *gringo,* he said. *"Para servir a Ud."* The other men laughed, I only wished I knew more than the little Spanish I'd learned in high school so I could tell him to fuck off and the rest. The driver got out of his truck and went over to talk to Justin.

"Same old shit?" the driver said.

"Same old," said Justin from his chair.

"We go from day to day."

"Speak for yourself."

The man stared at the truck, then at Justin. "You got the help though."

Justin said that he did, the driver smirked and went away to the toilet. I looked back at my car. The steam had gone away, it sat there in the heap and I only wondered if I would ever really be able to fix it. I dried the squeegee, the pimply-faced passenger pointed to the windshield. "Missed a spot," he said, and the other men laughed some more as if they understood him. And maybe they did, I thought, as I pulled the nozzle out from the tank. Maybe they understood the joke of my working here too, the foolishness of ever taking this job in the middle of so much dirt and sand. The man came out from the toilet buttoning up his pants. "Who do I pay?" he said.

"Pay the kid."

I put out my hand, thought it funny Justin would call me the kid when I was nearly thirty-five. But truth be told, I *felt* like a kid. A kid who needed to be where the water was blue and there weren't men in trucks laughing at me for filling their gas. The driver paid me and got behind the wheel, told the men to sit tight as he turned the engine. "Thanks," he said, and he pushed the gas and drove away.

Justin took the money and shoved it into his front pocket. "Border runners," he said. "They bring them up, then take them back, it's a goddamned assembly line." He shot me a glance. "The last help left when one of these runners offered him more money than I could ever pay him." The pickup disappeared down the road, Justin shifted in his chair. "You're not going to do that, are you?"

I went quiet just to see him squirm. "No," I said, finally. "I guess I don't want to be arrested."

He smiled widely. "Who does?"

"I'm looking for the beaches and not jail," I explained, and he nodded as if this made any kind of sense.

Justin popped open a bottle of Coke. "Why don't you sit down where it's cool?"

I sat on the bench next to Justin's chair and regarded the empty road. This wasn't how I'd pictured it, stuck nowhere sitting with an old man passing the time. I thought of the women I'd driven on the dates up to Twin Peaks, sitting in the cab beside them with the fog rolling over the city. "It's like a dream," I'd say, pulling them close. My hand would move along their back, I'd give the kiss and stare into their eyes. "This too," I'd say, holding my gaze. "Like just before waking."

Justin kicked his leg up onto his knee. "We'll roll the car into the station this evening," he said. "When it's cooled down."

"You have tools I could work on it with?" I asked, knowing in reality how little I could do. Driving a cab, I'd never had to fix anything, the mechanic always going in with his wrench and taking care of the problem.

Justin cocked his head, gave me the scowl. "Now what do *you* think?"

A piece of tumbleweed rolled by and Justin tossed the empty Coke bottle into its center. "Twenty points," he said. I leaned back and considered my car, then made the calculations as to just how long I'd have to stay here. Justin snorted, closed his eyes. The sun burned down onto the station and the only sound was his breathing. "Twenty points," he said again, and he drifted off to sleep.

■

THE NEXT DAY I cleaned the toilet with the brush and ammonia, washed down the windows with the towel. It was already noon and not one car had stopped, I wondered how it was Justin could ever get by. He'd told me that morning it might be slow at the moment but there were times when the cars were lined up. "I know you can't believe it," he'd said. "But we get people who come to look at the dunes."

"The dunes," I'd said.

"It's true, they travel from all over to see them." He told me these dunes were among the largest in the country, that some of the crests reached heights of more than three hundred feet. "So those mountains aren't mountains?" I'd asked, gesturing around us. Justin simply smiled. "Sand," he'd said.

Justin sat in his chair. He'd been watching me all day in between reading his newspaper, had shaken his head as I'd cleared away the tumbleweed and its empty bottle. But I was restless, my mind was spinning in this too quiet place. I wanted to be in Mexico, not here. But if I was going to be here, I wanted to do what I could to clear my head. "I've run out of work," I told him. "Tell me what else needs to be done. Clean the pumps? Water the plants? Just tell me."

Justin glared at me as if I'd emerged from the very newspaper on his lap. "You *want* to work even when there's no work to do?"

I said that I did.

Suspiciously, Justin said, "Tell me why."

I told him there was no reason, then mentioned that maybe there was one. "Tulum," I said. Then, "A girl told me about it and said it was something to see." And there it was, the very explanation for my being here, and what a ridiculous thing. Diana, who'd always wanted to go to Tulum. Diana, who'd shown me the pictures in the magazines, pointed to the blue water with the white sand. I pushed my shoe into the hard dirt, made the indentation. "This is what I get for listening to her."

"Yeah?" Justin said, his eyes now filled with something resembling contempt.

"Yeah."

"Women," he said, getting up from his seat and going to the door. "They'll either leave you bleeding or make your blood run is how I see it." He went into the shop, came out with a towel and broom. "I can see *you're* bleeding," he said. "Now I suppose I've got something I can give you to do."

"Fucking A," I said.

"Fucking A," said Justin.

He gestured toward an old, brown birdhouse in the far distance. "There's a beehive a couple hundred yards back," he said. "Those bees fly there and I don't have to tell you I've been stung more than once." He handed me the towel, then the broom. "Take the towel and douse it in gasoline, and burn that house down. Do you think you can do that?"

I said that I could.

"Those used to be where they lived," he said, directing me with his hand to a tree and burned-out car. "Notice the distance."

The tree was closer than the car, the car farther.

"I keep moving them back. After the birdhouse they'll have to pack up and leave."

"If you say so," I told him.

I went to the pump and doused the towel in the gas. Halfway to the birdhouse I glanced back at Justin and he waved me on. I could already hear the buzz in the distance when I stuck the towel on the end of the broom, lit the fire. Suddenly the bees were all around and I scrambled. All I could hear was the buzzing and I felt the stingers along the back of my neck when I tossed away the broom and towel and ran to the hose. The water leaked out all over, I still managed to spray the bees away, then to douse myself, and Justin's laughter echoed from the station.

"Son of a bitch," I said, and I went straight to him, my eyes already swelled.

"That hose leaks," Justin said.

"You knew."

"I knew you'd get within twenty feet of those bees and they'd come at you."

"I could kill you right now."

"Yes you could," he said. "And I bet you would, too." He pointed his finger straight up into the air, then at me. "But the truth is that in that one moment you weren't thinking of her. And in the next day or so as the swelling gets worse you'll probably not be thinking of her too much either. You'll think of the pain but not *her* pain." He produced a beer from beside his chair and held it out. "Skin pain is a hell of a lot less painful than heart pain," he said. "If I know one thing I know that much."

The old man was fucking nuts. But I also knew that out here in this nothing land I couldn't just walk away from this station. My ass was his—more so now, as a few of the bees had managed to sting me in this very place. I stepped forward and took the beer, held it in my hand.

"Ooh," he said. "They got you all right."

I twisted open the bottle and took a long drink, then another. The beer was gone and I felt a little better.

"Let me get you some aspirin then," he said. "And I have some ointment."

"Just get me another beer," I said.

He smiled and opened the door. "Like I said. Better already."

TWO DAYS after the bees Justin's son pulled into the gas station. His name was Rafael and he drove an old Mustang—a '65 or '66 coupe—had short, black hair and eyes that darted. He was shifty at best, around thirty with a voice that was more of a growl than anything. "You're the new sucker," he said, when Justin introduced us. Then, "I see the bees got you. They get everyone, eventually. This hellhole, these bugs." I had it in my head this wasn't going to be a good relationship from the start when he glared over at my car and then at me, said, "*Gringo* is a long way from home."

I noticed Justin rubbing the towel in his hands like a nervous habit, as if he was waiting for the other shoe to drop. "I live in San Diego," Rafael said. "Which I suppose is a long way from home, too. I mean, this gas station, which might as well be the black-and-white movie."

Justin threw down the towel. "Would you *stop* with that business?"

"I'm only saying."

"Yeah, sure you are." He picked up the towel and trampled back to the shop.

Rafael forced a laugh. "My dad gets mad because he thinks I'm squandering," he said. He scratched his chin, glowered back at the station. "Jesus, like *this* isn't squandering." In the distance a dust devil spun in its circle, Rafael turned and peered at me. "You do any runs yet?"

"Runs?"

"You know, with the illegals."

"I don't do that."

"Sure," Rafael said. "Not *yet*." He looked at my car, went to the pump and unscrewed his gas cap, stuck the nozzle in. "One of the perks."

He put in the gas while I made myself busy sweeping the front steps and walkway. "Remember," he said, and he forced the nozzle back into its pump. "If you ever want a little more money." Rafael got into the car and started the engine, Justin came back out of the shop still holding the towel as his son skidded away. I whisked the broom into the dirt, the gas cap skipped from the roof of Rafael's car and spun on the asphalt behind him.

THE MORNING was unusually cool when Justin pointed at the road and said that his wife had been one of the illegals when he'd first met her. "She'd been in the back of one of these very same trucks you see today," he said. "I looked at her and I just knew." A piece of tumbleweed blew by, Justin settled into his chair and told me the story. Her name had been Juanita. She had been the most beautiful girl he'd ever seen. He took out the picture from his wallet and showed me. Surely, she was beautiful. She had long, black hair, and dimples in her smile. Her eyes were sleepy in a sexy way and she wore a yellow dress and white sweater, held her sunglasses in a pose. "Very nice," I said.

"You bet your ass very nice," said Justin. "That's enough."

I handed back the picture.

Justin wiped the photograph's clear plastic encasing with his thumb. "Love of my life. She's dead now."

"I'm sorry," I said.

"Yeah, me too," he said, stuffing the wallet into his pocket with grunting. "She died in Mexico, went back to visit the family and was hit by a truck just inside the border." He shook his head. "She'd left in the morning. I'd kissed her good-bye. At least I'd done that much." He took out his handkerchief and blew his nose, I glimpsed at the road and the mountains of sand in the distance. "Ten years ago. Now it's just me and the station, the punk when he decides to come home."

"Your son."

Justin sneered. "The one and only."

A car slowed and pulled in, a Cutlass Supreme. I stood and went to the pump like the good soldier, asked what it would be. The driver was a gray-haired Mexican with a bushy black mustache below his broken nose. "Fill it up," he said in careful

English, and his dark eyes brightened. "And check the oil too, please." He got out of the car and Justin asked if he wanted a soda.

"*Gracias,*" said the man.

I stuck the nozzle into the tank and opened the hood, Justin went into the shop and came out with the Coke. The man drank it while Justin watched him, I pulled the dipstick out from its cylinder. "You're a little low," I said.

"Do what you have to do."

I added some oil and checked the radiator too, listened as the man told Justin about his farm down in the valley, how he'd nearly lost his whole crop from the unexpected rain the week before last.

"Yeah?" said Justin. "Well, we got bees."

It occurred to me that Justin didn't care to hear about other people's problems. Hence the bees when I'd mentioned Diana and her ideas about Tulum. And now, this man explaining his trouble with the crops and his waving the unfortunate incident away. I slammed the hood down, told the man how much it would be. He reached into his pocket and pulled out the money, wadded and damp. He paid me, handed me a peso as well.

"*Para buena suerte.* For good luck," he said.

I took the peso, held it up to the light.

"I know it sounds funny." He put down his empty bottle of Coke and smiled at Justin. "But I think it's always best to have a little bit of Mexican with you at all times."

"Agreed," said Justin.

I squeezed the peso in my palm, agreed as well.

"Your girl was Mexican?" Justin asked.

The man stared at me.

I didn't have to answer this question, the fact was I could drop-kick Justin and tell him to mind his own goddamned business. But I knew better than that, had been told by more than a few women I was the gentle soul. *Gentle soul,* I thought, and I could have almost said it with the laugh. I pictured Justin giving the man the knowing glance as I laughed for no reason as far as they could see, telling him as he walked him to his car to fetch the police, this one had finally cracked.

"Well then?" Justin said.

"Maybe it's his own business," said the man.

"It's no big deal," I said, only wanting them to forget about it. "She was Mexican American. From El Paso, actually."

"El Paso," the man said, thoughtfully. "*Amigo,* that's the toughest break." He looked at his watch, drew his keys from his pocket. "Leave behind a Latin woman and she'll follow you to the end of your days." He winked at Justin. "Of course I've had enough of them to know."

"That you have," Justin said. They'd talked about this often, it was the familiar territory they were only too glad to include me on. *Lost comrade,* I imagined them thinking. *Sad and forlorn, one could tell just by looking into the eyes.* But I wouldn't have any of it, I pushed the peso into my pocket and stepped around to the pump, wiped its glass.

"I'll probably see you in a week on the way back," the man said, separating his keys. "And you too," he said to me. "If you're still here."

"Oh," I said, pointing to the Buick. "It's broken."

The man nodded at Justin. "That explains it," he said, getting into his car. "In the nutshell." He started the engine, rolled down the window and gave the wave. The dirt rose from his tires as he pulled out from the station. We watched him drive off, the car disappearing on the horizon.

Justin turned toward the chair. "Well then," he said. Just over us I noticed two clouds, and it struck me this was the first time since I'd gotten here that I'd seen anything but the blue. Justin gestured to the shade, ambled over and sat down. "It's better here," he said.

I told him I was fine.

"Suit yourself."

The clouds made their way over the station, for the brief moment there were the shadows. The air cooled, I could almost imagine the better world where everything didn't shrivel and burn. Justin rocked in his chair, peeked up at the sky. The clouds hovered over us, and then just as quickly, passed.

I TOOK DIANA up to Twin Peaks the first night we went out. She sat next to me in the cab, the heater making its noise with the windows steaming. Earlier, before picking her up, I'd driven a couple of fares to the airport, one of them the well-to-do husband and wife from New York giving me enough of the tip to take care of the evening. The night was cold, the sky clearer than I'd ever seen it. "Usually there's fog," I explained. Diana cracked her window open and told me the story of how she'd ended up in San Francisco after finishing college and having nowhere else to go. "I taught back home for a while," she said. "I loved the kids but was so poor because the school barely paid me." She clucked her tongue. *"El Paso,"* she said, and I took her hand. That's when she told me about her father who'd left her mother and Diana when she was a child. *"Hijo de puta.* But still, my father."

The week before she'd been the fare. I'd picked her up from her downtown office and driven her down the dark streets, told her about moving to San Francisco from Sacramento so many years ago. *To find myself,* I'd said, like the tired line. *Well, here I am,* I continued, and she simply stared out her window. I asked her where she worked, she told me in a law firm indexing files. "But I'm not finding myself there, that's for sure," she added, distractedly. *No?* I said, and she talked about the attorneys and the ridiculous amounts of money they made, how the work wasn't exactly the intellectual challenge. I watched her in the mirror as she talked, considered the mole on her cheek and eyes that went deep a million miles. I told her this, said, *You have million-mile eyes,* and tried not to laugh. Something shifted in her then, she smiled. "A million miles is a long way," she said.

IT WAS THE middle of the night when I heard the scratching on the glass. I opened the window to find Rafael standing there, dirty with his jacket ripped and leaves in his hair. "Had a small problem," he said, and he glanced behind him. "I was bringing along the truckful when they stopped us." He bent down, breathed out in the whistle. "I made a break for it and here I am."

"You ran *away* from the patrol?" I said.

"Can you believe it?"

I told him to wait a moment, that I'd come to the door. Of course this wasn't good, I'd be harboring a fugitive if I let him stay. But I had little choice, I couldn't just leave the poor bastard outside for the police to find and take away. I opened my door, he stepped in and looked around. "I only need to wash up," he said, dropping his jacket onto the floor. "And borrow your car."

"My car?" I said. "I don't think so."

"Relax already. I'll bring it right back. I need to go to San Diego to take care of a few things."

I sat down on the bed. *No way,* I thought, knowing that once my car was brought into this I'd surely be a part of the equation. Rafael stood over the sink in the bathroom, turned on the water and cupped his hands. "You got yourself some mess in here," he said. "All your dirty T-shirts."

"Your dad gives them to me."

"Yeah, he used to give them to me too."

Rafael brushed the leaves from his head, went to the window. "So what do you say? Just a couple hours."

"No," I said. "The radiator is shot anyway."

"Shot, huh?" said Rafael. "Well my dad's got sealant somewhere. That will hold me over until I get there, at least."

"Sorry Charlie."

He dumped the leaves outside and turned to me. His face was still wet and made him look suddenly young, clean with the ruddy complexion. His eyes had gone still, lost their flitting quality. He sighed, sat on the bed next to me and I could smell the funk of his sweat. "I know you're thinking I'm a bum. I'm sure my dad has told you some stories."

I shrugged.

"I don't really like being caught in this racket," he said. "But this is the last time. I decided as I was running through the desert I couldn't do this anymore. That I've had enough now." He got up from the bed, went back to the window. "I never wanted any of this. I wanted to buy a house in the country, live the quiet life."

"What happened?" I asked, despite myself. It was late and I only wanted to go to bed. But I knew he wanted to talk, figured he didn't get to spill his guts very often. And here I was once again doing what I'd always done, the cabdriver listening to the person's sorrows, the impartial jury doing his best not to catch the passenger's eyes.

"You really want to know?" said Rafael.

"Try me."

"Okay," he said. "The truth is my mother was an illegal until she married my dad, let's just say it was a family affair." He put his face to the glass, peeked outside at the blackness. "I'd drive with my dad in the truck and the illegals hidden in the back, he'd tell me to cry like a baby if we ever got stopped. The police went a little softer then, a crying kid did the trick every time."

"Your father ran illegals?"

"He probably told you he met my mother in somebody else's truck."

I said that he did.

"You should know she's not dead either. She's living in Mexico, in a tiny town that I know you never heard of, and I hadn't heard of either until she wrote the first letter. My dad doesn't want to believe it, so he says she's dead. But the truth is she's doing just fine. She decided to stop making the runs was all, missed her family when she was here more than us when she was there, I guess." Rafael stepped from the window, crossed his arms. "My dad carries the picture around. If he could he'd probably make her a headstone."

I watched him go back to the bathroom and grab the towel from the rack, dry his face and throat. I wanted to believe him but didn't want to believe him—he was like his father, so unlikable one moment and a pal the next. But with Rafael there was an edge that I was sure Justin once had, the kind I'd seen in so many of the cabdrivers that lasted only the month or two on the job. He came back and picked up his jacket, told me, "I have a plan. You may not believe it but I do. I have a friend I helped over here two or three years ago. He said he can get me some work in a garden near Yuba City, an estate there."

"Gardening's not easy."

"But I'd be outside. And I'm ready now. Before I looked down on that kind of work. Now I crave it."

Suddenly, from the driveway came the sound of tires against dirt.

"Jesus," said Rafael, and he dropped his jacket and fell to the floor. "Play it like nothing's happened." He slid under the bed. "Shit man, you got dead bugs here. Okay, kick up your feet or something, act like you're almost asleep and that you don't know anything at all." The car parked in front of the station and turned off its engine, Rafael's hand shot out and snatched the jacket from the floor. We waited.

Five minutes, then ten. "Oh come on," said Rafael, and he shook his finger at the door. "Could you see what's the deal?"

I put on my shoes, tiptoed around to the front. I was nervous, that much was certain. But I'd faced so much worse. Like most everything else, I compared it to the taxi driving, how there had been the fares with the passengers you knew you should have never picked up. Once I'd had a metal pipe held to my head and been asked for money, another time a customer lit a fire in the backseat before running out. I rounded the corner of the station and did my best to forget how much could go wrong in the middle of this desert.

There, next to the pump was an old beat-up Volvo, a man and woman in the front seat. I walked to the driver's side, the man looked at me and rubbed his bleary eyes. He had a scraggly beard, broken teeth that he revealed in his smile. "We were trying to sleep," he said in his Southern California drawl. "You don't mind if we sleep, do you?"

The woman was already out, I smelled the alcohol on his breath and told him it was fine, to sleep it off, it was no problem. When I came back to the room it was completely quiet, if I hadn't known better I would have thought Rafael had never been there. But then I heard the crack of the floor. "What the fuck?" he said.

"Who's that?" I said.

"You know who it is. So?"

"It was some old hippies. No big deal."

"You sure?"

"I'm sure."

He slid out from under the bed, jacket first. "Where are the keys?"

I sat on the bed, peered at the dresser.

"I need to go. The next time it will be the cops." He peeked out the window. "Or Macco and Pree."

"Macco and who?" I said.

"They're the people who oversee this whole operation. Not counting Humberto, but then he's the head honcho. Anyway. You fuck up or try to run, they make it a point to find you. In that I fucked up, they'd like to talk about it with me. Just a talk, nothing more. What complicates matters is that I'd like to leave. They don't like it when you leave, although it happens."

"So they'd understand."

He put on his jacket, went over to the keys on the dresser and picked them up. "Yeah," he said. "What they wouldn't understand is my getting paid for the job I didn't do." He squeezed the keys in his hand. "Is there anything special I should know? Steering to the left? The blinkers work fine?"

"I'm going with you," I said.

"What's that?"

It was my car and God only knew if he would really bring it back, and I had to get to Mexico *someday*. Besides, I was actually feeling for him. Here he was simply trying to get to the next place, and I wasn't about to let him drive my car with its broken taillight and leaking radiator and exhaust that coughed and sputtered that would surely get him pulled over. I stood from the bed, he held his eyes on mine. "Let's go," I told him.

I KNEW that driving down this road with Rafael after he'd made the break was asking for it. Chances were the police were somewhere along the road, waiting. Not to mention Marco and Polo or whatever the hell their names were. But with me driving he stood something resembling a chance. Rafael found the sealant and poured it into the radiator, checked the hoses and belts for good measure. "We should be fine," he said, not too convincingly. "At least there and back. But you should replace this radiator, it's pretty much had it."

"Tell me something I don't know," I said.

Miracle of miracles, no one stopped us. There had been a few police cars, one patrol pulling over a black van. This van had very likely saved us, Rafael explained down the road. They could well have been waiting and pulling the suspicious vehicles over, and the vehicles didn't come any more suspicious than the vans. And this van was indeed filled with the illegals, as Rafael said when we passed. They'd piled out and were lined up against the side of the road, the patrol shining their flashlights into the men's and women's faces.

We were twenty miles from San Diego when Rafael asked me to stop. "This is where I keep it," he said, and he got out from the car. The traffic passed in its highway roar, the dirt whipped around him as he ran out toward the field. The sun was coming up over the mountains, the sky yellow and golden. Rafael bent down near a patch of sagebrush, ran his hands over the ground. Then he marched ahead until his body became a tiny pinprick in the distance. The sky was nearly blue when he finally returned to the car holding a shoe box covered with black tape. "Herein lies the world's secrets," he said, and he began peeling the tape off in bunches.

"Money?" I said.

"Not money. But where we go to *find* the money."

He opened the box and presented a can of green chile.

"This means we go to the bank downtown," he said.

"And if it was mole we'd go to the valley?"

"Don't laugh. I've had people tap my phones, steal my mail."

"If you say so."

"It's true."

I pressed the gas and the car hesitated, Rafael stared at me.

"Piece of shit Buick," I said.

"That doesn't sound too good."

I pressed the gas some more, the black cloud rose behind us.

We drove into San Diego straight for downtown, a shock after being gone for so long in the middle of the sand and dirt and nothing more. We drove past the piers, the beach stores. Everything was so clean, the grass was green and the water seemed to flow everywhere. "Goddamn," I said, pointing to the stores and their displays. "So much glass and money."

"And *gringos*," said Rafael, and he cleared his throat. "Present company excepted."

We pulled up to the bank, Rafael told me to wait in the car.

In an instant he was back with a wide smile. "We're good," he said. "As far as they know everyone is crossed over."

"And when they find out otherwise?"

"I'll be long gone."

THE SUN was high in the sky as we left the city. There were the mountains, and then suddenly the desert once again. Rafael gazed out the window, pensive. Earlier I'd waited in the car outside his apartment while he'd packed his clothes and gathered his belongings. He'd come down to the car with his bag smiling, joking. Now he was almost sullen as he glanced over at me and said, "You got a good thing going."

"How's that?"

"You get to ride like the wind. You know, no strings."

I snapped my fingers together. I'd heard more than enough cabdrivers announce this as their reason for taking such a job. No cares, no one to answer to except the dispatcher. *The good life,* they'd say, but not for always. After a while you couldn't help but get tired of it, the drunks, the rude customers, the danger of not knowing who was sitting behind you. After a while it just wasn't worth it, even with the pretty woman who'd occasionally end up as your fare.

"Lucky," Rafael said. "Not a care in the world."

"Yeah," I said. "Not a care."

Rafael leaned forward in his seat, turned on the air conditioner. "*You* may not think so," he said. "But you *are* lucky. There's a whole bunch of folks who would kill to be in your shoes. I've tried leaving before but the truth is I couldn't after being here for so long." He tapped his finger to his head. "Too many memories. You know?" He sighed. "Yeah, I got a kid. Why do you think I keep doing this?"

We passed the gas station and I could see the Cadillac parked next to the fence, Justin sitting out on the chair. He waved and made a puzzled face, Rafael pressed his hand to the glass. I knew I would have some explaining to do when I came back, watched in the rearview mirror as Justin stood from his chair.

"Old man," said Rafael.

I adjusted the air conditioner vents, a locust splattered onto the windshield. On the side of the road I noticed a bicycle as it glinted in the light, Rafael pointed with his thumb. "He gave it to me," he said. "The bicycle. Like I would ever need it way out here, I'd die before getting to any place." He snorted a laugh. "Maybe that was the idea."

"Bicycles can be dangerous," I reasoned.

"You know about these things?"

I remembered the time I'd taken Diana to Sacramento, my first trip home in so many years. My mother fussed and my father dithered, I only wished Diana hadn't talked me into coming. "But they're your parents," she'd tell me as if this explained everything. "*Sangre.* You can't turn your back on that." At dinner we sat at the table and my father asked how everything was—the cab driving too, mentioned with the usual disdain. "A cabdriver," my father said, and my mother took his hand. "To think when he was a boy he was almost *run over* by a cabdriver, and now here he is driving the cab." I nodded at Diana. *This is how it always is,* I wanted to tell her. *This is how some things never fucking change.* My father leaned back in his chair, considered the pictures on the wall of me as the child. "Luckily he just gashed his elbow," he said. "Fourteen stitches when it could have been so much worse."

After dinner Diana and I strolled up and down the block, I showed her the houses and yards, named the people I'd known in these places. Then we came to the corner where I'd fallen to the ground and torn up my elbow. "Only my dad got the facts a little mixed up," I said. "Number one, I was on my bicycle. And number two, I was the one who hit *him.*" I shook my head. "He was double-parked with his hazard lights going, for Christ's sake. But my dad wants to remember it the way he does because he likes to remind me I was never meant to drive the cab." I held out my arm, pulled back my sleeve. Diana stepped close, pulled the sleeve back farther. She put her thumb to my elbow, gently drew the smooth, pink line.

AT THE BORDER I drove into the lot where Rafael had parked his Mustang. I popped open my hood with the engine still running, Rafael lugged out his duffel bag from the backseat and set it on the ground. "Let's take a look then," he said, and he went to his car and checked its inside before opening the passenger side door. "All clear," he yelled, and I shook my head. *"What?"* he asked. "I have to be careful, they know what I drive."

I poured the plastic jug of water I'd brought along into the radiator, let the engine idle before I turned it off. The radiator cap was still hot to the touch as I screwed it back on, Rafael walked over and stood beside me. "So I guess this is where I hit the road," he said, picking up the duffel bag. "Is it still in one piece? The radiator, I mean."

"It still has some life," I said, running my fingers along the hoses. "The sealant helps, of course."

"Of course."

I slammed down the hood and followed him to his Mustang, he tossed the duffel bag into the backseat and got behind the wheel. "Tell my dad good-bye for me," he said, rolling down his window with some amount of effort. "Would you mind doing that?"

I told him I wouldn't mind.

"Tell him that I'll write. Tell him that I'll write as soon as I get settled."

"I will."

"Mister Ride Like the Wind."

He drove out of the lot and I went to my car. The can of chile rolled around the floor as I steered onto the road, the splayed shoe box and tape slid from one side to the other. I pressed the gas and the car hesitated once again, the black exhaust poured out as it lurched, then kicked into gear. The heat bounced off the road, behind me was the Mexico I would be driving through in no time.

JUSTIN was back in his chair when I returned. He listened as I told him about Rafael, sighed. I sat down next to him in the cool of the shade, thought of the picture of Juanita in his wallet and his telling me she was dead as if he wanted it to be true. "Your car is running?" he said.

"We used the sealant."

"The sealant," he said. Then, "He'll be back."

"I don't think so."

He nodded. "We'll see."

It was a slow day, the middle of the week and so hot the road went soft in the occasional places. The ground waved, crows flew low or simply sat in the shade where they could find it. Occasionally the customer would drive up, ask for the gas and tell me to put the water into the radiator too. This was the hottest day since I'd arrived, when I mentioned it to Justin he told me I hadn't seen anything yet.

He was right. The next day was even worse. I woke up in my room and the sheets were stuck to my chest with the perspiration. I took a shower and was dry the moment I turned off the water, my sweat soaked into my T-shirt and stunk like the worst thing. I tried to remember San Francisco and its cool breezes, the fog that would roll in with its chill most every day. Now it seemed another planet away as I shuffled out to the cars and checked under the hoods, the heat from the engines pushing up into my face while the sun boiled down. Justin watched all this and said it was just a matter of time until I'd break, I told him I would get through this heat even as I wondered.

■

DIANA spent her twenty-fourth birthday with me. We went to the Italian restaurant with the plastic grapes that hung down from the ceiling, I reached across the table and sang her the song in my quiet voice. "Her birthday?" said the host, with his beaming grin. He went to the kitchen, came back holding the bowl of ice cream with the candle. He placed it before her, lit the candle and the other waiters gathered around and sang. All this, while Diana stared at me over the table with those eyes that went so far.

I never meant for this to go on as long as it had, nearly a year and counting. I never meant to take her to my parents and to pick her up from her office nearly each and every day. There was her laundry that became ours, the telephone calls after she'd gone to work and left me sleeping. "Baby," she'd say. "Oh, did I wake you, baby? Oh, did I wake you?" Yes you did—*baby*, I'd tell her. Yes you *did*. But holding Diana's hand across that restaurant table, the waiters looking down as the flames from the candle danced up into her face, it hit me, God did it hit me, here was the first woman whose name I had ever put in the song.

On the drive home she asked how many other girls I'd been with on their birthdays, I told her one or two but that here was the one I would always remember. She laughed and I said it was true, and when she moved close I really believed it— she was my Diana, the girl I cared for so much. Then *I* laughed, told her it was funny the way things turned out. "Maybe," she said. "But sometimes things turn out the way they're supposed to, too."

■

AT NOON, Justin said he would go into town to pick up a six-pack of beer to cool us down, some ice and a new garden hose too. "We'll spray each other when it gets too bad," he said, pointing to the faucet and the old hose beside it. "I'll make it as comfortable as I can."

I sat at the station, kept myself in the shade and when that didn't work went inside to the shop. But the shop was no good either, worse when all was said and done with the fan that blew out the hot air. I went back outside, a car drove by, then another. The telephone rang.

"Hey partner." It was Justin calling from his cell phone to tell me the tire to his Cadillac had blown. "On today of all days," he said. "If you can believe it." He paused, the wireless line crackled. "So you think you could make it here?"

"Well," I said, thinking.

"I suppose I could call the tow truck but that seems like a goddamned waste when you're right there."

The fan rattled as I held the telephone to my ear, slippery from the perspiration, a cricket jumped from the dirty floor onto the desk, then to the windowsill. And I knew in that moment I would tell Justin I was leaving. I would tell him that evening, take my paycheck along with the jugs of water and bottles of sealant, drive down to Tulum and make the new start Rafael had made that was my time to make too. I would drive the car as far as it would go, walk there if I had to. I just had to make it to the Yucatán was all that I knew. The rest would be cake.

"I'll be there," I said, and I hung up the phone.

The spare tire was behind the shop. I tossed it into the backseat of my car, turned the ignition and opened the hood. The radiator looked fine, I unscrewed its cap and poured in some more water just to be safe. There were the hoses and belts soft and rubbery from the heat, I screwed the cap back on and closed the hood.

JUSTIN had said he was halfway to Calexico parked off to the side of the road, but with the glare of the sun I had to wonder how I would ever see him. I adjusted the visor, sat up straight to block the light. The car hesitated, and when I pressed the accelerator the black exhaust poured out in the cloud. The dashboard buzzed, the red lights blinked all over. The radiator, the oil, the engine smoked with the acrid smell of burning. I pulled over and got out of the car, kicked the door, kicked it again. That's when I began to walk back to the station.

A car came up the road, another followed. I stuck out my thumb, stood off to the side and waited. When the first car passed I yelled out. Then the second car, and I held my voice because I could already feel my throat closing from the heat. I continued to walk, the sun so bright I could barely see, everything blurring. Crows flew above and made their tiny shadows, the gravel kicked up from my shoes. And then, there was the bicycle in the ditch, broken-pedaled and flat-tired, the chain in pieces. I stumbled off the side of the road, stared down. It was in this moment that I began to see Diana, her face before me like the waves of heat rising. "Here's where it happened," I said, and suddenly we were back in Sacramento standing on the corner of my parents' street. "The bicycle. The cab." I pointed to the ground, Diana touched her thumb to my elbow, traced it along.

Another car, I lifted my arm with the effort and when I looked up it was the pickup roaring by. Filled with the men, the illegals. They hollered and screamed, the dust swirled into my eyes with its sudden breeze. And I could almost see it, the tiny dot that was the gas station but then again maybe wasn't—the likely mirage. Diana, oh Diana, I thought, and now we were standing at the door to her apartment as she told me what she'd seen as I'd driven by. *The fare,* she said. *The girl, sitting in the front seat right there next to you.* I put out my arms, I pulled her close, all I wanted was to tell her so much but I couldn't say a word. She held me, then pushed me. "You're the asshole," she said. "*El cochino.* The fucking pig." She turned and I followed her into the kitchen, she grabbed a glass from the counter and uncorked the bottle. That's when she poured the first glass of wine.

The heat came down, the dot wavered in the distance and I imagined the water from the gas station's faucet—blue, clear, like Tulum. And Diana should have been there with me as I stepped into the Tulum water. Diana should have been there with me with her body against mine. We would swim out and I could see it now, the white sand beneath our toes as the water lapped and rippled, the breeze coming through our fingers as we raised our hands. Because that night I'd awakened on her couch to the telephone ringing and the rain making its terrible noise. Because that night she had drunk the entire bottle of wine and the cab was gone and I'd already known. I'd stared out at the empty space where my cab had been, held the telephone to my ear and listened even though I didn't want to hear. *Rain,* the policeman's voice may as well have said as he'd told me she'd driven the cab into the tree. *Coming down like the cats and dogs to tear up the world.*

A car passed, I staggered. There was a skid and the car backing up. I ran and my knees buckled, it was Justin in his Cadillac as he got out and walked toward me. "Jesus Christ, what happened?" he said, and I pointed to where I'd left the car. He said that he'd seen it on the way here, that a neighbor from town had pulled over and ended up having a spare. "But you," he said. "Well it looks like your ride is pretty broken." He helped me to his car. "Just take it easy," he told me, and he set me down in the seat and placed the ice in my mouth, then the water from the bottle. I set my head back, a crow flew alongside the car before it flickered away. Justin pressed the gas. He adjusted his mirror and gazed down at me, turned on the air conditioner as high as it would go. Ahead was the gas station, the tiny dot changing from the glimmer to the actual, real building. I lifted the bottle and leaned farther back, poured the water down onto my face and closed my eyes.

Ross Willow's
New and Used Cars

Ross Willow watched the cars pass on the freeway as the sun made its morning shadows onto the field. On the ground were the scattered walnut shells, some still green. The air was filled with the pleasant scent of the soil in its fecund brownness, the trees themselves, so abundant. *I could just stay here,* he told himself. *Throw off my jacket and pick these walnuts until the trees are clean, go to the next town and pick their walnuts too.* He walked across the field and picked up one of the nuts, cracked it open before tossing it aside.

The world was crazy, that much was clear. There were the bombs in China, the president was sending the National Guard to the colleges and his son was dead in Vietnam, *dead in Vietnam* for God's sake, a country he'd barely even heard of until the news reports had started to come over, the pictures of the men in straw hats holding their guns, the American soldiers muddy and bloodied, looking much too young and confused.

"Oh, Thomas," he said to the trees, the sky. And he continued across the field, his boots crunching into the walnuts, pressing them down so that they became a part of the soil, disappearing beneath his heels. He went to his car, sat for a long moment as the traffic passed. And when he pulled onto the road he looked back to see the field that seemed smaller somehow, as if shrunken and put into some kind of box. The trees lined up in perfect formation, while from the field they'd appeared to be planted randomly, not arranged in any particular order. It occurred to Ross that here was the difference between walking and driving, that it put trees in lines and houses on blocks and so much could be passed over so quickly. Like his life, like Thomas's life, this son that he had hardly known, so much he'd taken for granted.

WHEN HE came back to the lot Tracy was there with his clipboard, escorting a couple through the maze of cars and checking off the things they would save if they decided to shop here. Tracy had thick glasses and dentures that clicked, and he put the buyer at ease by pointing to his glasses and teeth telling them, *Would this face lie?* Ross had recommended he tell the potential buyer this when he first started at the lot, because he knew that in actuality his glasses and teeth could be a liability, that they needed to play a little bit of this reverse psychology game when dealing with a face like Tracy's. The customers seemed to like it, taking some small pity on the man and telling him no, it wouldn't lie. There had once been the elderly woman who'd come back to the lot after she bought her car, offered Tracy some cookies and said, *You're not such a bad-looking man as all that.*

Ross went to his office and the goose honked from behind the building. *This goose,* he thought, and he reached for his pen and began signing the various forms. Thomas had found the goose waddling in the field behind the house, brought him over to Ross and said, "I think this bird is searching for a home." One year later Ross was using the bird in his commercials, had trained it to honk on command and stand still on top of the cars.

He pressed his pen down onto the carbons. They'd sold three cars already, and this was a slow day. The television commercials had helped tremendously, although they'd cost a bundle to run. But to *make* them, it was peanuts. He'd used the goose in each and every one, had told the investors, *How could we go wrong with animals?* as they sweated over the expense of putting these commercials on the air.

Ross stacked the papers on his desk and swung around in his chair, watched Bill sweet-talk a young, blond woman into buying a Chevrolet Impala. Bill was the better-looking of the salesmen here. Ross kept him in reserve for these younger women, knew that his smile could do more work than a thousand words. And Bill *did* smile, treated each customer as if he were taking them to the prom. *The seats in this number are the be-all and end-all,* he would say. Or, *Try the steering and you'll know what it's like to have wings.*

Ross only stepped out to the lot to do the selling now on

special occasions, mainly when they were short-staffed. Then it didn't take much more than his showing up, most of the customers so intimidated by having an honest-to-goodness television personality right there in front of them. He only wished real life could be so easy, that he could change minds and affect ideas with as much ease as he could here.

There was his family that wasn't his family, his wife who slept in the same bed but that was all that she did, his remaining son David who only talked to him in the mornings and evenings—not so much talking as grunting—on his way out the door. The boy was seventeen and all Ross wanted was to have a real conversation with him, but ever since Thomas died it had been as hard to talk to his wife and son as anything.

Ross signed the remaining papers, sat back in his chair and the blue and gold streamers beside his window glittered in the breeze. The goose honked, in the far distance were the mountains, the snow on their ridges. This snow, Ross thought, and he considered the river a mile or so away, across the road and behind the field. On some days he would smell the water, its scent of fish that would carry in the air. But not today, with the chill of autumn already upon them, the October morning and its sun that shone through the clouds.

HIS WIFE was sitting at the table when he got home. She had been crying, he knew this much, as she had been crying most afternoons these days, it seemed. *Six months since they got the telegram,* he thought as he closed the door behind him and gave her a kiss on the cheek. Ross went to the refrigerator and pulled out a beer, popped it open and had to wonder, when would this heartbreak end? He sat down opposite Cheryl and set his beer onto the table.

"Saw your new commercial," she said. "It was pretty funny."

"Oh come on," said Ross. "It was ridiculous."

"How'd you get the goose to wear the hat?"

Ross patted beneath his chin. "Rubber band."

"Still," she said. "It was funny."

Cheryl worked mornings for a real estate company. Until Thomas had died, she'd had the best sales record in the region. Ross was familiar with her technique, she had his same ability for the soft sell that put the buyer at ease. Because that was the trick, making the buyer comfortable. Once the seller had done that much, it was easy as pie.

But now the soft sell, or any kind of sell, was the difficult task. Losing a son scrambled everything up, made one rethink the priorities. Selling houses and cars seemed suddenly absurd, and Ross had come to terms with the lack of meaning in his job not long after they'd received the telegram. He'd reconciled himself to the news with the knowledge that everything was absurd, even this war—that wasn't so much absurd as tremendously sad. And he knew that his commercials helped, however slightly, to make the world a little less sad. There were the terrible news reports with the dead children and soldiers with wounds, and then his commercial with the goose wearing the hat, and perhaps this made people a little more hopeful, however slightly, for the fate of humankind.

David came through the door, went to the refrigerator and made his grumble. He was wearing his red T-shirt with the picture of the pinball machine, the seashell necklace. His arms were skinny and white and reminded Ross of broomsticks—he had on the usual pair of jeans and the Converse tennis shoes with the purple shoelaces. When he glanced at Ross the eyes had their same angry quality as always, the remnant of sadness. "Hey there," said Ross.

"Hey."

"How was school?"

"It was school," David said, as if this made any sense at all. He grabbed for a soda and opened the can, closed the refrigerator door and left the kitchen in his lifeless way. Ross stared at Cheryl, lost in her own world, drank his beer and turned to the window, the passing clouds, the breeze that slowly moved them along.

ROSS had an early morning meeting with Bill and Tracy the next day. They drank their coffee and ate their doughnuts, Ross with his feet up on the desk and Bill and Tracy sitting in their chairs. Saul out front hosed off the driveway, while Art wiped down a few of the cars. The meeting was about hiring new help. All in all Ross had fifteen employees, not counting himself. A good number, and chances were he would end up hiring more by the end of the year with the way sales were going.

Ross watched Art pick away at something on the windshield of the Malibu, Saul spray the driveway clean of some piece of paper when he could have simply gone over to pick it up.

"I ended up taking the Impala home last night," Bill said, chewing his maple bar.

Tracy regarded him, twitched a smile. "You don't say."

"A trip to the stars."

Ross clicked his boots together. Here was one of the fringe benefits of the job, meeting young ladies who saw you at your best. You made your jokes, you showed your soft side. Perhaps even talked about your mother, the fact that she had this very same car and that you drove her to the grocery market on Tuesdays because you enjoyed driving the car so much, and also to do her this favor.

Ross had met a few women this way in the early days, but it invariably left him with some sense of regret, spending the night and not having a word to say to them in the morning. He was a sentimental fool—he'd come to know this much about himself, even as a young man. He'd first seen Cheryl crossing the street from her university as his car idled at the light. She'd passed in front of him, dropped her books onto the ground. Before he knew it, he was outside with all the cars honking behind him, helping her and saying to wait on the side of the road, that he had something he wanted to tell her.

Tracy adjusted his glasses. "Perhaps this week I could get a few of the ladies?" he said.

"A few," said Ross. "But we need to consider the demographic," he added, delicately. Tracy knew his limitations, but still made the odd date from the job. Some women liked his goofiness, and his intelligence was obvious once they saw through his technique. "My downfall is that the only women who like me are the ones who end up knowing me too well to buy my cars," he'd once lamented to Ross.

They talked about the past month's sales, the new models expected in by the end of the year, the commercials and how many people mentioned them when they came in to the lot. Bill filled his cup with coffee, pointed out the window and said, "They sure like that goose."

Ross leaned forward and brought his feet down from the desk. "Of course they like that goose," he said. "He makes them smile."

WHICH MADE IT all the more alarming when Ross came into work the next day and found the goose missing. Gone from its cage and with Tracy in a state of panic, because two families had already come by the lot to look at the cars but when the goose wasn't there they'd left. Tracy walked alongside Ross in his nervous way. "So what do we do Ross?" he said, his dentures clicking. "What do we do?"

Ross went to the gate, its lock disappeared and door pulled open. "I guess we call the police," he said.

"Yeah, but what can the police do, really?"

"I couldn't tell you," Ross said. "Look for a few clues. Follow the feathers." He was concerned but not too concerned, there were other geese. But then he went to his office and there was the framed photo of the goose on the wall—the bird standing in front of the lot, snow white and crane necked with its wings spread and beak open as though laughing. And Ross realized there weren't really other geese, that here was a bird that could honk on command and wear hats without protest. This goose was trained, and he didn't know what he would do, the next commercial scheduled for shooting next week.

"More people coming and going," said Tracy, sticking his head into the office.

"There's nothing we can do," Ross said.

"It's awful."

The police found the goose run over in the fabric store's parking lot across the street. Apparently someone had set the goose down in the adjacent field before running away. Ross met the police officer in the parking lot and they both stood over the bird. The customers of the store gathered around Ross and the officer, the owner Mr. Sharma came out with his wife as the officer scribbled the information onto his notepad. "There's nothing as sad as a dead bird," Mr. Sharma said, and the wife nodded. Ross bent down and picked up the limp goose, held it to his chest and crossed the street back to the lot.

ROSS got the call from the police at the office, figured there were more goose details to be worked out. But there were no goose details at all, it turned out the police were holding David because he'd been caught stealing a *Playboy* magazine from the supermarket around the corner from their house. *"Playboy?"*

Ross said dumbly, and he realized yes *Playboy,* what else, the boy was seventeen and if he was going to steal, it seemed like that was what he would take.

"His mother wasn't home so we called you," the officer continued. He cleared his throat. "Your goose," the officer said. "Well Mr. Willow, sir. We have reason to believe, *evidence* actually, that your son let the goose out of the cage."

"The goose?" said Ross. He couldn't believe David would do something like that. Stealing girlie magazines, maybe. But letting his father's goose out of the cage? He felt the slight tear in his chest at the thought of it, David watching the bird make its way out.

"We found the lock in his pocket. And when we asked him what it was for he simply told us."

"He told you," Ross repeated.

"You should come," the officer said.

Ross remembered the goose in the lot crushed and lifeless with its white feathers all around, felt a flash of anger toward the boy. Then he imagined David in the police station probably scared out of his wits and realized what it was they were holding him for, that he had stolen a magazine, *a magazine,* for Christ's sake, and they had only come upon this evidence of the goose that wasn't between anyone really, but Ross and the boy. *They had no right,* he thought while he told the officer he would be right there. He hung up the telephone, gathered his keys, and went to his car.

■

DAVID sat on a bench in the station, his face calm and serene as if waiting for a movie to begin. Ross talked to the officer who had made the telephone call, a young man of no more than thirty with kind eyes and short, bristly hair the color of sand. "There were several witnesses to each crime," the officer said. "I know it seems like we're making it a big deal, and frankly, the only reason he's here is because the manager of the supermarket insisted we bring the boy in."

"Make him an example."

"That's the way it usually works," the officer said. He scratched his head, pulled on his ear. "So anyway, we found the magazine on him, and the lock, as I said, was in his pocket. A little girl saw him take the magazine, and he matches the description we were given by the people in the fabric store who saw him with the goose."

Ross folded his arms and glimpsed over the officer's shoulder at his son who hadn't yet acknowledged his father's presence. *Come on boy,* Ross wanted to say. *Now we can stop playing these stupid games.*

The officer handed over a form and explained how there would be a trial date, Ross signed it and went around the desk to the bench where David was sitting. He sat next to him and squeezed his thin arm. "Hey," he said. "I'm here."

David stared straight ahead, his face remained steady.

"We can go now," Ross said.

"But I'm under arrest."

"You're not under arrest. I took care of things."

He let go of David's arm and the boy stood, walked ahead.

Ross followed, thanked the officer although he didn't know what he was thanking him for, just that he had been reasonable about the whole matter, he supposed. The officer took a basket from his drawer filled with David's wallet, loose change, and the lock—its shackle cleanly broken.

"Do you want to press charges?" he said.

Ross regarded the officer. "He's my son."

"Yes," the officer said. "Still, I have to ask."

Ross took the lock and the wallet, the change and put it all in his pocket. When he came out to the car he gave David the wallet and change, opened the door. "You get the lock too?" David said, and Ross was shocked that the boy could be so cavalier.

"What the hell were you thinking?" said Ross.

David simply shook his head, stared up at the sky.

"The *Playboy* is one thing, but the bird? An actual, living being?"

David glared past his father at the clouds, the sun, the airplane passing in the far, far distance. His eyes were wet, and Ross saw that he was doing everything he could to keep from crying. "We can get in the car," Ross said, but it was too late, the tears were already streaming. Some police officers walked by and looked at Ross and the boy, then down at their feet.

"I never wanted it to get killed," David said.

"Okay," said Ross. He held the door open. "Let's get in and talk about it."

"I brought him to the field. I told him to fly away."

Ross leaned into the open door, felt his heart do some kind of turn.

"And he *did* fly, but he came back, and then the car ran over him." He wiped his eyes. Ross reached into his pocket and handed David his handkerchief. The boy flattened it into his face, smeared it into a circle. "I never wanted it to get killed."

Ross took the boy in his arms and a few more police officers made their way past them. *The goose,* he thought, and he remembered David coming by the lot more than once as a boy and insisting on feeding the bird the potato chips he'd brought from his lunch. A car honked and an officer yelled to his partner. A siren echoed, then another. "Let's just go," Ross said. David stepped back and wiped his face again, sat down in the car. They drove and were quiet, the only sound the road beneath them.

CHERYL hadn't much to say about the goose and David getting arrested for the *Playboy,* only that maybe he was giving them a cry for help, that this was his way of communicating with them. *No shit,* Ross had thought although he didn't say it. Cheryl had been talking this way a lot lately. She had quit her job at the real estate company, found work in a nursery across town. "This way I don't have to talk to people," she'd said, and Ross figured it was true, that she could water the plants and plant the trees and it would be so much easier for her to get through the day. His hope was that in devoting herself to the plants and flowers, she would come back around to this world, begin to find the ways to talk to him again.

Because it had been too long since they had talked, let

alone made love. Months and months, he couldn't even re-member the last time. One night he watched her as she breathed in and out in her steady way, her mouth slightly open. "Cheryl," he'd whispered into her ear, and she'd stirred. He'd run his hand along her back, then over her shoulder to her breast, pulled her close. "Cheryl," he'd said again, and she'd opened her eyes and turned toward him, considered him with the face that suggested this was what she had expected but didn't want, and that she didn't want to have to say it. He'd held her, slowly let his hand fall from her breast, they'd fallen asleep not long after.

And now they *were* talking, but he didn't like the way her voice sounded, as if he were some kind of child without an idea in the world about how to fix things. They sat at the kitchen table and she underlined several words in the notebook that had become her journal. "A cry for help," she said again, and she made a circle, then another circle around the circle. "I learned about this from Wanda at work," she said, gesturing to the illustration. "How we need to concentrate on the inside."

The inside, thought Ross, and he watched the way she tucked her hair under her kerchief, pulled the pens from the pocket of her denim skirt. She had started wearing the kerchief and skirt since the nursery, said it made her more mobile, less inclined to worry about the way she looked. She peered up at Ross. "I think he's trying to tell you to spend more time at home."

"But I *am* home."

"Not enough." She set the pens down, centered the notebook before her. He imagined the words between these pages: *the war, losing Thomas, everything that caused her so much pain.* She leaned forward. "Here's what I think you need to do," she said, with too much conviction. "Spend some time together. Just you and David. That would be the start of the healing."

Ross picked up one of the many pens, rolled it between his palms. "What about us?" he said.

"This is between you and the boy."

"It's between us too."

Cheryl pushed her finger over the circle in the notebook. "It's between you and the boy," she said again. "If I know anything, it's this much." Ross put down the pen. *If you say so Cheryl,* he could have told her, with the sarcasm. But he didn't, simply moving the pen across the table toward her. Cheryl stared at the pen, leaned back in her chair and sighed.

Ross shot the commercial alone, with no goose, needing fourteen takes just to get it right. "Without the bird I'm hopeless," he said. So when it came time to shoot the next commercial the following week, Ross borrowed a chimpanzee from the zoo. The monkey was trained to smile and jump, and Ross put him behind the wheel of a Ford Mustang as he told the camera, "Come on over already and don't monkey around, these deals are getting cold."

His fears that the cars wouldn't sell without the goose

were abated when even more people came to the lot after the commercial with the monkey ran. They asked about the monkey and Ross had to eventually purchase his own—a female chimpanzee—build it a pen and train it much as he had trained the goose. But dealing with the goose had been so much easier. Whereas the bird had simply needed the cracker for honking, the monkey demanded more, a hug or scratch behind the ear, sometimes a look at the mirror so she could see herself and make the faces. *"Primates,"* he'd sneered to Bill and Tracy.

DAVID was put on probation. The judge fined him two hundred dollars and said if he got caught stealing again he would end up in the juvenile detention center, recommended several sessions with a youth counselor as well. David had remained silent throughout the hearing, when the judge asked him if he had anything he wanted to tell him he shook his head.

Ross sat on the bench and thought about this boy taking the magazine and goose, just what it was he was trying to say to them, this *cry for help* as Cheryl had put it. Cheryl sat next to him and held his hand. The hand felt nice in his, reminded him of the old days and how it used to be. *Time,* he told himself. *All they needed was more time.* And he knew exactly what he would do, take the boy on a camping trip to Yosemite, where he and Cheryl had gone so many years earlier for their honeymoon. He and David would go away for a weekend, she would see how their differences had been resolved and that slowly, eventually, the differences between Cheryl and Ross could be resolved as well.

David turned from the judge and went to his parents, they walked out to the car from the courthouse. "So that could have been much worse," Ross said, trying to lighten things up. Cheryl cracked the window open, David sat in the backseat and stared out as Ross pulled from the lot.

"What we need is some time together," Ross said, watching his son in the mirror. David remained expressionless with his eyes fixed to the glass. "A camping trip, I think that would be the best thing." Cheryl put her hand to the boy and he reached out. Ross steered onto the freeway, realized she shared something with David he never could, and he felt an ache raise itself from his heart at this knowledge.

"It's something we talked about," she said.

"You talked about," David said in his quiet voice. "Well thank you for including me in the conversation."

"Come on," said Ross.

"We thought it would be a good tool for healing," Cheryl said, and when David glimpsed at his father in the mirror, Ross only wished she would be quiet. Lately, her friend Wanda had been lending Cheryl books about healing and making the best of grief, giving her pills to facilitate sleep, dark powders for milkshakes that were supposed to boost the immune system. Cheryl had begun to walk differently, with bigger steps as if she were trying out new boots, her voice had taken on a new cadence when she explained these new ideas her friend was sharing. He watched David and knew that here was an area his son agreed with him, that they didn't like this new person she was becoming, and this gave him some small comfort that they could share this much, at least.

"Healing is good," David said.

Ross veered past a hole in the road, swallowed hard against his sudden anger. "Healing isn't good. Talking's good. And we need to talk."

"I don't need to talk to you," said David.

"No you don't," said Ross. "But you will."

"You can't make me go."

"I'm still your father," Ross said, and Cheryl rolled the window down farther and let the wind blow into her face. Ross glanced at Cheryl and saw the walnut field behind her— the walnut field he liked to go to when things became too much. And if he didn't have his family with him he would have pulled over onto the field and gotten out of the car, raised his arms to the branches all around and shaken down the nuts that were so plentiful. "Walnuts," Cheryl said, following his gaze, and Ross said that they were, ready to be picked any day now. He gave the field one last look, and then they were past the trees and driving onto the off-ramp and the city streets toward their house.

ROSS made love to Cheryl that night. For one brief moment it seemed that perhaps she was back, that things were once again normal, that life would go on. But then she started to cry just before he came, and she pushed him away and told him not to touch her, then pulled him close and said there was no way they could keep going on. The next morning she drank her powders and took her pills, Ross read the newspaper but didn't read it, the words and pictures not quite adding up to anything he could understand. David came into the room, stood at the door with his hair dripping. His hair had grown long—the style these days—his face was spotted with the terrible acne that was as unfair as this boy's life had been. He sat down and poured his cereal and milk, Ross explained his plan for them to go to the mountains that weekend. David ate his cereal, Cheryl drank her milkshake and kept her eyes on the boy. Ross put out his hand and gently placed it on David's shoulder. "What do you say?" David chewed and slurped his cereal, didn't look up as he said, "What *can* I say?" before leaving the table.

ROSS bought the tent he'd always rented when he went to the mountains with Cheryl. Those days seemed so long ago now, and he supposed they were, more than twenty years and count-ing. Back then they had taken his father's old Dodge, driven along the Yosemite roads that were all dirt and gravel. There were fewer people then, the stars were larger and more plenti-ful. They would lie back with their heads outside the tent and begin counting, sometimes she would sing songs and her voice would be the only sound all around them. These were surely the most beautiful moments of Ross's life, the pine trees gently swaying and the stars glimmering above. He'd recently re-turned from the war, which wasn't so much returning from the war as its garages. He'd gone to Italy, then France, spent most of his duty under the jeeps and tanks that brought the men to the fields. He was proud of his work there, even if it was so much unseen. He'd explained it all to Cheryl and she'd put it best when she'd said he may not have fired a gun but he'd helped to carry a lot of bullets.

In addition to the tent, Ross bought the typical provisions. A flashlight, batteries, sunscreen, dried fruit. He made a point of picking up some of David's favorite candies as well, put them in a plastic bag along with the dried fruit. He loaded the car after dinner while David watched from the window, staring at him with his blank expression. He finally came down with his sleeping bag and placed it atop the tent, said to wake him in the morning, they had a long drive ahead of them, that much was certain. That night, Ross came to bed strangely happy, this new day laid out before them with its exciting possibilities.

"I think we're going to have a good time," he said to Cheryl. She sat in bed with the pillows gathered behind her, reading the book about pain and healing and the never-ending circle. She glanced up from the book with her dark eyes, tilted her head, and he remembered when he'd parked his car after helping her with the books, how she'd watched him with her head turned this same way as he'd headed over. Funny how that could seem like just yesterday, he thought, and these lines in our faces, this slight ache in our bones, that crept up on us this way.

Ross pulled off his boot, tossed it to the floor. "What?" he said.

"I already talked to David," she said.

"Okay."

"There's something we need to talk about."

"Okay," he said again.

"I don't know how to say this."

"You can say it," Ross said, and he could feel his stomach dropping, dropping, into some kind of hole. He knew what she was going to say even before she said it. But still, hearing the words had the effect of tearing at him in the way he never quite expected, the finality of it all, the fact that she could say it in her voice with the manner he barely recognized.

"I'm asking for a divorce."

He wanted to insist she couldn't do something like that, that they had too much between them. He knew what it was that made her cry, how she could laugh if he touched her in just the right place. He knew the stories of her mother who'd been the artist—making paintings of the lakes and mountains until she'd begun to lose her sight, her father who'd said more than once to Cheryl she wasn't worth the salt on his table—and when she'd told Ross this he'd held her and said she was worth all the salt in the world. *What about all we've been through?* he wanted to say. What about our boys and holding them when they were born? Standing next to you at the funeral and taking your hand and your squeezing it back and knowing, *knowing,* we were all that we had? *I love you Cheryl,* he wanted to tell her, but he stopped himself, knew that she would say he loved who she had been, that all they had were memories, that it was time to move on.

"Jesus," said Ross. He walked around the room, one boot off and one boot on. "You told David?"

"Right after dinner."

Ross thought of the boy tossing the sleeping bag into the car, considered it curious he hadn't mentioned a word about what his mother had said. But then what *would* he say? That he couldn't believe it had come to this? After all, this was no surprise, it had been coming for so long now. He went to the window and put his face against the glass.

"Don't be upset."

"That's easy to say."

"You're going through the stages is all."

"*Stages.*"

"It's normal is all I'm saying."

Ross turned from the window. "We could talk to people."

"I *have* talked to people. I know what we need to do."

He came back to the bed, put out his hand. "But can't we just try?"

"No," she said, shaking her head. "We can't. We really can't."

Ross cracked open the door to David's room and found him still awake listening to the transistor radio. "What's on?" he said when he came into the room. David removed the radio from his ear, sat up in the bed.

"Just music," he said.

"Anything good?"

"They play the same songs."

Ross took the chair from the desk and sat opposite David, crossed his arms. "So I hear your mother talked to you."

"About the divorce?" he said, and there it was again, the same careless attitude he'd shown with the lock outside the police station.

"Yes the divorce," Ross said. He wasn't sure what he'd even come in here for, maybe just to have the boy ask him to give it one more chance, to see if they could work it out. But David seemed positively calm and accepting of this new direction their lives were about to take. "I don't know," said Ross. "I guess I only wanted to see how you were doing."

"I'm okay," David said.

"So are we still on for tomorrow?"

"If you say we are."

Ross uncrossed his arms and looked around at the room— the dresser with the clothes sticking out from the drawers, the pinball shirt bunched on the floor near the closet. In the corner stood the fishing rod taken from Thomas's old bedroom, empty now except for the books and records piled on the floor. The fishing rod was green and corked along the handle, and Ross remembered taking Thomas and David fishing so many years ago, sitting in the boat with the water lapping up against the sides. Thomas had insisted they throw back each fish they'd caught, made him do it. "Their eyes are sad," he'd said, even as Ross told him that fish were dumb as dirt, dumber even, that he had no need to worry as he tossed the fish back anyway. But then had come the last fish of the day, a larger than usual bass and even as Thomas had cried for Ross to stop he'd knocked the fish dead against the side of the boat. David had laughed then, and who would have ever thought he would become the pacifist while the other went to war? *But what do we ever know anyway?* Ross told himself as he got up from the chair and slid it toward the desk.

"I thought you might want some time to yourself," Ross said.

"No," said David. "I'm fine, really."

Ross left the room and closed the door. He stood there and listened, David clicked the radio back on and he could hear the twangy sound of the music, peppy and glad with its dancing beat. Down the hall the light switched off in his bedroom and he knew Cheryl was close to sleep now, soon her even breathing would come. He stood in the hallway a moment longer, went to the table and picked up his keys and went out to the car.

THE TENT was up on the front lawn by midnight. Ross had done the job quietly, and therefore slowly, taking care not to wake Cheryl or the boy. When he finished, he kicked off his boots and went in. He lay with his head out the tent and gazed up at the stars, but there were so few, this light from the city making it difficult to see anything more than their traces. Funny, he thought, that when he'd come back from the war he'd stare up into this same sky and it would be absolutely filled with the dots of light. Time passed and the stars disappeared, and what a sad thing that was.

ROSS woke up the next morning with the sun shining into his eyes, the neighbor from across the street regarding him from the sidewalk and giving him a wary hello. He blinked hard and sat up, the tent teetered before falling down upon him. When he checked his watch he could see it was already past eight, that he had slept much too late and that he had to go and wake David.

He crawled out, gathered the tent and stuffed it into the car before going back to the house. At the front door he heard the hiss of the shower, he walked past his bedroom to see Cheryl's nightgown draped over the bedside chair. "David," he yelled, and he went to the boy's room but he wasn't there. He sat on David's bed and listened to the sound of the water from the bathroom, picked up a handful of pennies from the nightstand and tossed them onto the floor.

"Cheryl," he said quietly to himself and he stood and trampled over the change, went to the bathroom door and cracked it open. "Who's there?" Cheryl said. Ross hesitated, said it was only him as he stepped inside. He took off his boots, then his pants, unbuttoned his shirt.

"We saw you out on the lawn," she said.

"That so?"

"Yeah. We figured the camping trip was off, even though I told David to go ask you." The water splashed against the steamed shower door. "Did he ask you?"

"No he didn't," Ross said. He took off his shirt, then pulled down his underwear, tossed his socks into the pile of clothes.

"That's too bad," she said. "But did you want to go?"

"I would have," said Ross.

"I'm sorry," she said, and he could tell that she really was, her voice genuine and real as it had once been, Cheryl as he had known her. He padded onto the bathmat and quietly opened the door. When she saw him there naked as he was, her eyes shrank back but he joined her anyway. He moved under the faucet and she told him, "Well I'm getting out then." But he held her and when she tried to break loose his grip was strong. "Let me go," she said, but he didn't, and when she finally relaxed he relaxed too. The water came down, she pressed her head into his chest. "I just wish it were different," she said, her words gurgling into the water. He held her, pulled her even closer as the steam swirled around them.

ROSS moved out of the house, took a hotel room across from the lot. It was strange, looking out from his window and seeing his picture on the billboard with the monkey, the streamers blowing in the wind. He had named the monkey Dumpling, not so much for the apple or sugar, but the dumps that she took and threw at the walls of her pen—although he never told the public that. She seemed to become even more popular, this most recent advertisement with her wearing aviator goggles sitting behind the wheel of an Oldsmobile. They had filmed the latest commercial only the day before last. In it, Dumpling wore a hippie wig and sunglasses, made a peace sign while Ross told the audience, "Get with it, come on over to Ross Willow's New and Used Cars."

Cheryl continued her work at the nursery, joined a peace group and even spoke to the newspaper about how wrong she thought this war was, that she'd lost a son and for what? Ross

was proud of her for doing that, even if he wasn't sure he nec-
essarily agreed. It was complicated was all he knew, with no
right or wrong in this mess that was tearing people up all over.

Then came the news of the My Lai massacre. Ross heard
about it from Tracy, who heard about it from Bill, not so much
because of the sadness of the event but because of his son burning the American flag in front of the high school to protest
what the soldiers had done. The fact that David took to doing
this was bad enough, but that the television reporter described
the boy as the son of Ross Willow of Ross Willow's New and
Used Cars made it all the more awful.

Tracy brought the television into the office, Bill plugged it
in and told Ross to watch what came next. And sure enough,
on each station there was his son in the red pinball shirt holding the flag as it burned, and the police handcuffing his wrists
to take him away. Tracy turned down the volume after the reports were through, Bill folded his arms and said, "What do you
do with a boy like that?"

And the truth was, Ross didn't know. Burning the flag was
wrong enough, not to mention the whole issue of the flag being public property as the news anchor had pointed out. But
this My Lai business of killing women and children—he
couldn't find much to defend in that. Ross grabbed his keys
and was on his way out the door even as the telephone was
ringing and Tracy picked it up, yelling at him that it was Cheryl
and she was at the police station, to come on over. "I'm over,"
Ross yelled over his shoulder. "Tell her I'm over."

■

271

A DIFFERENT OFFICER was watching the desk, much older with a gritted jaw and way of regarding Ross that set him in an immediate state of unease, as if *he* had been the one who'd burned the flag. The officer asked Ross to empty his pockets and Cheryl to leave her purse. "We have him in Cell Three," he said.

"You put him in jail?" Ross asked.

"Follow me," said the officer.

They found David there, his hands still smudged from the burnt cloth. The boy seemed even thinner than the last time Ross had seen him, his hair was long and scraggly. He got up from the bench and came to the bars, the policeman stood nearby. A few other prisoners watched from their cells, some pretty tough-looking customers. "He'll have to stay here until the judge determines bail," the officer said to Ross through his teeth. He seemed utterly pleased to be telling him this, and Ross found himself wanting to push this officer into the very cell that was holding his son.

"And how long will it be until that happens?" he managed to ask.

"Morning," said the officer.

"Morning," Ross said to David through the bars. His mother reached for the boy's hand, gave it a squeeze.

"I'll be fine," David said.

"But all night?" Ross asked.

"I don't make the rules," the officer said. "If I did, it would be two nights. Three even."

"You can't talk that way," Ross said.

"No?" said the officer.

272

Cheryl took Ross's arm and they walked out of the cell area together. The officer returned Ross's wallet and Cheryl's purse without the word, they agreed to meet back at the station in the morning. The entire way home, Ross heard the news reports that mentioned his name and the son who'd burned the flag. That evening when he turned on the television, each news report started with the film of his son holding up the flag and the flames licking its center.

BAIL WAS POSTED the next morning and the judge said that from this time to the trial date the boy should think long and hard about what it meant to burn something that people held dearly. David wore the gray suit his mother had brought from home, his hair neatly parted. But Cheryl had forgotten the shoes, and the judge considered David's Converses with the purple laces. "You wouldn't like it if I burned your shoes and you had to walk over glass," he said, as if this made any sense. Wisely, David said he wouldn't and the judge banged his hammer.

David went out ahead of his mother and father from the courthouse, they met him at the bench by the tree that was the sapling. Cheryl sat down, then Ross. The boy loosened his tie while Cheryl rifled through her purse for her pen and notebook, presumably to get down her latest thoughts on the war or First Amendment rights or whatever it was she felt the need to get down. Ross stared up at the sky, its clouds and one patch of blue in the far horizon, glanced over at the two of them, then back at the sky. "You know you screwed up," he said.

"I did what I believed," said David.

"There are other ways to express your dissatisfaction."

David got up from the bench. His eyes shone and his breath clouded before him, round little puffs that drifted upward. "*What is it?*" Ross asked, and then Cheryl asked it too. David walked away to the lawn, then circled back, went to the sapling and pulled at the leaf that had started to go brown. "Sometimes I just don't believe you," he said, quietly.

"What's that?" said Ross.

"Dissatisfaction," David said, and he tore the leaf from the tree and crumpled it to the ground. "*Dissatisfaction.* We line up women and children in a ditch and shoot them like wet dogs. We burn down their village and take their babies—*their babies*—and shoot them too."

"I'm only saying there are other ways."

"Other ways?"

Ross stood. "Yes," he said.

"Well I tried the best way I knew how."

"And probably ruined me in the process."

David paced away from the tree, back onto the lawn. "Ruined you," he said with the sneer, and when his son stepped close it surprised Ross to see that he was almost as tall as he was. *When did that happen?* he thought, and then David said, "That's all you care about anyway."

Cheryl got up from the bench and tugged at her son's arm. "Come on," she said. "It won't do any good telling him that."

"What is this?" Ross said. "Is this what you say about me?"

"We don't say anything," said Cheryl.

"It sure doesn't look that way."

"Let's go."

"He burned the flag," Ross said. "That doesn't make for good customer relations."

"Like he said. He did what he believed."

"What he believed?" This was too much. David's age almost excused his actions. But Cheryl? It took everything in Ross's power not to walk away and leave them standing there, accessories in their stupidity. Instead he breathed deeply, told them, "Well I might want to dance naked in front of the courthouse because it's what I believe. Does that make it right?"

Cheryl smiled slightly. "Maybe," she said. "Maybe not."

"Oh, come on Cheryl."

"Dad," David said, his voice the warble. "The problem is you think of money before you think of principle." He looked at the courthouse, then at Ross. "When I let the goose go it was because I wanted to show you something. Then the goose died, and I realized my point was sorely missed. But I wanted to show you, that's all I really wanted."

"This is bullshit," Ross said.

"Thomas found that goose. And then you took it and put it in that tiny cage and used it in your commercials without ever asking him."

"I asked him."

"No you *told* him. One day we woke up and the goose was gone and that was it, he was living at the lot and in the commercials." He turned and headed across the lawn with Cheryl, stopped while his mother continued ahead. "There's more than money," he said.

That's what it took for Ross to lose it, holding his temper in all this time. "Oh yeah?" he yelled, as they walked across the parking lot and got into Cheryl's car. He followed them to the lot, stepped up to the car as Cheryl turned the engine. "Oh yeah? Well my *money* got your ass out of jail."

They backed out of their space, drove past Ross and the attorneys with their briefcases and expensive suits pointed. He could make out some of their words. *Huckster* and *flag burning,* and when he peered up he could see the clouds thicker now, smell the moisture in the air. He pulled the keys from his pocket and trampled to his car, knew that it was going to rain by the night.

AND IT RAINED all right. Rained like the end of the world. The television news kept playing the film of his son burning the flag and everyone saw it because people had no choice but to stay indoors. At the lot business came to a standstill, Tracy and Bill made concerned faces and the other employees tried their best to appear busy doing nothing much at all, surely hoping Ross would find the way out from this unfortunate turn of events.

Then the commercial with the monkey wearing the hippie wig and glasses began to run. Like some kind of answer to the employees' prayers it brought the customers back, this advertisement so cheeky and glib while never quite naming the object of its obvious scorn. Of course there had never been any object of obvious scorn when Ross had shot it, but the public didn't know that. And as long as it brought them back, that's all that mattered as far as Tracy and Bill and the others could see it.

This was the final straw for David, any hope for Ross of salvaging their relationship long gone now. The boy took the commercial personally, even as Ross tried to explain to him he'd made it before any of the mess with the flag had ever happened. "Like I said," David said before hanging up in Ross's ear. "Money before principle."

Ross began to spend time with Bill and Tracy, they occasionally went to the bar around the corner with its stale popcorn in the wooden bowls. He would go home and brush the kernels from his teeth, fall asleep on the stiff couch by the push-button telephone. It was on those nights that he would consider calling Cheryl but he'd always stop himself, know that if she picked up he wouldn't have anything to say to her, after all.

It was a Saturday when Tracy dropped by with his fishing pole to ask Ross to come to the river with him, explaining that the fish were out in record numbers. He adjusted his glasses onto the bridge of his nose and his dentures clicked when he said, "Life's a bitch and that's why there's fish."

"I don't have a pole," Ross said.

"Yes you do," said Tracy. And he produced a pole from his large bag.

They went to the river, put on the yellow waders and went

out just beyond the shore. Tracy reeled out his fly, bright feathered green, Ross let the water pull his line along. The water was cold but it felt good to stand out in this quiet, the currents streaming between his legs. Occasionally the fish would run into Ross's ankle, swim dumbly past him and he would think here is my life, moving in the water and bumping along as the world crumbles around me. He looked down and watched as a trout swam in circles before him, held the fishing pole under his arm and reached to scoop the fish from the water. The fish breathed in the air with its beating gills, its teeth stuck out tiny and jagged. Ross held the trout in his hands.

Tracy glowered at Ross, truly exasperated. "Well it's yours," he said, pushing back his glasses with his wet thumb. "Put it in the bag already."

The fish went slack, the gills slowed. Ross could feel its life leaving, see the eyes cloud. He gently let the trout down, slipped it back into the water. The fish hesitated for a moment as it gathered its bearings. Then it darted. Once into his leg, then away and toward the bank, then the rocks, tumbling over the edges and into the dark, brown pool. Tracy shook his head and reeled out his line. "I don't know what the hell you did *that* for," he said.

Ross stared past the rocks, the fish gone from sight. He trod to the shore, kicked off his waders and set his pole onto the sand. The sun was warm against his cheek, he squinted against its light. He imagined his family standing there with him, David and Cheryl, Thomas too. How often he'd imagined this scene, all of them back together as if nothing terrible had ever happened. But here he was fishing with Tracy, and it was funny where people could end up, so far from where they thought they'd be, a million miles. Ross sat down on the bank. Birds flitted from tree to tree, the breeze rustled in the leaves. Tracy waded farther upstream and reeled out his line. The green fly bobbed and weaved, moved in the river and its dark currents.

Wedding Dance

Benjamin Strickland's wife and son left him the day before his sister's wedding. Now here he was sitting in the courtyard at the wedding reception and waving to his sister as she danced with their father. The relatives and friends watched from the side, there were the Christmas lights that hung along the fence that created their colorful effect. His mother turned to him, put her hand on his arm. Her hand was powdery soft, and Benjamin couldn't remember when it had taken on this consistency. "His heart," she said. "I'm worried about his heart."

"You don't have to worry," Benjamin said, and it was true, he knew he had his tablets, had been with his mother earlier in the evening when she'd asked his father whether he had them in his pocket. His father twirled his sister in front of Benjamin and his mother. The song played on—Glenn Miller's "In the

Mood." The horns quieted before their final hurrah, the music came back and his sister and father did their spins.

His father parted from Benjamin's sister and came over to sit down on the chair. "You're okay?" his mother asked him in her concerned way. He nodded and said that he was never better. Friends and relatives embraced Benjamin's father, he wiped the sweat from his face and laughed.

"Hey Mr. Bojangles," came the voice that was Aunt Trudy's. Aunt Trudy was his mother's sister who'd come all the way to Sacramento from North Dakota, a woman in her mid-fifties with large, round glasses that made her eyes look twice their size. Her mouth made its toothy smile as she shook her head. "I didn't know you had wings," she said.

"Only on special occasions," said Benjamin's father. He gestured to Benjamin. "But there's a boy who can dance. Why don't you ask him?"

"I don't want to," Benjamin said.

"*Of course* you want to."

"No," said Benjamin. "I don't."

Aunt Trudy took his hand and he reluctantly stood, because if there was one thing a person could never do, it was to refuse an aunt a dance. They went out to the floor, he turned her around and his sister Emily sidled up beside him. "Tear it up," she said into his ear, and he said that he *was* tearing it up, as he spun Aunt Trudy around again and saw that most everyone was on the floor. Aunt Trudy clapped to the beat, Benjamin thought how funny it was that he could dance like this while Leah was with her mother across town.

He stomped his feet, looked back at his father and mother who were talking to the assorted relatives. Leah used to say that family was the only thing that kept people from floating away, that without brothers or sisters and fathers and mothers everyone would be moving through the clouds. What a load of crap, he'd said to himself when she'd explained it all those years ago. But funny how what was once crap could almost seem sweet and appealing so many years later. He'd learned this much, that adulthood offered up the fluidity of facts, that people changed and what once seemed true was often its very opposite.

The song finished and his aunt gave him a kiss on the cheek, went back to the table. His sister turned to him. "Well then, how about you?" she said, and suddenly their cousin Randolph was asking for her dance. "It's okay," Benjamin said. "We can dance later."

"Yeah?"

"Yeah," said Benjamin, and Randolph took Emily's hand. He walked off the floor, his Uncle Edward came up to him.

"Too bad about the wife not being here," he said.

Benjamin rested against one of the white, lacquered posts surrounding the dance floor. Here were the words he'd been waiting for, and funny that it had taken this long to hear them, past the ceremony and well into the reception. "Yeah too bad," he said, staring down at the feet of his sister as they moved below the gown.

The uncle shook his head. He was Aunt Trudy's husband, a man that had only recently begun to age after thirty years of looking exactly the same. His eyebrows were now gray with

the eyes as stern and authorial as ever. "Couples have problems," he said. "It goes with the territory. After all, we're born
alone into the world."

Benjamin wasn't sure what his uncle meant by this, in that
nobody was born alone since one's mother was right there and
it didn't get much less alone than that. He shrugged, watched
Randolph glide his sister from one side of the floor to the other.

"I only wanted to say rough waters inevitably occur."

"Thank you."

Uncle Edward leaned into the other side of the post and
folded his arms together, turned to face Benjamin. His pointed
eyes shone in their intensity, reminding Benjamin of some bird
of prey. "I cheated on Trudy once," he said, the side of his
mouth quivering into some kind of smile.

Benjamin had heard the stories of his Uncle Edward and
this revelation was no surprise, although his willingness to share
it always struck him as odd. His father used to tell Benjamin's
mother how peculiar it was that Edward wore this infidelity on
his sleeve like some badge of honor, as if it showed how much
Trudy loved him. *If it wasn't their own problem,* his father would
inevitably add, *I would show him a thing or two about honor.*

"But now look at her," Uncle Edward said. "Dancing with
you like Ginger Rogers out there."

"She can dance," said Benjamin.

"She sure can."

Uncle Edward moved away from the post, Benjamin strode
past his sister's and husband's friends as they offered up their
hands. He grabbed a glass and bottle of red wine from the table.

When he got to the parking lot he circled to the back of the building, stood behind the fence. The music and the laughter wafted through the air, his father's voice audible above the din. He poured the wine into the glass, took a long drink.

BENJAMIN married Leah two months before she had the baby. He liked to think this was why things had fallen apart, that he hadn't been able to consider what he was getting himself into. He'd been twenty-six, and he could already see that he was younger then, that his view of the world had been just a little smaller.

Leah had been an old soul in so many ways, had figured out most everything was bullshit, as she liked to say. "But here's something that's true," she'd told him on their first date as she'd taken his hand. And she went on to explain that here was a significant moment, hand against hand, as people had done through the ages, perhaps when all was said and done, since *before* the ages. Monkeys in caves for instance, fire not known, but still, hands holding hands in all their hair-leathery splendor. Corny yes, Benjamin had thought as he'd imagined the primates sheltered in the cool rock from the various dangers. But wise and funny too, and what more could anyone want than someone who saw the world in such an obvious way?

He leaned back against the fence and poured another glass of wine, listened to one of his sister's friends say that she was happy for Emily, that she looked more beautiful than any person had a right to look. *Samantha,* thought Benjamin. He would recognize her glib asides anywhere. He drank the wine and listened as she went on about her book she'd been writing for the past three years, the one about men and women and how it was they talked without talking. *Samantha the expert,* he muttered, gazing up at the sky. Samantha who was single and had been single for as long as he could remember, who was one year away from getting her doctorate in psychology and opening an office in Manhattan. There was his sister's whoop and her husband's laugh, the break in the music and the deejay getting on the microphone. "Benjamin," he said, and feedback crackled from the speakers. "If you're out there your sister wants to dance with you now."

Benjamin stood and a pair of headlights flashed against him. He raised his glass to the driver, the car pulled out of the lot. "Benjamin?" came the deejay's voice through the air. "She's waiting." He stared down at the glass in his hand, sat back down on the curb and drank the wine.

WHEN HE FINALLY returned to the courtyard, many of the guests were leaving. His sister was upstairs changing into her honeymoon dress, the husband Gabriel sat at the table with Benjamin's mother and father. Gabriel pushed back his hair that was already going gray despite his being only thirty-three, when he saw Benjamin he got up. "My main man," he said, and he smiled.

"Hey," said Benjamin as he approached the table.

Benjamin liked Gabriel, considered him funny and kind.

He worked for a computer company writing the latest software programs. Gabriel had described his job to Benjamin on countless occasions—Benjamin still wasn't sure what it was that he did, but knew that it involved great masses of numbers. It was so much different from what Benjamin had ended up doing, being an artist and drawing for magazines, teaching the occasional community college class.

"Emily was looking for you," Gabriel said. "Where'd you go anyway?"

Benjamin patted his chest with the hollow thump. "I needed to get a breath of fresh air." He gestured around. "What, with all these people."

"It's too bad. She wanted to dance with you."

"He was hiding," said Benjamin's father from behind Gabriel.

"I wasn't hiding," Benjamin said. "Like I said, I just needed fresh air."

"We got on the microphone. You would have heard."

"Fresh air," said Benjamin.

"Uh huh," Benjamin's father said. He gave Gabriel the conspiratorial glance, and it occurred to Benjamin they might well become closer than he and his father ever had. His father straightened his tie, cleared his throat. "Well I suppose I should say my good-byes then."

"Me too," Gabriel said, standing.

Benjamin's father strolled out into the crowd, stretched out his arms to the priest who had said the wedding.

"That was a nice speech, by the way," Gabriel said, adjusting his cuffs.

"It was nothing, really," said Benjamin.

"Maybe," Gabriel said. "But you should know that your sister really liked it a lot. She was getting all teary, and let's just say you didn't hear that coming from *my* mouth." He ambled from the table, shook the hands and gave the hugs as he weaved through the guests. *All teary.* Benjamin just wanted to go home now, be in his own bed with the crickets outside and the cool breeze coming through the window. Only now there wouldn't be Leah next to him, and the pain that filled him upon this realization surprised him, its truth almost too strange. Samantha was talking in her loud tones, the friends gathered around her. One of the friends gave Benjamin a wave. He waved back and Samantha caught his eye, she broke away and came up to him.

"Hey brother of the bride," she said.

"Hey."

She took his hand, gave it a slight tug. "Last dance."

"So it is."

"So you should be dancing."

"I'd rather not."

"Of course you'd rather not," Samantha said, and she pulled him onto the dance floor, let him go. *The wine,* Benjamin thought. Had it not been for the wine, he would have never ended up on this dance floor with the friend of his sister's who'd always struck him as nothing more than tragic. Samantha put her fist into her hip. "Don't just stand there," she said.

"I'm dancing."

"You're *moving*," she said. "There's a difference between dancing and moving."

Benjamin closed his eyes and concentrated on the rhythm, kicked up his feet.

"That's better."

The music got louder, a few other couples joined them on the floor. Samantha smirked at him. "People are waiting for your next move," she said.

"Nothing up my sleeve," said Benjamin.

"There's always something."

"No," said Benjamin. "Nothing."

Samantha put her hands to his hips and held him tight. "Okay glum boy," she said. "Hold on." She spun him around and the dizziness hit Benjamin immediately. *The wine,* he thought again, and he could feel its numbing redness slosh against his insides. He tried to stop but she kept on spinning him and when he tumbled to the ground she was laughing as if his falling down was the funniest thing she had ever seen. She knelt over him, when he glared up he could see that everyone else was laughing too. "I didn't mean for that," she said. "Really."

Benjamin blinked hard.

"You okay?"

He put his head back onto the floor and closed his eyes.

"Are you?"

"I'm okay," he said. "Just leave me here, I'm okay."

EMILY came down the stairs from the changing room and her brother was sitting alone at the table. How sad he appeared, she thought. All hunched over in his gray suit, his face in its frown with the water glass in his hand. "I heard you fell," she said.

"Like a tree."

"You're okay now?"

He nodded without giving her so much as a glance, she sat next to him in the chair. Benjamin was a good four years older than Emily, but he seemed younger so often. Like now, not even being able to look into his sister's eyes because of the happiness he might find there.

"Your speech was lovely," she said.

"It was nothing."

"You're wrong," said Emily. "Speeches at weddings are never easy."

Benjamin crossed his arms together. Emily stared down at his ring, said a tiny prayer that she would never find herself in her brother's shoes with his broken marriage and felt suddenly terrible for even thinking it. Before the ceremony he'd come over to their father's house as she was putting on the gown, taken her hands. "I'm happy for you," he'd said, but the words had sounded empty, as though he was reading them from a page.

"It turned out to be a nice evening," Benjamin said.

"I'd say so," said Emily.

"Dad sure danced. I don't think I've ever seen him dance like he danced tonight."

Emily stood, remembered when they were children and how he'd once tied string to her leg and his, their running down the street and his telling her this was the only way they would ever be able to run again, that they were part of the chain gang escaped from prison, that they were connected until the end of time. She began to cry.

"Emily," he said. "Stop."

"I can't."

Benjamin rose from his chair. "Marriage is only a piece of paper. There are many pieces of paper. This for instance," he said, handing her a napkin from the table.

"It's *not* only a piece of paper," she said, taking the napkin and holding it to her face. "It's more."

"It is?" said Benjamin. "Everything else is only a way to make it feel like it is."

Emily held the napkin to her face, the people outside stared and she didn't care, she only cried more. *Hug me you fool,* was all she could think, but Benjamin simply stood there with his hands in his pockets shifting his feet.

"Emily," he said. "People are looking."

Arms around her, she closed her eyes and pushed her face into the chest that was not Benjamin's but Gabriel's, and she figured this was how it should have been anyway—he was only her brother and it was her husband who was supposed to come to her in these kinds of situations. Gabriel pulled her close, she squinted at Benjamin. "I know you were hiding," she said, as they moved away.

BENJAMIN'S father Derek was sixty-three years old but tonight felt half that age. His heart seemed fine, his breath was even and steady. It would have been the perfect evening, the best night ever, had it not been for Leah leaving Benjamin as she had. He didn't understand how someone could just leave another person like that. People did stupid things, his sister's husband Edward was the fine example. And God knew that he'd had problems with Katherine, that there had been the rough-and-tumble fights when he thought they wouldn't last another day. But to leave her? Or for her to leave him? It just seemed out of the realm of possibilities.

He had plans about what to say to Benjamin. Tomorrow he would drive over to his house, sit down with him in the kitchen and explain that it was true he'd mucked things up all right, that fact was as plain as day. But he would also tell him that he knew this much, that everything was a lesson and that in time the point of all this sadness might even become clear. *In time,* he would say. Everything, *in time.*

Benjamin came up next to his father and they stood in the courtyard together and said good-bye to a few of the relatives and friends. Katherine was talking to her brother by the entrance, moving her hands in the circle as she did when she was excited by what was going on around her. From here she looked as though she were describing the art of hog tying, the hands going circular again and again.

"Niagara Falls," Benjamin said.

"What's that?"

"Niagara Falls. Emily. She's a regular Niagara Falls crying like that."

Derek shot a glance back at the dining hall. "She's crying? Where?"

"In the kitchen. Gabriel took her to the kitchen."

"That's not good." Derek turned his eyes from the dining hall to Benjamin. When had his son become so cold and unfeeling? As a boy, Benjamin had been more sensitive than any child he'd ever seen. He used to cry when another child cried, put his hands to his ears and hold them there when Katherine would scold Derek. When Emily had come along he'd never leave her side, the two of them inseparable for the first couple years of her life. Then Benjamin started school, and the other children were cruel to him because of his teeth that stuck out. *His teeth.* Funny that Derek could chart the course of the boy's misfortune in this way, how it had started the instant he'd come out into the public world.

His chest tightened for a tiny moment, he figured this was the spasm from the dance, nothing really, then a pain swept up from nowhere like some fist closing. He stepped away from Benjamin and reached into his pocket, took out a pill from the vial and placed it beneath his tongue. He sat down on one of the nearby chairs and the pain left him, drank a glass of water and Benjamin asked him what was the matter.

"Nothing," Derek said. "My dancing legs decided to give out is all."

"You're pale as a ghost."

"Like I said. Suddenly tired."

Emily came from the dining hall and Gabriel had his arm

293

around her. Her face was wiped clean and Derek could see the puffiness of the eyes even from this far away. He poured himself another glass of water, Benjamin sat down next to him and leaned his elbow into the table. "She seems pretty torn up," Derek said as he slipped the vial of pills back into his pocket.

"It's an emotional day," Benjamin said.

"Oh, Benjamin," said Derek, and he wondered if he should have told him about his heart but decided against it. The evening had been so wonderful, he didn't want to spoil it with the pains and aches he'd known for so long. Benjamin and his problems, he could follow the trajectory of the boy's life pointing him toward this very moment. *The teeth. The goddamned teeth sticking out over the too red lips, wet like dew, the apple.* The orthodontist had said to be patient, they would give him the braces as soon as the boy grew just a little more. *But what was a little more?* Derek had asked, knowing Benjamin would have no easy time of it. He remembered the first day the boy had come home from school with the cuts and bruises, asking Derek why the children had pushed him as they had, laughed at him like that. Of course he'd had no explanation, Derek had simply held him because it was the only thing he could do.

He waved to Emily, Gabriel saw him and waved back too eagerly. Gabriel was a good man, but there was something in his nature that put Derek off, however slightly, his need for approval. Gabriel gave Emily a gentle nudge, they slowly made their way across the courtyard. "She really wanted to dance with you," Derek said to Benjamin, the sadness of this missed opportunity hitting him as he watched Samantha give Emily the spin.

"It's just a dance," Benjamin said.

"It's a *wedding* dance," said Derek.

"No," Benjamin said. "It's just a dance."

LEAH'S MOTHER put her daughter up in the guest bedroom that had been Leah's as a child, Nicholas in the corner on the mattress she'd dragged from the garage. Nicholas was fast asleep, breathing heavily with the occasional murmur. The boy was still too young to really understand what had happened, but how curious it must have seemed, to leave the house in the middle of the night half-asleep as he was. *It's time we visited your grandmother,* Leah had told him as she'd carried him to the car.

She pulled the blanket up over the boy, imagined the wedding that was happening right now. She'd wanted to be there—she loved Benjamin's mother and father nearly as much as she'd ever loved Benjamin. But there had just come the point when she'd had to leave, Benjamin making his telephone call so late in the evening to tell her about the moon.

Her mother rapped lightly on the door. "You okay honey?" she whispered, and Leah said that she was. "All right," her mother said, more loudly, and when she opened the door the light from the hallway poured inside. She came into the room and sat on the mattress. "But, really," she said. "Are you really?"

They sat listening to the sound of the boy's breathing, and all Leah could think was here was her life in this room, everything that would be and had been, her mother holding her hand like she was six all over again. She didn't want to cry and so she didn't, but this one memory kept returning, Benjamin swimming out into the middle of the river and waving his hand, telling her to come join him.

"We swam," Leah said, and her mother offered her smile as if she understood what she was talking about. "In the river, and the stars were just coming out and he took me in his arms." And Leah remembered drifting along with Benjamin in the darkness, the water babbling all around and sensing this was the moment in her life she'd been waiting for, the happiness welling in her throat at the realization that here was the most peaceful feeling she'd ever known.

Her mother squeezed her hand. "Everything passes," she said. "Your father. My brother. Even me. It's the way these things work."

All they had was each other, her mother was supposed to go on to explain. This was the thing that kept us from simply floating away. Leah waited but her mother remained silent, and she felt sorry to think this onetime maxim was seemingly no longer. So Leah said it, just to hear it, to remind her.

"Family is what keeps us from floating away," Leah said, and her mother got her faraway look, held her hand steady.

"Into the clouds," her mother said. "Into the clouds and up into the stars."

"IT'S GLUM BOY," Samantha said to Benjamin in the parking lot. She put her arm in his, walked him to her car and opened the door. "We're all going out for a drink," she said. "And you're coming along as the bride's brother who needs to get happy."

"I'm pretty tired."

"I don't want to hear it."

"I am."

Samantha glanced at Benjamin, rubbed one eye and then the other. "I don't really know any of these people anymore," she said. She blinked, gestured to her rented Geo. "Just come along." And there he was in Samantha's car as she steered out of the lot and rolled down the windows. Benjamin stuck out his arm and felt the air blow around him, looked over at Samantha. She was pretty, and wasn't it funny he would notice this now as if he had never seen it before. Her hair was silky and brown, her skin luminous in the oncoming headlights.

"What?" she said.

"Nothing."

"Yes, there's something."

Samantha slowed down, parked the car along the side of the road and turned off the engine. She reached over and put her hand alongside Benjamin's cheek. She held the hand there and moved close. Her breath was warm against his face, the fragrance of her hair tart and flowery. A car passed, then another, and it was suddenly, completely, dark.

THE GIRL had been in Benjamin's class, he'd seen her at the art store buying the paintbrushes. He was waiting in line when he'd felt the tickle on his elbow, turned around to pretend surprise as she held the paintbrush before him and said, "Mr. Strickland? It's me, Shelley your old student from the year before last."

They got to talking, he accompanied her to her car, then to the café across the street where her work was hanging on the walls. Her medium was oils. She was talented, painting fields and horses and boys in trees. There was the painting of a prepubescent girl standing naked on a roof, a man in a white T-shirt and jeans coaxing her down. "Nice," Benjamin said, and she nodded greedily at the praise. They sat at one of the tables and she told him about her life, how she'd moved out of her mother's house and it seemed she was experiencing everything for the first time.

"I try to paint it," she said. "Capture it because sometimes I feel like it's boiling up inside."

"And what's with the naked girl?" Benjamin asked.

Shelley smiled. "That's me."

"And the man?"

That's when she took his hand.

Of course he shouldn't have gotten into her car and gone to her house. Of course he shouldn't have let her close the door and turn the blinds and light the candles. He should have told her that it was wrong, that he was nearly fifteen years older than she was, nearly too old to be her brother and old enough to be her father for God's sake. But when she'd let her skirt, the red skirt with the white flowers and tiny black buttons fall down to her skinny white ankles, it was as if he couldn't form the words.

And afterward when she'd dropped him off at his car and it was dark with the moon coming up over the art store, he stood there in the parking lot and wondered how he could have done such a thing. He had her smell on his hands, in his hair, and he knew that when he got home he would have to go straight for the shower and wash every inch of his body. He stared at the moon and imagined Leah at home, curled up in bed with the pillow held tight to her chest. The moon would come in through the window, its light shine down onto her face in all its peacefulness.

"The moon," he said. "The goddamned moon."

He went to the telephone and dialed the number. His head was swimming, heavy. One ring, then another. And then her sleepy voice. "Benjamin?" she said. "What is it Benjamin? Where are you? It's nearly ten o'clock."

"I'm looking at the moon," he said.

"What's that?"

"I'm looking at the moon and I'm thinking of your face and I am so sorry for what I've just done."

ANOTHER CAR PASSED, the headlights shined into the interior and he could see the tender quality of Samantha's eyes, the concern in her face. The trees around them moved and rustled in the breeze, Samantha held her hand steady against Benjamin's cheek. "What can I do?" she said.

"Do?"

"Just tell me."

Benjamin pondered the question. Outside the frogs bel-
lowed in a cacophony of deep song—the darkness settled once
again around them. There were the tiny stars above, pinpricks.
"I can think of one thing," he said.

"Go on."

"You're going to think it's crazy."

"Tell me."

"You're sure?"

She nodded.

"Well," said Benjamin. He paused, felt the twitch of her
thumb, its pulsing. "Would you mind driving to Leah's
mother's?"

Samantha's hand dropped from his cheek.

"I told you it was crazy."

But then she smiled as if this were the biggest joke in the
world. "There is no crazy," she said. "Bad childhoods, terrible
genes, chemical imbalances and brains that didn't develop the
way they should have. But crazy?" She reached for the ignition
and started the car, gunned the engine so that it kicked out the
exhaust behind them. "Let's go then," she said.

LEAH and her mother watched Nicholas sleep. The light from
the hallway filtered into the room, Leah considered the boy's
eyes that moved under his lids, his murmur. Then her mother
sneezed and the boy stirred. When he opened his eyes and saw
his mother and grandmother beside him, his face darkened.

"What is it?" he said, and his grandmother took his hand as Leah switched on the lamp on the nearby table.

"We were just watching."

"Watching what?"

"Nothing," she said. "Just watching."

Leah and Benjamin used to watch Nicholas sleep. Benjamin would make his drawings in the middle of the night because this is when he said he did his best work. Then he would come to bed and rouse her, take the flashlight from the drawer. "Let's go see the boy," he'd whisper in her ear, tell her that in a year there would be a different child asleep in that bed, that actually in *six months* there would be a different child asleep in that bed, children changed so quickly. "Like clouds," he'd tell her. "Moving into their different conglomerations."

It was only in the last year *she* began to insist they look, to remind Benjamin that the world was more than sad. Benjamin was drawing less and other younger artists were doing his work at the magazines for half the price, the teaching jobs had dried up at the nearby colleges and universities. Leah had taken work at the frame store around the corner from their house to supplement the income, but it wasn't enough money. They were barely getting by and it was only a matter of time until Benjamin would have to find something besides his occasional work at the magazine.

"I'm nothing," he would tell Leah as he'd drink his beer. And she would tell him that he was *not* nothing, point to his drawings and the boy Nicholas. On those nights she'd wake him as he used to wake her, take him to see their son changing into something more wonderful each day, everything they'd ever wanted, life would work out, this much she knew.

Nicholas sat up and rubbed his eyes, Leah's mother leaned over him and placed her hand on his head. "Dear child," she said, this grandson new and unusual to her having had only two girls but never a boy. "How would you like ice cream?"

"It's late, Mom," Leah said.

"So it's late," said her mother. "He's awake anyway."

Nicholas was already out of bed and on his way out the door to the kitchen. "I want chocolate," he said. "Chocolate with nuts and marshmallows."

"Rocky Road," said Leah. "He wants Rocky Road, it's what Benjamin always gets him."

DEREK AND KATHERINE drove home and talked about the evening, agreed that all in all everyone had had a wonderful time, that it'd been a most tasteful affair. Unlike Benjamin's wedding, although they didn't say it. Benjamin's wedding with Leah so pregnant Derek was afraid she might have the baby right there in front of the crowd, Benjamin's wedding where Leah's mother wore the tight dress that made her arms go pink, her nipples stick out beneath the fabric. No, thought Derek. This wedding had been exactly how he'd pictured his children's weddings would be. Katherine took his hand, he steered onto the freeway and she sighed. "Now that it's over," she said. "I don't know what we're going to do with all our time."

But Derek knew the time would fill quickly enough, his going back to the affairs of the hospital where he worked as the administrator, Katherine as the speech therapist. They would slowly immerse themselves in their work once again, become reacquainted with the various dramas. For instance, the boy from Katherine's session who couldn't pronounce his consonants. Derek would stop by the office and Katherine would introduce the boy with the unfortunate name of Tennessee. "He calls himself E," Katherine always told him. "But you can call him by his full name."

Derek would shake the boy's small, loose hand, give him a good-natured rub of the hair. Then the boy would say a few words that sounded more like one long, slurred groan to Derek, move on to whatever book or puzzle he'd spread across the table. And for the rest of the day, Derek would see this boy in his mind, know that wherever he ended up this early childhood would shape him, create its permanent damage.

A motorcycle passed his right and Derek changed lanes. Benjamin was likely home in bed now, drifting off to sleep or perhaps watching the television in that same way as the terminal cases in the hospital, seeing but not really seeing, their eyes washed over. He turned onto the off-ramp and glimpsed over at Katherine, reached out for her and she took his hand.

THEY'D STOPPED to fill up for gas, in that Samantha's tank was nearly empty and they had the drive across town. Benjamin held the pump and she leaned into the car. "So what do you think you'll tell her?" she said, and she put her fingers to her chin.

"I'm not your patient," he said.

"I'm only asking."

Benjamin finished filling the tank and put the cap on, replaced the pump in its holder. "The truth is I miss her," he said. "The truth is I miss her and if I don't see her tonight I think I'll dry up and blow away."

"That's how it usually is," Samantha said. "Like the stages of death. If I had to wager I'd say you're at the point of bargaining."

"What happened to denial?" said Benjamin.

"Well, that too."

Samantha pulled out of the station and they were back on the dark road in no time. Soon there were the bugs in the headlights and the reflection of the passing trees. "It's probably extra hard with the kid and all," said Samantha.

"You could say that," Benjamin said, knowing that she had no idea how hard it was, that even considering the possibility Nicholas might not be a part of his life any longer made his vision blur, his legs go weak.

"I mean, that's a lot of history there," Samantha said.

"Yes it is," said Benjamin.

Benjamin knew Samantha's history, and it wasn't pretty. Her mother was on medication and lived in Sacramento, regularly called her daughter in New York to tell her that she was going to kill herself. But she never did, instead went to the nearby park to fall asleep in the sandbox. Samantha would get the call from her stepfather, according to Emily it was only at Christmas that they saw each other anymore.

Samantha accelerated onto the long and dusty road toward Leah's mother's house—in the middle of the day the road gave the illusion it would take one to the end of the world, its grade so flat it seemed to meet the sky. She turned to Benjamin and then back to the road, suddenly a rabbit jumped out in front of them and there was the bump—its pounding rattle—beneath the tire. Benjamin swallowed hard. She'd run the animal over, he had no doubt in his mind.

"Sweet Jesus," Samantha said. "Did I do that?"

Benjamin placed his hands on his knees.

She came to a stop. "I mean, did I just run over that rabbit?"

He didn't answer.

"No, please God, tell me I did not."

"But I think you did."

She looked behind her at the road, electric red from her brake lights.

"I could feel it as we went over."

Samantha stared straight ahead and rolled down her window. "I didn't," she said. And this, Benjamin figured, was the way she'd gotten through the various catastrophes of her family life—this denial—telling herself they didn't happen in the hopes they would simply go away. As he'd done with Leah this last year of his marriage, all of their problems piling up into her finally leaving. He looked at the rising dust all around them, Samantha covered her face with her hands.

LEAH AND HER MOTHER sat at the table with Nicholas. It was past midnight and the first time he had ever been up at this hour. He was excited by the dark and quiet, the new surroundings. He swung his legs from the chair, licked his lips. "I like ice cream when it's dark outside," he said.

"Even when it's not ice cream?" said his grandmother.

"Corn flakes are good," said the boy.

Her mother had lactose intolerance so she didn't have ice cream, even as she swore up and down she'd had a carton but that she must have tossed it away. Her mother poured the cereal into bowls, Leah thanked her but said she wasn't hungry. "Suit yourself," her mother said, and she added the milk for Nicholas, Lactaid Milk for herself. She placed the bowl before Nicholas and he spooned the cereal into his mouth, Leah dabbed the milk from Nicholas's chin with a paper napkin.

She had called the frame shop earlier that day to tell the manager she wouldn't be working there anymore. It was a part of starting her new life, her plan to take classes at the community college. She had to believe this was all for the best, that now she could begin to tend to her own needs. That's what her sister had continually told her to do anyway, and she knew that she would get her credential in teaching, work with second graders because that's what she'd always wanted to do.

"It's for the best," she told her mother and the boy.

They glanced up from their bowls of corn flakes.

"Now I can tend to my own needs."

"But where's Daddy?" Nicholas said, as if seeing right through this proclamation to its missing element.

"Daddy is tending to his needs, too."

Leah's mother took a bite of her cereal, gestured for Nicholas to do the same. They ate their corn flakes, the refrigerator made its hum and then went silent. "Well now, it's like a tomb here," her mother said, wiping her mouth. She reached for the radio. "Want to hear what music sounds like when it's this late?"

The boy licked the milk from his lips, said that he did.

"Well listen to this," she said, and she clicked the knob. A violin and oboe crackled through the speaker, the various strings. They listened and Leah considered how it was that music sounded different in the middle of the night, more intimate, giving the impression it had been created especially for them. She leaned forward in her chair, rested her head in her palm and closed her eyes.

DEREK saw Katherine off to bed and went to the kitchen, opened the bottle of brandy. He normally didn't drink alone in the middle of the night, but the evening had jangled his nerves, left him restless. He stared out the window at the stars through the trees. So many years ago he would watch Benjamin and Emily from this very same window, run out whenever a car sped by too quickly. As if he could do anything after the car had already passed, the leaves swirling and exhaust in the air. But he knew what it was that could happen, had seen the tragedies that occurred in other people's lives. Like the friend who'd lost his nose to cancer, then a child and wife to a car accident two years later, and it turned something deep inside Derek to know the directions life could take just like that.

He took a drink from the brandy, walked out the door to the porch. *Please let Benjamin find his way through this mess with Leah,* he said to himself. *Please let Emily and Gabriel be happy.* He closed the screen door behind him, went to the lawn and gazed up. *Stars like ice,* he thought, and he laughed, because this is how Benjamin would describe the night sky as a child. When Derek would ask him, *Why ice?* the boy would make his flabbergasted expression as if it were the most obvious thing in the world. "They just look cold is all," he'd say.

He felt the slight twinge of tightness, and when he reached for the vial of tablets they weren't in his pocket, because his pocket was in the jacket draped around the chair in the house, and goddamnit he should have known better than to leave them anywhere than on his person after the pain that had come earlier in the evening. He took a step back, dropped his glass, and felt the twinge that had become the fist, an even larger wallop. Then another. And suddenly he was down on the ground staring up at the stars, and the pain was so large he could only imagine how much it would have hurt if he wasn't already blacking out, his head going far away.

He thought of Benjamin, then Emily, of course Katherine. What a shame that she would find him out here on the lawn like this, how he wished he could have at least been with her in the final moment. Because this was no surprise, he knew it had been coming for the longest time. He said her name in his mind, willed her to hear it so he could hold her. Then the children. He wanted them to be safe was all. He wanted them to have a good life, not to have these terrible things happen that inevitably would, as they happened to all of us, this very heart bursting—the evidence at hand.

The last thing Derek Strickland saw were the stars in the sky, but he saw the stars as snow, thinking of Benjamin and how he had called them ice. And this reminded him of his own mother and father, taking him out to the ice rink as a child, putting out their arms and standing next to each other and waiting. And there he was, back in Minnesota skating toward them with the organ playing its music and the tiny lights hanging from the ceiling, his mother telling him he could do it, he could do it, just a little farther. Derek pressed his head back into the grass and saw the face of his son there before him, on the skates and heading for his arms. The smile, there was the boy's smile, the eyes bright and shining. "Oh, Benjamin," he said.

SAMANTHA AND BENJAMIN got out of the car, went back to where the rabbit had been. Only they'd found no rabbit, just a bump in the road that led the both of them to consider the possibility, however unlikely, that she hadn't run over the animal. Benjamin picked up a twig and peeled at its bark, they stood out in the middle of the road with the red light from the car illuminating them. Samantha faced Benjamin, stuffed her hands into her pockets. "I sure don't see any rabbit," she said.

"Maybe it got away," said Benjamin, not believing it for a minute.

"Do you think?"

"It's possible."

"But what about the bump?"

"It could have been the road."

Samantha nodded. "Then maybe I didn't kill it."

"Maybe."

She did a twirl. "That makes me very happy."

They walked back to the car and their shoes crunched into the gravel. Samantha pointed to the light coming from around the bend. "Leah's mother's house?" she said, and Benjamin had to wonder if it was. The light was curious at this late hour. He tossed the twig onto the ground and they got into the car, Samantha drove away. Benjamin could see as they veered the corner that the light was most definitely coming from Leah's mother's house. "Is that it then?" Samantha asked, and Benjamin said that it was. She slowed down. "Looks like they're still up."

Benjamin checked his watch, it was almost one-thirty and the lights were on in the living room. "Yeah," he said. "That's kind of funny."

"Maybe it's a late night of gin rummy."

"Not this late," Benjamin said.

Samantha dimmed the headlights and coasted down the driveway. Benjamin peered up at the house, felt his stomach spin. As he'd imagined this encounter he'd never really taken it farther than pulling up to the dark house, turning away after seeing that everyone was sleeping. But now here they were, and the next step was of course, going to the door and knocking.

"Well?" said Samantha.

"I'm thinking."

"Okay," she said. She switched off the ignition, looked out her window. "It sure is quiet out here."

"It's the country."

"You can hear things," she said. "The insects making their noise."

"They're out there."

Samantha reached over Benjamin's lap matter-of-factly. "All right, then," she said, and she opened the door. Benjamin got out of the car and marched toward the house. The light from the windows shined brightly, illuminated the grass and shiny metal sprinkler that sat in the middle of the lawn. He stood at the door, hesitated. When he glimpsed back at the car Samantha waved. "Okay," he mouthed, and he turned to the door and rapped lightly on the screen, then more loudly. The curtains rustled, Leah's mother's face suddenly appeared. "Benjamin?" he heard her say through the glass. Then, "It's Benjamin, Leah. It's Benjamin right here."

Leah's mother opened the door holding Nicholas, and Benjamin was about to ask what was the deal with the boy up at this hour when Leah appeared behind her mother in tears. "Benjamin," she said, and she opened the screen door and let him into the house, took him into her arms. He let her hold him, sob into his chest. This wasn't what he'd expected at all, such remorse and grief, an abundance of emotion.

"Hey now," he said. "I'm right here."

"Daddy," said Nicholas, and when Leah's mother put her hand on his arm, he could see that her face was broken. Nicholas shook his head and it suddenly occurred to Benjamin that something more was wrong than Leah's leaving. He nudged Leah away, asked what was the matter.

"Sit down, Benjamin," Leah's mother said.

AT THE FUNERAL Nicholas sat between his mother and father. The ceremony was short, the irony of the wedding having taken place days before not lost on anyone. Afterward they all gathered at Benjamin's mother's house. There were the flowers from the wedding mixed in with the flowers from the funeral, Benjamin greeted so many of the same relatives he'd just seen.

"A shame on the very same day," said his Uncle Edward.

"Yes," Benjamin said before moving on.

Leah sat on the living room couch with her mother and Nicholas, she glanced up at Benjamin and gave him a weak smile as he walked across the floor. They had talked the evening before about his coming back and their trying again, she'd told him she wished she could only let it happen. "Especially now," she'd said. "It must be so hard."

Must be so hard? he'd thought, the words seeming distant and not the sort of thing one's wife would say to her bereaved husband. He'd agreed that it was hard, reached for her hand and noticed how the touch had changed slightly. Like his mother's hand, the different consistency.

"The truth is I don't think I can be with you anymore," she'd said, and he'd asked her why as if he didn't know the answer. She'd only glared at him with her hard eyes, then at the glass in her hand filled with the water. "I want to be a teacher," she'd said. "I have a plan."

"I can help," Benjamin said, the waver in his voice betraying him. He'd told her he was ready to take any job now, that he wouldn't let his pride prevent him from going for the meaningless work that had nothing to do with his drawing. "I'll make hamburgers," he'd said. "I'll clean bathrooms. Just let me come back."

She shook her head, frowned down at the glass.

"Come on, Leah," he'd said.

"No."

He'd found the blackness rising in his throat, couldn't believe she would leave him at such a terrible time as his father's death. "I need you," he'd said faintly, and she'd looked at him with those same hard eyes and it scared him because he could see she'd already gone away.

"Too many bad things have happened," she'd said, finally.

And now here he was at the reception for his father's funeral, and his wife was smiling at him as she would smile at the neighbor's child or the mailman as he handed her the mail. He wanted to pull her into his chest and tell her, shout it out loud, that he was as sorry as any man had ever been and for her and the boy to stay with him. Leah's mother excused herself for the bathroom, Benjamin sat on the couch. "Do you mind?" he said, and when Leah didn't answer Nicholas climbed over his mother and sat on Benjamin's lap. The death had all been explained to the boy, he seemed to understand it as young children did. That his grandfather was in the better place, that he would be happy now for always.

"Howdy partner," Benjamin said into the boy's face. Nicholas's breath smelled sweet, he had the powdered sugar on his lips from one of the many cakes and pastries the friends had brought over. "How you holding up?"

Nicholas didn't answer.

"We've done better now, haven't we," he said.

"You can stop that," said Leah.

"I'm not saying anything."

"But you are."

They sat on the couch, silent in the middle of all the talking. Emily and Gabriel shuffled through the people. Benjamin noticed the way Gabriel ran his fingers in a circle along Emily's back, how he offered her this small comfort. "Here we all are," Emily said when she came up to him. She placed her hand on top of Nicholas's head, the boy turned into his father's chest.

Leah stood. "We should probably get back to Grandma's," she said. "He's pretty tired."

"I would think," said Emily, and she stepped aside.

Leah reached for Nicholas. "Here we go now," she said, and she placed her hands under his arms. But Nicholas held on to Benjamin's neck, his tiny fingers pushing hard into the skin.

Leah leaned close, tugged at the boy. "Tell him to let go," she said. "Tell him."

The boy held fast to his father.

"It's plain that he wants to stay," said Benjamin.

"It's not *plain.*"

But he knew better, that to tell the boy to let go would mean cooperating in this madness, helping to end everything. Leah pried the fingers on one hand, then the other. Nicholas was strangely quiet, his mouth clamped shut and eyes wide open. When the boy's fingers finally released there were his nails scratching along Benjamin's neck, but he didn't care. *Let him scratch,* he thought. *Let him scratch me to bleeding.* Leah gathered Nicholas into her arms. She staggered back, then forward.

"That wasn't necessary," she said.

Benjamin reached out for the boy's arm, squeezed it tight. "You know that I'm sorry," he said, and he held on. "At least *you* know that." Leah jerked Nicholas's arm away just as her mother came out from the bathroom. "We're going," she said, and they moved through the crowd. She stopped before Benjamin's mother and hugged her, then Leah's mother hugged her too, and they walked out the door.

"She took my boy," Benjamin said.

"Just across town," said Emily, even while she was thinking this was some kind of curse she didn't want to consider. First her brother and now her mother too. Alone, the both of them in one fell swoop. Her mother eyed her from across the room, Emily raised her hand to let her know everything was all right even though it most clearly wasn't. "Just across town," she said again, and Gabriel's fingers moved along her back.

THEIR MOTHER walked through the living room toward them, her face composed. The night of her husband's death she had torn at the grass where he'd died, cried into the ground as if it had taken him from her. In the backyard were the brown patches that she'd pulled, she'd stared at them the next day and thought how funny it was that the grass would grow back while Derek would be gone forever.

"Hello there," she said, placing her hands together. "Are we doing all right?"

"We are," said Emily.

She glanced from Emily in her chair to Gabriel and Benjamin sitting on the couch. "We're sure?"

Benjamin nodded. "We're sure."

Uncle Edward wandered up and offered his condolences, the neighbor from across the street did the same. "You know that we're here for you," she said, stepping close to their mother. "Just call if you need anything at all. Really now Katherine, you know that I mean it."

"I will," their mother said, and the neighbor gently nodded, walked away with Uncle Edward. Uncle Edward took a cookie from a plate, gestured to the picture on the wall of Benjamin and Emily as the children. "I knew these kids before they were even born," he said. "Back when they were inside their mother's stomach kicking and turning."

"That's something," the neighbor said.

"It is," said Uncle Edward.

Their mother shook her head. "The strangest part is knowing we danced with him only three days ago," she said, and Emily remembered the dip from her father's arms, the music that filled the courtyard all around them. He'd laughed and told her, *I wish it was always like this.*

Emily got up from her chair. "Let's play some music," she said.

"What's that?"

"Some music. Get some people dancing."

"I'm not so sure," said her mother. It's a funeral reception, after all."

"All the more reason," said Emily. Gabriel stood, patted her arm. "It might not be the best thing to do," he said, and she pushed him aside. Benjamin watched as his sister went to the stereo and Gabriel followed, talking into her ear. She searched through the tapes and compact discs and her mother came up beside her. They quietly argued back and forth, Gabriel came back and sat down next to Benjamin.

"Your mother doesn't think it's a very good idea," he said. "She says there are your father's brothers and sisters to bear in mind, not to mention the priest." He folded his arms together, slouched into the couch. "I think I would have to agree with your mother on this one. I mean, music is one thing. But dancing?"

Emily headed back to Gabriel and Benjamin. "Dad wouldn't have liked it this way," she said, and she sat down between them. She sighed, leaned back and fingered the pearls that hung from her neck. "But I suppose it's the living who make the rules for the dead. You know?"

There was music and Benjamin looked across the room to see his mother at the stereo. She nodded to the rhythm, its piano and tinkling bells, the cymbal. It was Ella Fitzgerald—her "Night in Tunisia"—the song their father played so often when Benjamin and Emily had been children. The bass rolled in and thrummed alongside the piano, followed the notes in the swinging time. And then the voice, as light and playful as Benjamin remembered it being. *The moon is the same moon above you,* the voice sang. *Aglow with its cool evening light.*

"Ella," Emily said.

"His favorite," said Benjamin.

And when his sister took his hand he could feel his heart lift in its tiny flutter. The dance he thought, the *wedding dance* as his father had put it, those three short nights ago. Emily jittered her knee and he remembered the evening, his father turning her on the floor as they moved around and around. She clicked her heel, he made the tap with his foot and she glanced over. "Benjamin," she said, and he imagined her there before him, the dip and twirl, the stars above. The music filled the room, he slid his shoe and she made the scuffle. "Benjamin," she said again.

About the Author

MATTHEW IRIBARNE earned his MFA in Creative Writing from San Francisco State University in 1997, has been the recipient of the Joseph Henry Jackson Literary Award and Nelson Algren Prize for his fiction. He lives in San Francisco.